SCHOOL'S IN

Compiled & Edited by
Ben Thomas & D Kershaw

BERTIL

rlett
Chicaaa !!!
R IT

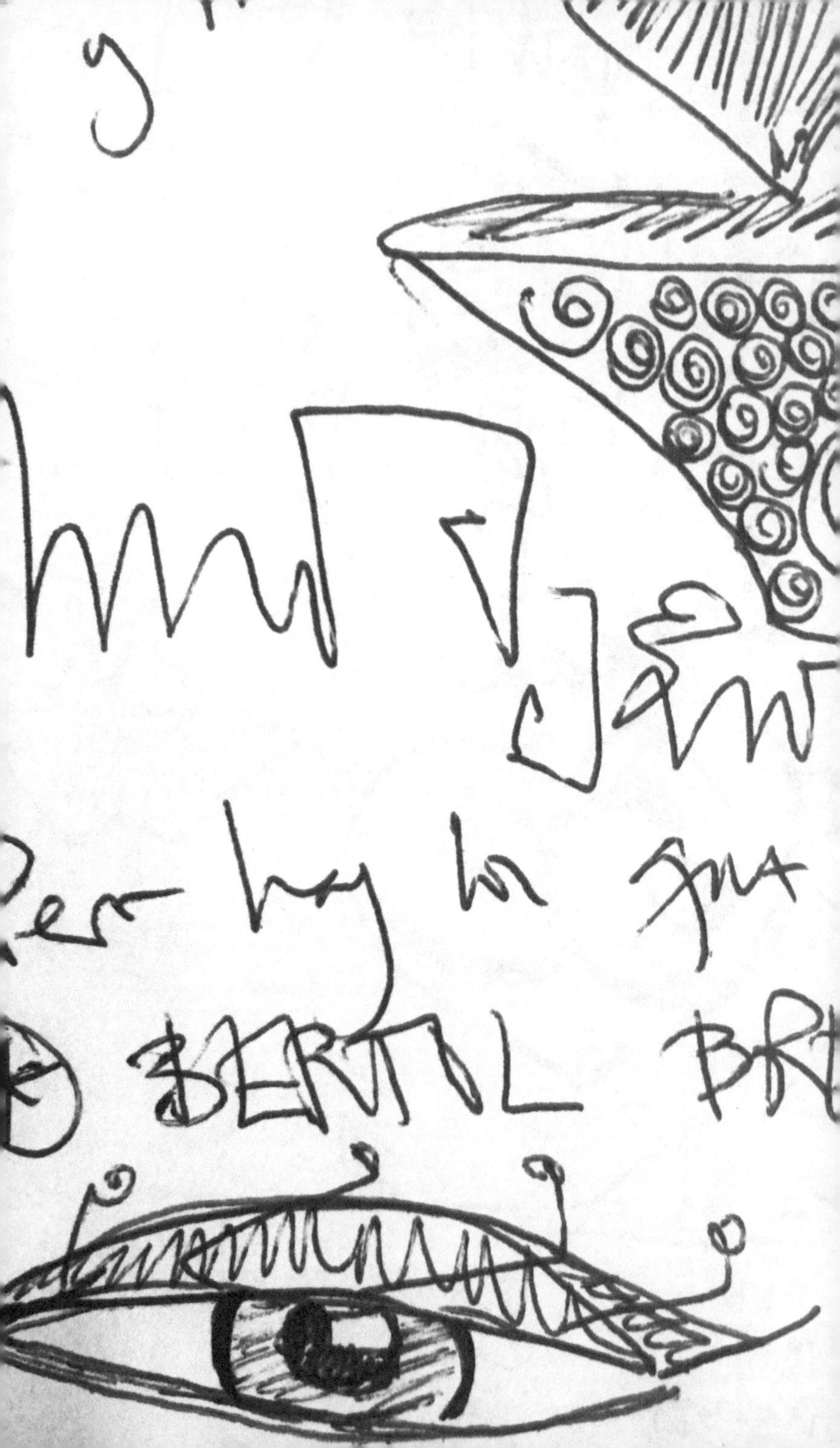
BERTOL
BR

Also available from Black Hare Press

DARK DRABBLES ANTHOLOGIES

WORLDS
ANGELS
MONSTERS
BEYOND
UNRAVEL
APOCALYPSE
LOVE
HATE
OCEANS
ANCIENTS

BHP WRITERS' GROUP SPECIAL EDITIONS

STORMING AREA 51
EERIE CHRISTMAS
BAD ROMANCE
TWENTY TWENTY

OTHER VOLUMES

DEEP SPACE
WHAT IF?
DEEP SEA
KEY TO THE KINGDOM
BEYOND THE REALM

Twitter: @BlackHarePress
Facebook: BlackHarePress
Website: www.BlackHarePress.com

Table of Contents

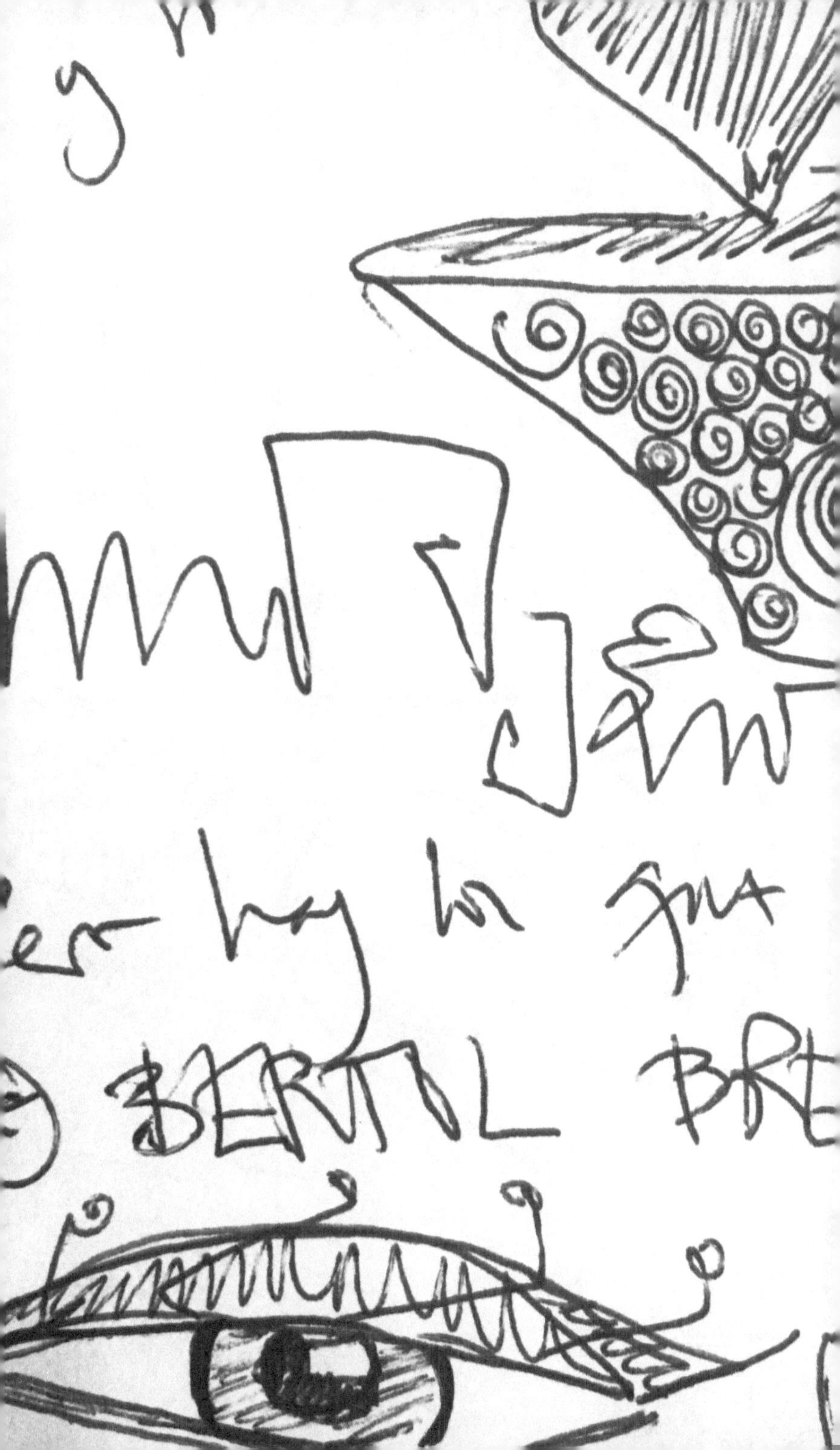

BERTOL BRE

rlett
chicaaaa !!!

FOREWORD

School's in, school's out,

Why do the kids all jump and shout?

Is it the monsters beneath their desks,

or evil teachers in their nests?

Maybe those kids wreak with fright from shadows flitting through the night…

Ideas forming in their minds, transforming into special finds

To put their thoughts down on a page, pencils racing in their rage.

Chairs are clacking, exams are done,

Students free to have some fun.

Back they come but something's changed;

Energy gone and eyes are glazed.

Teachers uneasy with their prey

What happened to the kids they will not say…

Jo Seysener

THE SECRETS OF LOCKER 4D

by K.B. Elijah

Everyone knows the lockers at Kedron Vale High are haunted.

The teachers are invariably quiet as they pass the foreboding rows; their eyes downcast, feet treading a well-used route down the centre of the corridors. The parents, all ex-students in this tiny town, take the long way around to the gym for the Saturday basketball games, preferring the muddy path behind the library to facing the looming metal boxes that fed their nightmares throughout their teenage years.

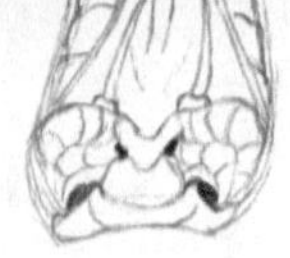

The current students ignore the lockers, choosing instead to carry around their stuff from class to class. It's easier for this generation: one tablet ain't nearly as heavy as the thick textbooks we used to have to laden ourselves with. I have often wondered if each of them individually had an encounter with the monster in the lockers that gave them such sensibility, or whether it's a herd mentality, a knowledge of self-preservation without the reasoning behind it. But then I would lay a hand on one of the lockers, the metal far colder to the touch than steel should be, a gelid touch that bites at my fingers accompanied by a creeping sense of horror, of eyeless creatures and slithering darkness and the tang of blood. And I would know, as the kids know, that there is an otherworldliness to the metal, the song of death and despair, and my whole body cries out in primal fear.

That is why the students stay away from them, save for the occasional convenient disposal of some unwanted item or another—a report card, a stolen item too hot to sell, an ugly jumper given to them by their grandmothers.

For the monster in the lockers is not a monster in a locker. It is in all of them, a gaping maw of death that somehow jumps between the rows of separate metal structures tucked against the walls of the fourth and fifth corridors between ancient classroom doors. It's a single

entity, split into a dozen parts, devouring anything which is abandoned inside any of its hundred metallic mouths.

When playing the game, you have ninety-nine lives and one certain death, a Russian Roulette in which there are no prizes for winning but your life. For you never know, when you open a locker door, if that will be the one which the monster is occupying at the time, green eyes gleaming with fevered hunger.

Not that many others in Kedron Vale would know the colour of its eyes.

I guess I'm lucky that way.

Yet I'm still plagued almost daily by the icy nightmares that brush against my thoughts as I'm polishing the gym floor, repainting the window frames of the science classrooms, fixing the air conditioning in the teachers' lounge. Dusting the lockers.

Timmy likes that, I believe. Me in my handyman's overalls, weary lines stretched across my forehead, rubbing a clean cloth across the worn facades of the rows of the lockers. Paying extra attention to locker 4D, making sure its handle is shiny and free from rust. Tears running down my weathered cheeks as I hear him slithering through his metallic domain, hissing at my fingers from the other side of the doors.

Yes, he likes to see me so, broken and beaten,

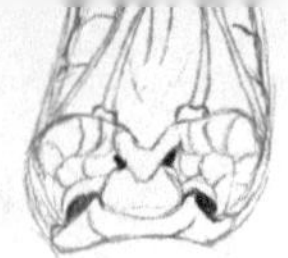

keeping him gleaming in my supplication and guilt. I'm the only one who dares to even touch the metal, but for the kids who use him like a personal disposal unit. They're lucky Timmy hasn't yet become wise to their tricks, content to consume the morsels of rubbish they supply him with rather than biting their very hands as they dump inside their unused lockers whatever item they have bored of or wish to hide. It's always gone, of course, when one reopens the door later, no matter how short the amount of time which has passed. This is the monster's domain, and it devours all.

Including the weekly sacrifices I bring directly to its maw, in a desperate effort to satiate its hunger and protect the students. It's why I'm here, a Grade-A student with scholarships to a university of my choice, destined for greatness…forty years a handyperson at my goddamn old school.

I stand before locker 4D. It's always locker 4D. I unzip the satchel at my hip, my fingers probing into the damp darkness within.

"Darren?"

I start, my fingertips brushing matted hair.

"Darren, is that you?"

I turn to find the new Principal of Kedron Vale High striding towards me down the corridor. He's brash, and

he's loud, and I don't like him.

"Darren, it's good to see you here so early! You set a fine example for the rest of the staff. If only the teachers would follow your example, Darren."

Why is he using my name so much?

I shrug. "I just…ya know. Wanna make sure everything's all good for the start of term tomorrow."

"Ah yes, the return of the students," Pierce says sagely, nodding as if it's a nugget of wisdom he's bestowing on me. "The school never feels the same without them."

I turn my hide to hide my expression, faking a cough. The man was only here for a week before the previous term ended as a result of the previous principal experiencing an unexpected medical emergency, yet he's making it sound like a lifetime.

I have spent a lifetime here, in these four walls. I should know what one feels like.

"Are you alright, Darren?" Pierce takes a concerned step towards me, and I wave him off as he wrinkles his nose. "What on *earth* is that smell?"

"Uh, had to clean the boys' toilets 'gain," I say, pressing the bag at my side closed with one arm. "Saturday's loss to Hurvale High must 'ave upset them physically as well as mentally, if ya know what I mean."

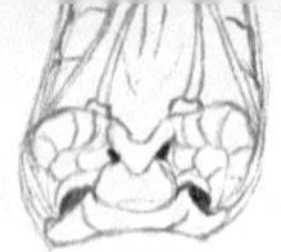

The principal makes a disgusted noise in his throat. "Well, I'm glad I caught you. I wanted to ask one more favour before the start of term."

"Yeah?" I ask wearily, abandoning my plans for a hot cup of tea in favour of spending some pointless hours attempting to scrub graffiti off bathroom walls or filing initials from the surfaces of desks. But I'm not prepared for what Pierce has in mind.

"These old things," he says cheerily, slapping a palm against the lockers. I wince, waiting for the inevitable gasp of horror and surprise as his flesh meets the metal. But there's…nothing. "I'd like them gone."

"The…lockers?" I say slowly, convinced I'm mishearing.

"What do you think I mean? Of course, the lockers. They take up far too much room, and clearly the kids don't use them. Don't you agree that we could do a lot of things with these corridors if they weren't here?"

I blink up at him, at his tall lean figure with the gleaming smile. "Like what?"

"Like…" Pierce falters. "You know, things. More wall space!" he practically shouts, obviously struck by an idea. "We can put up new posters about the dangers of cyberbullying and online harassment, *that* type of thing."

"I can probably find a noticeboard for the foyer," I

offer, but he's already talking over me.

"To be honest, it doesn't really matter what we will do with the space. But filling it with useless hunks of metal is no longer an option," Pierce says, jutting his square chin. He reaches out a finger to stroke it along the top of the lockers, obviously expecting to be met with a thick veneer of dust.

But Timmy doesn't like dust, and that means I keep them very clean.

"Hmm," Pierce says, brushing his finger gingerly on his pressed trousers as if trying to convince me that it's filthy. "So, you'll get on it, then? Good man."

He turns away and starts moving down the corridor with the power and speed of a man thirty years my junior.

"Wait!" I call, caught by surprise of the abruptness of his departure. "No, we shouldn't move them—"

The principal sighs, coming back to me. "Darren, I'd like us to be friends. I really would. But if you are going to push it, I will remind you that I am your boss, and I am telling you to get these darn things out of here."

I shake my head. "It's not about you. It's the lockers."

"What about them?"

"Don't you *feel* them?"

Pierce lets out a soft snort. "Not you, too."

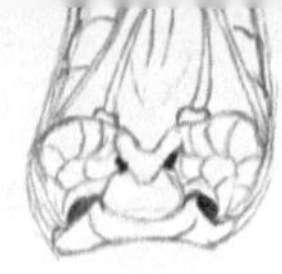

"So, you do—"

"I've tried to have this conversation with two other members of staff before you, Darren. Each of them turned as white as a ghost and refused to even discuss the lockers. What is it with this remote little town and its stupid superstitions?"

"The lockers are special," I say carefully, but he just raises an eyebrow.

"The lockers are lockers. Nothing special at all."

A rumble reverberates through the air, an angry snarl that makes me take a step back from locker 4D. Timmy's in that one now, I know it.

I look up at Pierce, feeling a flash of grim triumph, but he's still frowning at me in a condescending sort of way.

"Honestly, Darren, I thought you had a more sensible head on your shoulders. We've got to think forward, think efficiency, not be stuck in a *'it's what we've always done'* loop. Every school I've worked at, the kids hang around the lockers. They decorate them, make out against them, swap them in bets. Here? It's like they don't even exist!"

"Or they're haunted," I offer helpfully and am rewarded with a withering stare.

"Term starts tomorrow. I want them gone."

Locker 4D growls again, but the principal doesn't

notice, his eyes fixed on mine in the question he hasn't asked.

"Sorry, Pierce," I say, my heart sinking. I'm going to get fired for this, but it's worth it. Pissing off the monster will only get more people dead, myself included, if I'm the one trying to move the lockers. Timmy is very protective over his domain, his grave, and any attempts to dispel him over the years have always turned nasty.

Just looked what happened to that exorcist the geography teacher tried to hire.

Maybe if I'm fired, I can make a copy of my keys. Sneak back in here every weekend to feed the monster until Pierce realises his mistake and begs me to return to take care of the school. With no one else daring to touch the lockers, and the lockers needing to be maintained, it's a deadly paradox which only I can resolve, my lifetime of penance for the mistakes of youth.

But Pierce doesn't say anything about my employment this time. He whirls on his heel and yanks open a random locker door.

Random, but it's not. Of the hundred lockers he could have opened, he opened locker 4D. The tall, thin space located dead centre between the physics classroom and one of the girls' bathrooms, unremarkable from the outside but for small initials carved into its glistening

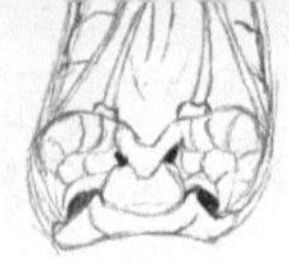

handle—*T.W.* The locker whose metallic insides are covered in the blood of thousands of dead hares, the remnants of a gory weekly ritual which has kept the monster relatively quiet for the last forty-nine years at the cost of my promising career, my sanity, and my life.

And that would have been terrifying enough to this upright young man with his fresh haircut and big ideas, but in another cruel twist of possibilities, it's also the one of the hundred lockers in which the monster now lurks, ready for its weekly meal. Darkness looms as green eyes flash and blood-drenched fangs extend, set to a backdrop of the sound of Pierce's screams. I blink, and by the time my eyes have opened again, they come to rest on a shred of inky blackness chewing noisily on the remnants of Pierce's neck, an exposed artery enthusiastically decorating the faded linoleum with bright scarlet lines.

The monster watches me with those big green orbs, eyes that stare at me accusingly from my nightmares. Timmy's eyes, once set in a round chubby face instead of a gaping maw of horror.

It slurps up the spurted blood and, wrapping its jaw around one of Pierce's wrists, pulls the corpse into the locker. A man shouldn't be able to fit in there—a boy, for certain, but not a man—yet Pierce's body disappears nonetheless, consumed by the supernatural bending of

space that the monster somehow possesses. In moments, the darkness fades, and I'm once again looking at a bloody metal box housing mere square inches of space.

I'm certain that if I threw open the doors of each of the lockers in Kedron Vale High, I'd find the principal. Perhaps in more than one locker—an ankle here, a finger there. But why would I be stupid enough to go *looking* for the monster?

I dip my fingers into my bag and toss the dead hare into locker 4D, slamming the door shut on the grisly sight.

Biting my tongue until it leaves iron in my mouth, I scuff a spot of blood on the floor out with my shoe, planning to bring bleach down later and scrub the whole thing clean. As I turn from the imposing visage of locker 4D, all of the lockers rumble with what sounds like laughter, and I scowl, hobbling away under the weight of a bad back and worse guilt.

It's been forty-nine years since the monster arrived at Kedron Vale High.

Perhaps others wouldn't remember the number of years so well, but I am incapable of forgetting.

For it has been forty-nine years since a bunch of friends and I stuffed Timmy White into his locker as a joke. Forty-nine years since we opened locker 4D an hour later to find him dead, his green eyes blazing into me with

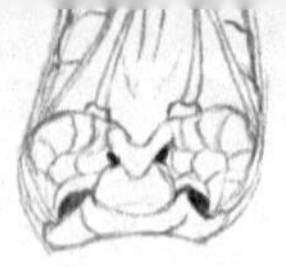

the promise of eternal damnation as his lifeless body fell to my feet.

SCHOOL'S IN

BLACK HARE PRESS

THE GIRL WHO HATED SHAKESPEARE

by Tim Mendees

"It's just not fair," Cassie pouted, it was the first day back after Christmas and she wasn't happy. Not in the slightest. "How come *she* gets to do it and I get stuck with *Macbeth*?"

John winced theatrically, "Shouldn't you say *The Scottish Play*?"

Cassie cut him with a look that could sever limbs at fifteen paces. "Don't be such a fucking nerd!" she snapped. As her current boyfriend, John had quickly grown accustomed to her savage outbursts. "I'm in the top

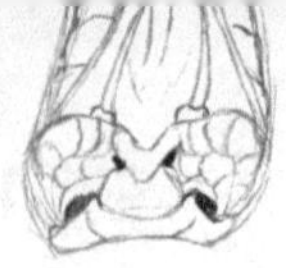

set for drama, why don't I get to do the interesting play?"

John knew he was skating on thin ice, but his mouth opened despite his brain telling it not to. "*Macbeth* is pretty interesting, Cass. I don't see the problem. Hey, you might even get to play Lady Macbeth!"

Cassie's eyes flared with anger as her whole body bristled. Her golden hair, thick with hairspray, seemed to writhe like a nest of vipers. She drew herself up to her full five-foot-seven and stated flatly, "I hate Shakespeare." The calmness of her voice betrayed more than just a hint of underlying malice.

Thankfully, for John, the bell sounded for the next lesson. He had woodwork and Cassie had French; this took them in opposite directions. John jumped at his window of escape, pecked her on the cheek, and ran off down the corridor trailing his tatty rucksack behind him.

Cassie barely noticed he had gone. She was glaring at the drama notice board with the new term curriculum. She couldn't believe that she was lumbered with Shakespeare…again, while her sister, Cammie, got to do something cool and new despite being in the B-group… It just wasn't fair.

The Chambers sisters, Cammie and Cassie, were identical twins. Though, their similarities were purely cosmetic. Cassie was brilliant at everything. One of those

people who didn't even have to try in lessons to end up with good grades. She could practically sleepwalk through exams. Cammie, on the other hand, had the reverse Midas touch… Everything she touched turned to shit.

Cammie's frustration at being worse than her sister at literally everything academic had driven her down a path of rebelliousness. The way she saw it, everyone thought she was a loser so why try to be anything different. Ironically, it was this attitude that had made her extremely popular. She strutted around the school in the shortest of skirts with a clique of friends and hangers-on. Cammie only had to click her immaculately manicured fingers and the boys, and a smattering of girls, would come running.

Despite being identical in looks, Cassie never garnered the same attention. Most of the school found her overachievement and arrogant sense of entitlement distinctly off-putting. The jealousy ran both ways—Cammie was jealous of her twin's success while Cassie of her twin's popularity. It didn't help that Cassie's last boyfriend had called her Cammie during an amorous encounter. That was the seed that grew a sibling rivalry into outright loathing and animosity. In her troubled mind, she was convinced that even John was only with her

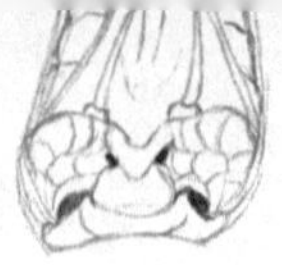

because she looked like her sister.

"You coming, Cass?" her friend Sharon asked upon seeing her standing motionless while everyone ran around her like headless chickens. Sharon was one of Cassie's only friends. She too was stamped with the unenviable label of being a teacher's pet.

"Eh?" Cassie blinked. Sharon's question jolted her out of her brooding reverie. "Oh, yeah. What period is it?"

Sharon looked at her dumbfounded. "Period five. French!"

Cassie excelled at French—surprise, surprise—and wanted to go and live in the country someday. She smiled at Sharon and swung her bag over her shoulders. This was a welcome development, Cassie had been using an app on her phone and was pretty much fluent, so while her classmates bumbled around for the correct tense, she could figure out how to get herself moved to the same drama group as her wayward sister.

One way or another…she would be doing *that* play.

***

In the end, switching groups proved easier than expected…

"Are you ready?" Cassie stage-whispered to John.

He was up in the rigging on lights. He shot her a thumbs-up and waited for her to get in position, fingers poised over the spotlight controls.

They were rehearsing Act Five, Scene One where Lady Macbeth, Cassie, loses her mind. She was directed to "sleepwalk" over towards where Mr Davies, her teacher, was standing. As usual, he had draped his jacket over one of the chairs and was pacing up and down, waving his arms around like a demented windmill.

Cassie directed a sly wink to the lighting booth once she was directly in front of her teacher's chair. John dexterously dragged all the sliders down simultaneously, plunging the room into darkness.

"John! What the hell are you doing, boy?" Mr Davies boomed.

"Sorry!" John waited as long as he possibly could without sparking suspicion and turned the lights back up. "Sorry, sir! I think I pressed the wrong button or something." He hoped to God Cassie had been able to pull off her part of the subterfuge undetected. She was back on her x of tape as she should be and had the faintest hint of a smile on her lips… It was looking good.

"Not to worry, John." Mr Davies smiled. "That's why we have these rehearsals, so you don't 'press the wrong button' on the night." He waved his hands at the

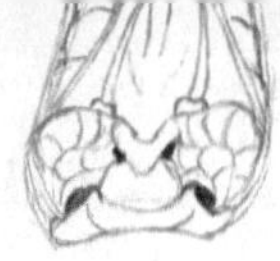

players. "Okay, let's go back to Act One, Scene Five. Lady Macbeth," he addressed Cassie, "Let's see some real fire when you deliver the line 'Leave all the rest to me', okay?"

After the final bell rang, Cassie gathered her things and waited for John to retrieve his things from his locker. She made sure that everyone saw her be the last one to leave the drama studio. She thought up some questions pertaining to the dialogue to ask Mr Davies, then left school via the back gate.

"Did you get it?" John asked once they were sure that they were well out of earshot.

Cassie grinned triumphantly and reached into her blouse. "Sure did." She laughed as she fished Mr Davies's phone out of her brassiere.

"So, what now?" John asked.

Cassie gave him a coy wink. "Leave all the rest to me…"

***

Two days later, Betyls Cove High School was hit by a tsunami of scandal…

Cassie had taken the phone belonging to her drama teacher home and put her own number in his phone book. After googling the sort of things a man of his age might

say to a young girl, she sent herself some decidedly lascivious text messages.

The following day, Cassie had John slip the device into Mr Davies's drawer in his form room and bury it under paperwork like it had been there all along. Meanwhile, Cassie turned on the waterworks and let the crocodile tears flow as she skipped class and went running to her mother's place of work.

Mrs Chambers did what all outraged mothers would do after finding a load of filth on her daughter's phone from a teacher. She marched down there, hellfire sparking off her high-heeled shoes, and proceeded to kick up one hell of a fuss. Within minutes of her arrival, the police were summoned, and half the school was calling Mr Davies a *nonce*.

Luckily for Mr Davies, he had noticed the theft almost immediately after the lesson and had popped into the police station to report it as stolen on his way home…before Cassie sent the messages.

In the end, the phone was found, and it was put down to being the work of a prankster. It didn't matter either way as it had achieved the desired effect, Cassie and John had to be moved out of Mr Davies's class. Ironically, the whole debacle was laid at Cammie's door. Even her parents were convinced that it was her sick way of getting

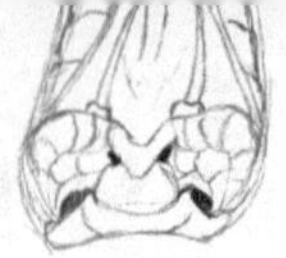

back at her sister. To have their golden girl moved out of the top set was a disgrace… Cassie was delighted.

***

Delight wasn't what you could call what John was feeling after his first couple of lessons with Mr Castaigne. "I was happier doing Shakespeare," he grumbled after the eccentric French drama teacher had chewed him out over the hue of the lighting for the fifteenth time that period. "I don't even know what the hell is going on. This play makes zero sense!"

Cassie gazed through him at the wall and said distractedly, "I hate Shakespeare." Her mind was elsewhere. It had been elsewhere since she had been hurriedly cast in the lowly role of "courtier."

John looked at her in a mixture of concern and irritation. "Is that it? *You* hate Shakespeare. This guy is a fucking lunatic!"

It was true; Mr Castaigne was definitely unstable at the very least. At worst, he was a raving madman. He seemed to be obsessed with the play. It was an honour, he trumpeted on many occasions, to be the first school to do *The Yellow Play*. He never spoke the true title of the piece, like it was some huge cosmic secret. Even the scripts, of

which they were only allowed Act One, had the title roughly scrubbed out with a black marker.

Every time he called it *The Yellow Play*, his face contorted into a bizarre grimace that could either have been one of mirth or despair. John could never quite put his finger on his unease, but he knew one thing for certain… He would rather be back in the other group.

"Mr Wilde!" Castaigne boomed up to the lighting gantry. "Are you awake up there?"

John had been daydreaming. Cassie's trance-like state was mirrored by the rest of the class. He was the only one, it seemed, that wasn't under the spell of the bombastic teacher. "Um, sorry, sir," he called back down.

Castaigne grumbled to himself as he fanned himself with the script. His eyes darted from pupil to pupil before settling on Steve Scott, Cammie's boyfriend. "You"—he indicated with a stubby finger—"Can you perhaps get the colour yellow to follow the main character, unlike that idiot up there?"

Steve answered in a flat monotone, "Yes, Mr Castaigne." John noticed that his eyes were glazed and bloodshot like they had just witnessed some unimaginable horror.

"Very well." Castaigne clicked his fingers with a theatrical flourish. "You two swap places." The two boys

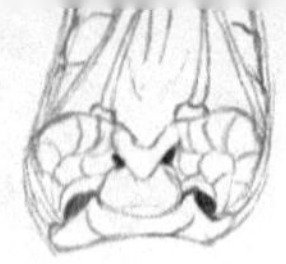

did as instructed. "Let's see if you can act better than you press buttons and twiddle knobs, hmm?"

The glare of the yellow light burned into his retinas as it reflected off the script that had been hastily thrust into his hands.

"You have very few lines," Castaigne briefed him enthusiastically. "But it is the most important role. You are honoured, don't forget that."

"Yes, Mr Castaigne." As he spoke, he could feel his girlfriend's eyes burning holes through his back.

***

Cassie, at once galvanised into action by John's promotion, had almost instantly started a campaign of diabolical proportions to get herself the lead female role. It was *her* role after all. Cammie was cast in *her* perfect role as the lead's twin sister. It was too much like fate for her to ignore. And then there were the names…

The girl in the lead role was one of her sister's cronies, Victoria Worthington. She was a tall, muscular girl, who could beat up most of the boys, never mind the girls. So, intimidation was out of the question.

Since changing groups, *The Yellow Play* had become her bible. That short first act, with its evocative chorus

parts and brooding nature, spoke to her in ways that other literature never had. Every waking moment, she ruminated on the message within the play. Even when she slept, her dreams were bathed in yellow.

As she sat alone at the edge of the football field one wet lunchtime, Cassie happened to spot a forlorn-looking figure on the opposite side. The field was out of bounds during wet weather and it wasn't a teacher that stood there. All she could make out was a figure clad from head to toe in a tattered yellow gown. She couldn't see its face, just a gaping black void under a drooping hood.

Cassie found herself mesmerised by the apparition. As she sat clutching her precious script to her chest, shielding it from the downpour, the figure pointed a long bony finger at her.

The sky seemed to shift in fast forward. The shadows of the trees that bordered the school shifted and danced on the grass. As she stared, transfixed, on the figure, the shadows split from the trees and gathered around the figure in yellow. Visions of twin moons and a still black lake flashed into her mind. The shadows now spread from under that tattered yellow robe. Writhing and squirming like tentacles.

Peeeeep!

"Chambers! What are you doing on the field?"

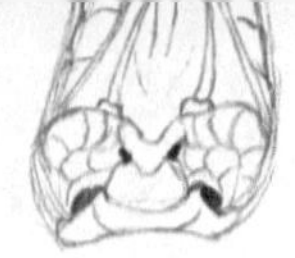

The shrill whistle and the even shriller voice of Mrs Green, the PE teacher, startled Cassie and she looked around. The teacher was coming her way, reaching for the detention slip. When Cassie looked back, the figure had gone.

After a sound rollicking from the headmaster, Cassie headed to class. On the way, Mr Castaigne pulled her aside and handed her the script for Act Two.

***

After suffering through the worst fate known to a student, double maths, Cassie had gone to the gym to serve her detention. As was usual in these situations, Victoria was also there. This was normal… Her demeanour wasn't.

The usually cocksure girl was shaky and pale looking. Her eyes were filled with an emotion that Cassie didn't think she possessed…fear. In front of her, next to the sheet of lines she had been instructed to copy off the board and printed on lurid yellow paper, was the second act of the play.

Cassie waited until Mrs Green had left them alone to attend to some other matter, then retrieved her own copy from her bag. It wasn't long but what was written changed

Cassie's life in an instant. She chuckled to herself as she turned the pages. Her laugh getting more and more manic with every word she read.

Across the cavernous gymnasium, Victoria stared at her in terror. Her hand was scribbling words on the page in front of her without her even knowing. Suddenly, Cassie stopped laughing and fixed her with a look that wouldn't have looked out of place on a vulture.

Tears started to roll down Victoria's face as Cassie reached for her pencil case. Never once taking her eyes off her prey, Cassie unzipped it and took out a yellow highlighter pen. With a savage swish of the pen, she drew a strange symbol on the paper she had been given.

Victoria cried and gibbered as Cassie held up the paper. She gazed at the symbol in abject terror before taking her fountain pen, holding it to her left eye and slamming her face into the desk.

Cassie screamed because that's what people are expected to do in the situation. Victoria's eyeball popped with a sickening *splat* and the pen drove into her brain. She leapt from her seat as Mrs Green came back into the room and pocketed the page that Victoria had been working on.

After she had spoken to the police and her parents had taken her home, Cassie unfolded the blood-spattered

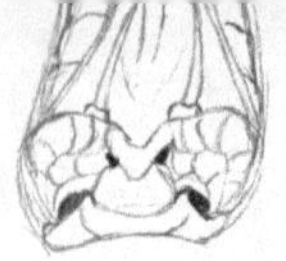

page and smiled. On every line, Victoria had scribbled "Have you seen the yellow sign?"

***

Finally, the big day arrived. Though it wasn't going to Cassie's plan, she had indeed been promoted but to the role of "Camilla," while her sister was playing *her* role as Camilla's sister "Cassilda." *It wasn't right, dammit. It just wasn't.*

She had fumed at John, but he hadn't listened to a single word. He was far too busy preparing to be "The King."

They had finished the first act, the last time "Camilla" made an appearance, and it looked like Cassie's dream of landing *her* role was about to be forever dashed. As she sat and sulked, shooting daggers at her sister, Mr Castaigne walked over and handed John a "prop" that he would need shortly, a box knife.

Castaigne was about to leave when he saw the rage in Cassie's eyes. He handed her a "prop" and said "You know what is required?" with a lopsided smile.

As the lights came back on, the crowd gasped at the ghoulish appearance of Cassilda. It was a full house and they were hanging on every word.

Cassilda crossed to where The King stood amongst the courtiers. Everyone onstage wore a mask. The play insists that everyone wears a mask…everyone.

Cassilda spoke to the King, "My Lord, Hastur. Will thee not remove thy mask as I do?" She gripped the corner of her mask and peeled it off with a disgusting *slurp*. The audience gasped once more as the figure under the pallid mask was revealed to be that of Cassie, her face caked in her dead sister's blood.

The King spoke in reply, "My darling, Cassie. I wear no mask…"

As the courtiers gasped in unison *"No mask! No mask!"*, the king lowered his hood.

John's face was gone. In its place was a gaping maw that seethed with a mass of squirming tentacles.

The crowd screamed as the ghastly form of Hastur unleashed his dreadful plague of madness and death upon all those in attendance. One by one, they murdered each other as Hastur took Cassilda's hand.

Finally, the room burst into flames as the lighting rig exploded. Laughing, the dreadful couple returned to dim Carcosa…

The papers put the tragedy down to a faulty gas pipe. No copy of the script was ever recovered.

BLACK HARE PRESS

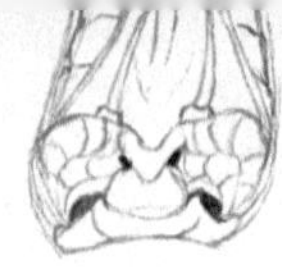

A BRAND NEW ME

by J.W. Garrett

The air clings to my skin, heavy, drops of sweat already dripping down my neck with zero exertion here so far, waiting for my ride. My hair and the trace bits of makeup I wear wilt from the humidity. *Sigh.* Lifting my head, I slit my eyes against the sun, anticipating the grinding screech of the brakes from the school bus as it lumbers from one stop to the next.

Soon…It'll be here soon enough.

To keep my mind busy, positive, and away from thoughts of the upcoming day, I tick off a few of the things I like about here. There aren't many. Beignets equal heaven… Po'boys…The French Quarter…Mardi

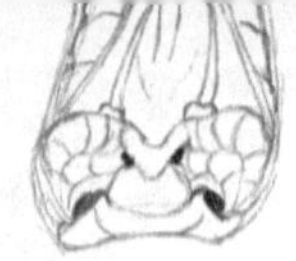

Gras…Definitely not hurricane season. That's pretty much the complete list. What I hate about here makes for a much longer tally.

Some people tell me I'd get along better here if I was more lady-like. Made an effort to fit in. I don't believe them though. All that's pretty much worthless when fists pound your face.

Still waiting, I kick a rock and watch as it arches high, then plunges into the putrid stench of the nearby canal, where all sorts of disgusting things live and breed. The constant malodour used to make me gag. Like everything else, I've gotten used to that too. Fresh air—another useful commodity—bites the dust, in this my sad reality.

I hear the bus approach long before it gets here. So I'm mentally prepared when the vehicle downshifts and rolls to stop just past me. Stepping in and heading to the back, balancing as it lurches forward, I eye my seat from last year, which I forgo.

People watch as I pass, no doubt recollecting scenes from the prior school year, but they don't know what I've become in the months since then. I don't meet their eager gazes; instead my breathing eases and the tension releases from my shoulders. Hers is the next stop…the very next one…

The bus grinds and hisses to another halt, and more students file down the aisle. One particular pain in the ass parks himself in the seat behind me and leans in, warming up, talking smack, before he sees *her* and beats a path farther back.

Sloan greets me like one of her crew, with a handshake, gripping my palm as we move through the motions; then she takes the seat opposite me. "Sara," she says, flashing a side eye to the guy in the back, who knows to stay put or face the wrath of our posse. His gaze slides to mine before anchoring straight ahead. *Smart.*

A smile lifts my lips. That's a first for me on a school bus in this city.

The yellow monstrosity makes its final stop on this leg. *Here we go.* Lines of students file into the high school's hallways, an animated weaving of arms and legs, as greetings and confrontations follow. My leftover feeling of fresh meat from last year still hangs like a weight around my neck. The crowd sums me up but does a double take, seeing Sloan beside me, my upgrade from over the summer. When did school become so much fun?

We pass by a hall I'll never forget. My gaze drifts to the corner, where I remember my face had been smashed against the wall, unable to move as two girls pound their fists into my gut. Another, a guy, watches, daring me to

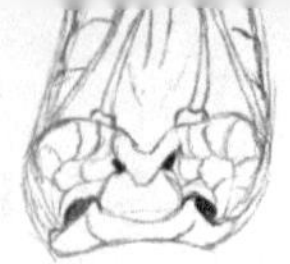

move or scream, which I don't, since I can't drag in a breath, and I'm pinned down tight.

Stan. His cocky smile, seared in my mind, served a purpose over the summer. Funny how your mindset changes when you're not at the bottom of the food chain any longer.

The school day slogs on. Nothing new there. What's different? Word has gotten out that I'm under protection now, and the students who used to get off by giving me a hard time now give me a wide berth when I pass. And as the minutes in the last period of the day dwindle down to the final bell, a tiny victory chant rises inside me. The day is almost done. I made it through.

So far.

Outside I go to Stan's favourite spot—the one where he taunts students as they leave the building, before hauling off the few he chooses for extra attention.

Today he's already there. A sneer lifts his lips as he tracks my progress, his gaze hungry for the conquest.

I don't have to turn around to know two of his buddies follow, flanking me on both sides, wordlessly guiding my path, the point of a blade pressed against my back, encouraging me along.

We're a few feet away from each other when I stop. Stan's eyes cut to mine, and I realise that he already thinks

he's won, that I'll leave, broken and in tears, like last time, if I leave him at all.

There shouldn't have been a last time.

My crew files in behind me, still out of my sight, yet I know the exact moment Stan ID's them.

An array of emotions passes over his face as he processes his tenuous situation, and I enjoy watching each one cruising by. He's surrounded, his back up now wisely cut and run. Sloan and four others from my gang hang back in a circle, ready, but understanding I want this for myself.

I close the distance between us and can't help my smile as my hands touch his face.

His breath draws in, startled by the gesture.

My fingers glide over his eyelids, hovering for a second, enjoying the moment of the punk's stunned stillness underneath my hands.

It's then I move.

I shove my thumbs back hard, through the tissues over Stan's eyes, mashing through the resistance, as he gropes air, until one eyeball bounces free, hanging just outside the socket.

The one good eye looks at me in a terror-filled shock as he screams. A crowd forms, greedy for the promise of ruins in the aftermath. Sliding through the gathered, I blur

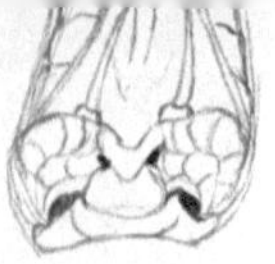

into anonymity, focusing on my crew waiting for me at the edge of the chaotic scene.

I suck in a deep breath and release a long exhale. Maybe today I've fallen off Stan's hit list for good, the same day he's crossed off mine.

Sloan lifts her chin, and I follow.

School, day one, in the books.

# SCHOOL'S IN

Stay away from the girl's bathroom!!!

THE GIRLS' BATHROOM

by Johann van der Walt

Tommy waited until his dad fired off a snore, packed with such gusto that the ceiling vibrated when his dad inhaled, before attempting his escape. If he wanted to open his rusty window undetected, he would have to slide it up in unison with one of his dad's famous roars. Once he successfully unlatched the window and pushed it upwards, he climbed out onto the roof and slid down the gutter. Piece of cake. It wasn't his first time sneaking out, although the previous times had not included a mission of this scale. Johnny and Kip usually didn't need to be asked twice to sneak out, but a little persuasion was in order for this particular run. Mainly due to the fact that they had to

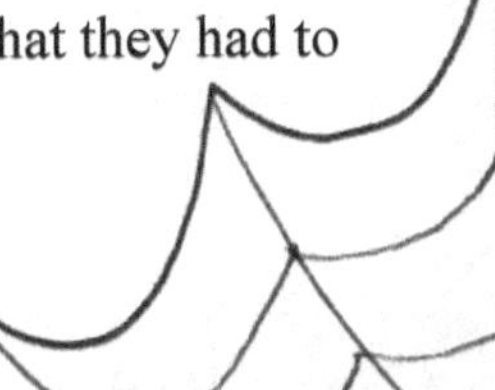

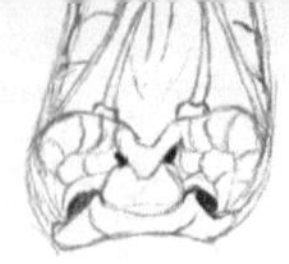

sneak into their school—after midnight.

He made his way to the park in the centre of town unnoticed and waited a few minutes for Kip and Johnny to show up.

"Geez, took you guys long enough," he said as they approached the bench where he crouched like some kind of creature. He pulled his hoody backwards and combed his fringe out of his face.

Kip caught his breath before he spoke, "My mother wouldn't go to sleep. So when she finally passed out, we ran all the way here."

"I was about to chuck a stone through your bedroom window," Johnny said and shouldered Kip playfully.

"Never a dull moment with a neighbour like you."

Tommy had always been jealous of the fact that his two best friends lived right next to each other. Sometimes it made him feel like the odd one out in their group of friends, and although sometimes they fought like cats and dogs, they always remained good friends, from kindergarten right up to their freshman year.

"Are you sure you want to do this?" Kip seemed concerned. It wasn't surprising, as he had always been the guy on edge, the responsible kid who was best described as a real momma's boy.

Tommy sighed. "We have been through this at

school today, and now you want to debate it again?"

Kip bit his lip.

"So you guys are really gonna force me to be the guy to mention the other thing?"

"What other thing?" Tommy frowned. A flicker of irritation reflected in his eyes.

"Martin and Jessie's sudden disappearance?"

Johnny rolled his eyes dramatically—the actor among them.

"Semantics. Surely you don't believe that story?"

Kip didn't seem convinced. "I mean I guess…"

"Why come along then?" Johnny asked.

"I guess I didn't think I'd be this freaked out, but look at how dark it is out. You guys can't tell me you are not at least a little afraid? Think of what the school will look like at night? What about that thing in the bathroom?"

"The undead cheerleader?" Johnny said, about to break out in laughter.

"That's just garbage seniors tell freshmen to scare them," Tommy intervened. "Come on, let's go."

"How do you explain their disappearance then?"

Tommy and Johnny exchanged glances.

"Anything could have happened."

"Why do their friends say they went to school at

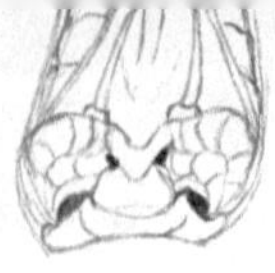

night and…"

Tommy wiggled his nose, a clear sign that he was getting even more agitated.

"That they went into the girls' bathroom on the second floor and was never seen again? You expect us to believe that?"

"What else then?" Kip's eyes were wide open. He was a gullible guy.

News of the two boys' disappearance spread like wildfire, and some grownups around town, as well as a lot of pupils from their school, couldn't stop talking about it. People connected their disappearance, as well as a few other kids throughout the years, to a tragic event that had happened at school eight years ago. A girl slashed her wrists in the upper girls' bathroom after being cut from the cheerleading squad.

Ever since her death, it was believed that she haunted the school. Whenever kids went missing, her story was brought up again and people freaked themselves out.

Over the years, a few people have actually tried to find her but no one had ever been able to provide concrete evidence of her existence.

What mattered most in a digital age such as this was proof, and nobody was able to provide any. It was rather alarming though (to Kip at least) that the janitor also

refused to be on the school premises after dark. He had talked about the dead girl to some kids and teachers, being the one who had found her, but as usual nobody had believed him. When he started complaining about her having come back from the dead, people thought that he had finally lost his mind.

"Your mother should let you watch less movies and partake in the real world a little more, Kip," Johnny said and smiled. "Honestly, we are too old to believe in such things."

"There is no undead cheerleader in the girls' bathroom, Kip. If Martin and Jessie had been murdered, so to speak, it was probably by a very sick and *human* individual. If you want to see a monster, just look at your neighbour."

Johnny and Kip stared at each other.

"Well I don't mean it literally you guys," Tommy said and stepped away from the bench.

"We have no choice, we have to change our scores. If we fail math, we stand a good chance to repeat this year; it's not like my other grades can make up for it." Tommy supressed a yawn while he spoke. "Why does our school have these stupid random tests that make up the biggest percentage of your grade anyway?"

"It's a new system to have kids participate more in

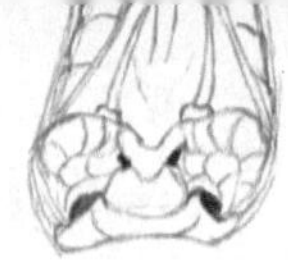

class and also to keep them up to date."

An uncomfortable silence surrounded them briefly and the only thing that they could hear was the sound of crickets. Kip swallowed hard. He just had to be the one to make things even more awkward.

Tommy finally spoke up and broke the silence, "Well, I have not been *updated* in a while."

"We kind of have to do this," Johnny added reluctantly, "even if I don't want to either."

"Did Kip get you all scared and gooey as well? Hey, if you guys are okay with a below-average grade, then go home. My parents will skin me alive if I let this happen."

"I did okay on the test," Kip said. Tommy and Johnny stared at him with blank faces, and he felt silly for making things awkward, yet again.

"Of course you did, psycho. Well, we gotta do this," Tommy said and tested his flashlight. He replaced the batteries that afternoon already. If it wasn't an emergency, he would have never wanted to enter school after dark. And he would be caught dead in that place without a light, although he would never admit to the others that he was, undead cheerleader or not, a little scared himself.

"So? Are you coming along or what?"

Kip sighed. "Oh what the hell, I didn't get dressed back into regular clothes after midnight for nothing.

Besides, I would rather die than let the two of you have an adventure without me."

They pulled their hoodies over their heads and made their way to the high school.

Once there, they climbed over the fence and walked across the football field. Tommy suddenly stopped midway. The others turned towards him.

"What is wrong?" Johnny asked, looking confused.

Tommy switched his flashlight off before he spoke.

"Do you guys feel that?"

They glanced at each other briefly. The dim light from the moon barely illuminated their creeped out faces.

"As if we are being watched?"

Tommy nodded. "For now I will keep the light off."

Kip started to panic. "You guys are freaking me out."

"You don't feel it?" Johnny asked.

A brief silence. Kip sighed.

"I do. Guys, something is definitely watching us alright. Maybe…"

"Don't you dare say it's the undead cheerleader," Johnny interrupted.

"I left the window open in Ms Bunton's class," Tommy said. "Let's get this done quickly and get the hell out of here."

They approached the building quietly and walked to

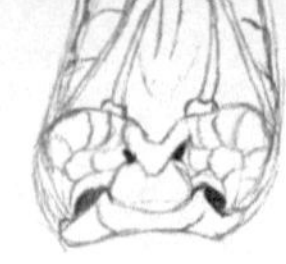

the open window.

Tommy climbed through first. He could barely see his own hands in the dark. Johnny followed after him.

"Guys, I can't do this," Kip said, breathing heavily. "Something is here; I can feel it."

"Then wait here," Tommy said annoyed, and then to Johnny, "You ready to go?"

Johnny nodded. They passed through the classroom and entered the hallway carefully.

Tommy switched the flashlight on. The beam cut through the thick darkness.

Being at school during the day was already uncomfortable enough, but to be there at night was borderline crazy. Both of them felt something different in the air but they didn't want talk about it.

It didn't take long before they reached Mr Norman's math class. Tommy cringed before opening the door. As if he didn't hate math enough now he was confronted by it during his personal time as well.

"There," he said and aimed the beam of light at the file cabinet behind Mr Norman's desk. "Let's be reasonable and give ourselves Bs."

Johnny nodded.

"Yes, and then we make like the wind."

"Bet your ass, this place is creepy as hell."

When Tommy found their files, he placed them on the desk. He was about to amend their test scores when Kip yelled from down the hallway. *Was he inside the school?*

"Guys? Where are you?"

Tommy felt his heart climb up his throat.

Johnny broke out in a sweat.

"What the hell?"

They stared at each other wide-eyed. *Was it real?*

"Guys?" Kip called again. "Where are you?"

"What is he doing?" Johnny whispered.

"Go check it out. I'll finish up here and put them back. He is making too much noise.

And don't go wandering off," he whispered.

Johnny carefully exited the classroom and disappeared into the darkness.

Tommy changed their scores and took a moment to observe his work. He even aced Mr Norman's handwriting. "Excellent," he thought aloud.

He entered the hallway but found it empty.

"Johnny?" he whispered.

No answer.

"Johnny," he called out a bit louder.

"Here," Johnny answered at the other side of the hallway, somewhere behind a thick curtain of darkness.

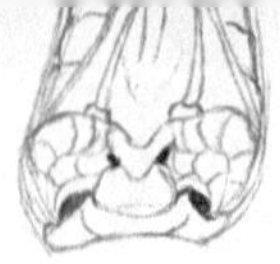

Tommy aimed the flashlight beam at Johnny.

"What are you doing down there?"

"What?" Johnny put one hand against his forehead to direct the light from his eyes.

"Why are you there?"

"Kip went up the stairs. Come on. Let's be quick, I want to get the hell out of here."

Suddenly the light started flickering. Tommy slapped the flashlight to no avail. "Damn it."

It went dead.

He made his way down the hallway slowly with his arms stretched out ahead of him, hoping he doesn't grab hold of something ghastly.

"Johnny?" he whispered just below his normal voice tone.

The only light, too dim to be of any real use, was the *exit* sign above the doors on the other side of the staircase down the hall.

"Guys," Kip yelled. His voice came from far away. Upstairs to be exact.

What is he doing on the second storey? Tommy thought and warily continued towards the staircase.

"Johnny, cut the shit. I fixed our scores. Tell Kip to get his ass down here."

"Kip?" Johnny called, already halfway up the stairs.

"Where are you?"

"Here," Kip answered. "Come check this out."

Tommy stopped at the foot of the staircase. The dim red light shined onto the first four steps only. He looked up at the thick darkness hovering a few inches in front of him, contemplating Johnny's present position.

"Johnny?"

A long silence followed. Tommy could hear his heartbeat vibrate in his eardrums.

"Tommy," Johnny answered finally, his voice far away.

A rush of fear wash over Tommy. He felt a sudden discomfort which he couldn't explain. He wanted to call out again, but simply was too scared. Looking down the hallway at the little bit of moonlight seeping onto the floor from Ms Bunton's classroom made him confused. Her classroom seemed farther away than usual.

How long was this hall exactly?

He thought about running back to that classroom and jumping out the window but he couldn't leave his friends behind.

"Tommy where are you?" Kip yelled, his muffled voice coming from very far away. "Come see this."

"I'm coming," Johnny called out. His voice a bit closer. His footsteps echoed down the stairwell. "Tommy,

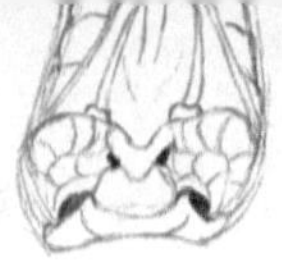

where are you?"

"I'm here," Tommy answered reluctantly.

He made his way up the stairs, breathing heavily. His feet felt like lead. The dark was so thick, he struggled to breathe properly.

Slowly, with palms anchored against the walls, he made his way to the second storey.

The light from the girls' bathroom a few feet down the hall was switched on and a little light rolled out into the hallway from underneath the door. Tommy inhaled and his lungs burned.

It was all just an elaborate hoax, he tried to assured himself, slowly putting one foot in front of the other.

"Come check this out," Kip yelled. His voice coming from inside the bathroom.

"You have to see this, Tommy." Johnny fired quickly after. Both voices coming from inside the bathroom.

Tommy didn't move. He was sceptical as to what was going on. The cynical member of their group.

Then Johnny opened the door and light gushed out into the hallway.

"Dude you won't believe this, come check it out," he said and disappeared back into the bathroom.

Tommy walked up to the bathroom, slowly. Having seen Johnny, without him looking distressed, soothed

Tommy to the extent that he could proceed somewhat comfortably. Kip and Johnny laughed aloud.

What was it? Did they both play a prank on him?

Tommy stuck his hand out and touched the handle. Without further hesitation, he shoved the door open and stepped inside.

No sign of his friends anywhere. He took another step and the door slammed shut behind him.

Then the lights went off.

"Guys, what the hell?"

No answer. He grabbed the door and tried to pry it open but it was locked.

"What is going on?" he cried. Everything was pitch black.

Footsteps started up behind him, slow at first, but faster as they closed in on him.

He felt two cold hands grab his neck and yank him away from the door.

"Don't you know you are not supposed to enter the girls' bathroom, Tommy?" a girl's voice whispered in his ear—her breath ice cold and rancid.

Her hands tightened around his neck. He shrieked.

One swift movement and his neck snapped like a twig.

***

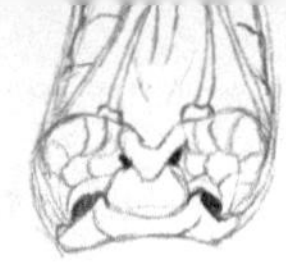

Johnny followed Kip's voice back to Ms Bunton's classroom. Kip leaned in through the open window.

"What's wrong?" Johnny asked.

"Dude," he said desperately. His breath was short. "We need to get out of here. Where is Tommy?"

Johnny climbed out. "He is changing our scores. Why, what is going on?"

They stepped back a few feet and Kip pointed towards the windows of the girls' bathroom on the second floor. The lights were switched on.

"Look there, we need to get Tommy out of the building now. There is somebody there."

Peeking at them from the window upstairs was a girl. Something about her seemed wrong though. When they tried to head back to the open window to call for Tommy, their bodies suddenly froze up. She stared at them with green glowing eyes, penetrating them with fear, and an insidious grin with rotten yellow teeth reflected against the glass. She had rendered them helpless with shock.

The lights went off and they heard Tommy's gut-wrenching scream followed by loud crack that echoed through the schoolyard.

When the two boys gained their strength, they got up and ran away.

BAD SEEDS

by Patrick Winters

Bad seeds lead to bad crops. Her father used to say that to her, in between the beatings and working the fields. *And there isn't any good in a bad crop.*

Miss Anna Baker had been made to take that thinking to heart in her twenty-nine years. And now, looking at the class before her, she believed her father to be absolutely right.

All the *shouting*. All the *complaining*. The *entitlement*. The smug, know-it-all *attitudes*.

But the poison she would put in tomorrow's milk would fix that. Fix it for good.

Her kindergarten class would not be another bad crop.

 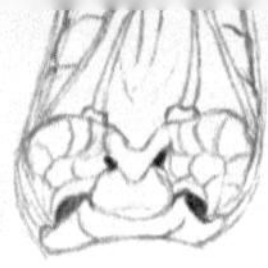

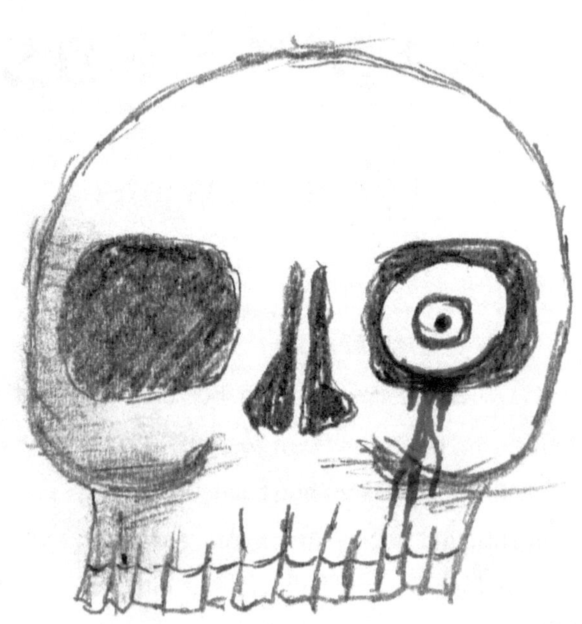

JOSHUA'S LAMENT

by Stephen Herczeg

Joshua stared as the group of senior girls tormented the skinny ninth grader. He'd seen her around. Her name was Shannon. A nice name that should belong to someone with a solid start in life and a bright future. Sadly, Shannon came from the wrong side of town. Her school uniform was a hand-me-down. Her shoes old and scuffed. Her hair long and matted from lack of care.

Shannon reminded him of his own journey through high school. He shared her station in life. He also shared her persecution. That's how it had been for him. Always the object of intimidation. Always at the wrong end of a beating. Not anymore. He'd ended it on his own terms.

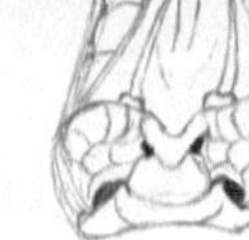

Now he only wished to help others like him.

Joshua's heart went out to Shannon as she bore the brunt of the girls' torment. He wanted to help, but his attention lay on the leader of the bullies: *Eve.*

Eve was the typical alpha girl who presided over all before her in the tiny goldfish bowl of life that was high school. Her family was rich. She wore the best clothes, the best shoes, always had the latest phone. She was pretty, which immediately put her above the average student, just through the power of authority drawn from attractiveness. She was cruel. Anybody that crossed her. Anybody that didn't come up to her standards. Anybody that wasn't her became the object of her wrath, rained down like a hail of insults.

Joshua had watched Eve's power grow over the years. She had started out with just words. Insults and barbs hurled at her victims, but of late, there was a creeping nastiness in Eve's intent. Usually, Eve would act out her own version of nastiness by herself, but now she brought others with her. Two of the bigger girls from the senior year flanked her. Held back in readiness, either for protection or worse.

Joshua wasn't sure of their purpose, and more he didn't care. What he did care about was justice. The girls subjected to the vicious verbal assaults from Eve had done

nothing wrong. They were just in the wrong place at the wrong time. Usually there was no violence, just a verbal dressing down with an intense shrillness to Eve's voice.

She was unhinged, Joshua was certain of that.

And then there was Shannon. Shannon was actually pretty. She didn't display it. Her tired old clothes, and lack of makeup, hid the fact. She shuffled around school, her head held down, to avoid any risk of drawing attention to herself.

On this fateful day, they had accidentally crossed paths. A simple coincidence as both turned a corner. Shannon had tried in vain to steer out of Eve's path, but the other hadn't even noticed her until they collided, and all hell broke loose.

Eve had unleashed such a torrent of abuse at Shannon that even Joshua had been surprised. The flood of words bordered on the deranged, a maddened outpouring from a psychotic mind. The other two girls even drew back at the unbridled vehemence that discharged from Eve's mouth. Once finished, Eve had indicated that it was their turn. They didn't hold back.

Shannon was pummelled with a rain of blows to dull what was on show of her pretty face. In the end, they left her, bruised and bloodied.

Joshua just looked from afar. Shocked at what he had

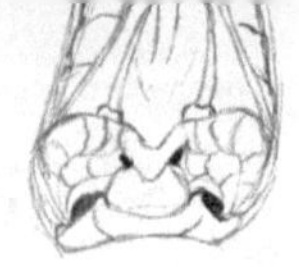

witnessed but knowing in his soul what had to happen next.

He followed Eve around the school for hours, waiting until she was alone and vulnerable. He wanted unfettered access to the despicable girl.

It was when she broke away from her two bodyguards and headed for the bathroom that he knew his time had come.

Joshua followed, quietly, unseen.

He waited until she was washing her hands and primping and preening before the mirror.

Then he sprung his trap.

He quietly stepped up behind his despised target, readied himself to spare the world of one more tormentor. Images of the boys that had assailed him flashed across his mind. He smiled at the realisation that the revenge that had always eluded him was about to come true.

He raised the long chef's knife he held in his right hand and slammed it down through Eve's head and neck. All the movies he'd seen. All the horror magazines he'd read held explicit images of what to expect. Sliced flesh. Exposed brains. Blood exploding forth like a torrent.

In reality. Nothing.

Eve shivered as if a chill had run through her. She shrugged and left.

Joshua simply stared at his reflection.

He dropped the knife; it dissipated and was gone.

Anger welled on his face. He balled a fist and punched at his reflection, hoping to shatter the glass. His hand simply passed through and disappeared into the wall.

He dragged it out again and stared at his open hands. The same hands that had ended his own life. His wrists no longer showed the deep gouges or the streams of blood caused by his final act, but the scars still remained deep within him.

His eyes lifted to stare at his sorrowful face. He had hoped to escape and help those in his position. The innocent. The tormented. The oppressed. The bullied. It was only now that he realised how helpless he had become.

As in life, so in death.

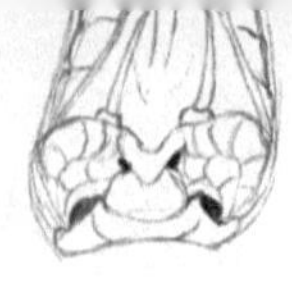

BLACK HARE PRESS

SCHOOL GIRL CRUSH

by Trisha McKee

Amber strolled through the hallways, not bothering to stop at her locker to get her books. The next class was History and that meant she sat in the front row, locking eyes with Mr Jacobs the entire time.

"Okay, everyone," Jacobs called out as the students sat in their assigned seats. "Papers due today."

As he reached Amber, his hand weakly hanging in the air, she leaned back and stretched out her bare legs. "Noooo," she purred. "I got home really late last night." She giggled as the red crawled up his neck to his face. "I'll turn it in on Monday."

As expected, Jacobs asked her to stay after class. But

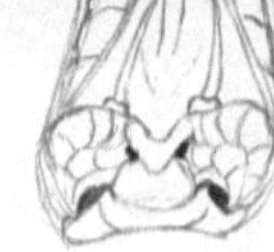

instead of pulling her into his possessive embrace, he hissed, "You have to stop this!"

Amber drew back with a scowl. "Excuse me? Ron, you want this to stop? You weren't singing that tune last night."

"No," he sighed, his tone softer. "You know I don't mean that. But if we don't want attention called to this, you cannot be acting like that in class. You can't expect special treatment."

Leaning in so that her lips were almost touching his, Amber breathed, "Oh, but I do. I expect the most special treatment."

She turned, her fiery red hair brushing against his face before she strolled out of the classroom. She paused in the hallway, tilting her head to regard Megan, a quiet blonde with a plain face standing right outside the door.

Megan stared back with no expression, and then she sidled past Amber into the classroom. Hanging back, Amber tried to hear the conversation, but Megan spoke softly, and only Ron's plaintive "No, I'm sorry. It's over."

"It's over." That could mean a number of things. It could mean the deadline for a paper. It could mean signing up for track. Or it could mean that Megan had something going with the teacher too, and he ended it.

That last thought sent her to the football field where

her ex, Brice, was practising. He was the quarterback, destined for a full scholarship to any college he chose, and bound to succeed despite his lack of intelligence. When he saw her in the bleachers, he smiled, losing focus and getting tackled, hitting the ground hard.

She had broken his heart, humiliated him in front of their friends, but he could not resist her. And Amber wanted to prove that no man would ever get the best of her. She destroyed hearts; she did not lose hers.

And that night, as Brice crawled out her window, his eyes already starry, she thought she saw a shadow move along the edge of the yard, but she told herself it was the wind blowing the branches around.

The next morning, Amber stumbled through the hallways, cringing when she saw Ron waiting by her locker.

"Wanted to talk about your late paper," he said loudly, and then he leaned forward, his dark hair falling into his eyes. "Where were you last night? I tried calling and texting."

"Busy."

He reached out and grabbed her arm in a vice-like grip, and she had to work to keep the shock and pain out of her face. She'd be damned if she showed a man he'd hurt her. "Busy, huh?" he spat out, his mouth close to her

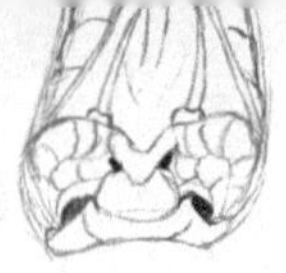

ear. "I heard you left here with Brice."

"What business is it of yours? I saw Megan in your classroom."

For a brief moment, panic flooded his face, but then he straightened. "I'm a teacher, Miss Barnes. Of course there are going to be students meeting with me. Grow up."

By using her last name, he was sending a message. She tossed her hair over a shoulder and smiled. "Anything else…Mr Jacobs? I really have to get to class. Mr Miller is offering me extra credit. And I'm such a dummy when it comes to chemistry… I need all the help I can get." She brushed past Ron, making sure her hips swung as she walked away.

After lunch, the news came. Brice had never made it home. He was missing. They pulled Amber into the office where police were waiting to ask her questions. Word travelled fast, so they knew she had left school property with him. She was honest and told them about their evening. He had been seen leaving her yard, and someone else had seen him walking into town.

And when his body was found later that day, Amber remembered the shadow moving outside her window. She tried to shake that nagging suspicion. That fear that pinched up her spine.

After class, Ron motioned for Amber to stay in her

seat. He looked sombre, his lips pressed together, his fingers squeezing her shoulder as he sat next to her once the class had emptied out.

"I heard. Amber, how are you doing?"

His deep voice lulled her into a sense of safety. He was a kind man, passionate, and the best kisser she had ever experienced. He couldn't kill.

"I'm okay. A little in shock. A lot, actually. And I hear the whispers. I was the last to see him."

Ron got up and knelt in front of her, pulling her to him. "No. You weren't. There were a few witnesses that saw him walking away from your house alone." He pulled back and traced her lips with his finger, their eyes locking…

There was a slight noise, a clearing of a throat, and the couple broke apart to see the principal Mr Styller glaring at them. "Ms Barnes, could you leave us? Stick around though. I might have some questions for you."

Amber escaped into the hallway, her heart pounding, the angry tone of Mr Styller following her. Her face was flushed, and for a moment, she turned one way and then the other, her mind racing.

"What's going on?"

She spun around and faced Megan, her fuzzy blonde hair framing that long, drawn face. "Oh, I bet you know!"

"What?"

"Did you go running to Mr Styller because Ron didn't want you anymore?" Amber spat out, her upper body arched forward.

Megan's eyes grew wide, and she backed up a step. "What? No! I—no."

"You liar!"

"I didn't!" Her face was red, and to Amber's horror, she started to cry. "I don't want Mr Jacobs to get in trouble. I wouldn't do that to him. I love him."

Amber glared at her, unwilling to feel for this plain girl that somehow posed as a competitor for Ron's affections. "He doesn't love you."

"I wouldn't be too sure of that." The fierceness that pushed the words out of her mouth stunned Amber, but she straightened and flipped her hair.

Mr Styller came out of the room and walked past them, his eyes straight ahead, his steps heavy, and he did not see them. Megan gave her one last withering glance before scurrying away, and before she could gather her composure, Ron was at her side, his grip on her arm tight. She had to bite her lip to keep from crying out.

"What did you say to him?"

"What? Nothing!"

"This is my career we are talking about!"

She stared at him, at a loss for words. Finally, she managed, "I don't want to get in trouble either! Maybe it was Megan."

He sneered, twisting her arm slightly. "Megan? She would never do anything to hurt me. Look, I'm not going to let a little tramp take everything from me! Keep your mouth shut! Because now they're going to do an investigation on me. I might be let go. Do you understand?"

Amber yanked her arm out of his hold. "If you grab me like that again, I'll scream so loud, they won't even bother with an investigation. Do you understand me?"

Amber managed to walk calmly away, but she escaped to the girls' locker room as soon as she was able. That was where her friends met to smoke and drink and relax unseen by any teachers. No one bothered them here.

Joyce and Penny took one look at her and merely handed her the flask.

Penny brushed back a strand of perfectly styled brunette hair and asked, "You okay?"

"No."

"It's crazy. I mean Brice. Who would hurt him? I think it was just a crazy person out there, and if that's true, we're all in danger."

And right on cue, the lights flickered a few times

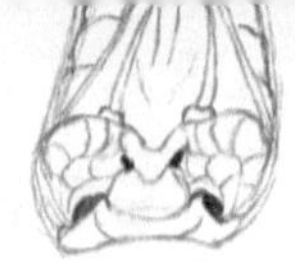

before shutting off completely. Outside of the locker room, they heard screams, and instinctively, they huddled together, yelping in surprise.

"Wait," Joyce breathed. "Should we hide? Can we fit in the lockers?"

Before they figure out a plan, Megan burst into the room, wild-eyed and sobbing. "Mr Styller was…he had a knife in him—murdered—"

"What?" Amber cried out before Penny covered her mouth.

"Ssssh. We need to get out of here."

"I tried," Megan informed them. "The doors are locked. We're locked in here."

"Oh, I think it was Mr Jacobs." It was a quiet statement, emphasised by the trembling in Amber's voice. "He and Mr Styller were fighting. I mean, he was about to lose his job because Mr Styller…"

Megan nodded. "I think I saw him leaving the office. I—"

Ron ran into the room, the girls screaming at the sight of him. He stared back, his eyes adjusting to the darkened room. "Amber! Amber, are you okay?"

She jumped up and let the other girls pull her back, still screaming. "Get away. We have a gun." It was an idle threat. He knew she didn't have a gun. But she was

desperate.

"Amber, no! No, it wasn't me. I...I thought maybe you—don't look at me like that."

Amber looked around the room, searching for something, anything that could be used as a weapon. But there was nothing. She opened a locker and saw only dirty gym clothes. "You need to leave. The cops will be here any minute. We called. You can still escape."

He cursed, advancing slowly, the slight sunlight from the high, narrow window in the corner highlighting his lined face. She wondered how she had ever found him attractive. He was cheesy with the gold chain and over-styled hair.

"Amber, this is me. I wouldn't hurt you. I didn't hurt him. Or Brice. No."

"You did! You saw Brice leaving my house."

"No! I was nowhere near your house. Okay, maybe I drove by to see if he was there, but it wasn't me! I...I'm falling in love with you. I wouldn't hurt you!"

At that, Megan let out a high-pitched scream and dove forward, bringing out a knife from the front of her pants. She plunged it into his chest over and over, and his mouth opened in a silent scream before he fell over.

As she pulled the knife out of his chest for the last time, she jumped up and turned to the girls who were now huddled in the corner. "Dammit! Why you? Huh? You're such a slut! You're like so overdone with the makeup and ridiculous hair. I mean, why is it that full? Extensions?"

Penny pushed the girls to the side. "Run!"

They made it to the hallway, almost tripping over the body of a student. "Just run!" Amber screamed, feeling the breeze of the door swinging open.

"Get back here!" Megan screamed, close behind the girls as they ran and turned down another hallway. "I was in love with him, and you had to ruin that! You even had a boyfriend! Stupid Brice just followed you everywhere. So yeah, I made sure he paid the price."

Joyce was in track, the star runner, so she ran ahead and tried the doors to classrooms. At one door, she peered in and then pounded on the door. "Ms Patton, let us in! Please!" She cursed and yelled, "You were my favourite teacher, you bitch!"

Finally, the last door at the end of the dead-end hall opened, and Joyce ran in, peeking out and screaming for them to hurry. She jumped in place, inching the door closed. Amber jumped forward, tripping into the room just as Megan grabbed Penny by the hair and yanked her back.

Joyce shut the door and locked it as Amber screamed out, "No! We have to get Penny!"

Joyce turned and shook her. "Get her? Megan is killing everyone. We have to save ourselves. Help me pile the desks against the door. Now, Amber!"

"Hey, come out here and save your friend!" Megan screamed, and Amber made the mistake of looking at the window of the door to see her friend with a knife against her throat.

"Please," Amber cried. "We can't leave her out there."

"We have no other choice." Joyce pulled the blind down on the window and then raced to the other side of the room. She grabbed a chair and busted out a window. "Amber, come on!"

Amber was frozen to the spot, hearing the screams of her friend and then suddenly silence. And she knew she had to save herself. Penny was gone, and it would not be long before Megan figured out their plan. She ran to where Joyce had already crawled out and followed suit, her arm scraping on broken glass.

They were immediately surrounded by police, and Joyce took charge, telling them what had happened. Amber was unable to speak, even as they ushered her into the ambulance to tend to her cuts. She heard them mention shock and stitches, she heard the police shout orders, trying to save other students from the hell going on inside.

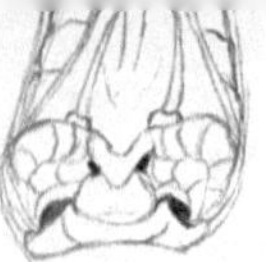

"We're taking you to the hospital," one guy informed her, but she could only stare up, unable to respond. She felt cold and empty, shivering as she tried to block out the images of all she had just experienced.

"Wait! I want to go with her. We survived this together."

Amber was flat on her back, images and sounds mixing together and not making much sense. But then she recognised the voice and struggled to sit up just as they shut the doors. And there, with a grin on her face, was Megan.

CYBEROACH

by Sabetha Danes

"You're going to love it here," Sharon told John as she drove him to his first day as a senior at Pearl Valley High. "They are rated one of the best schools in the state. Every room is equipped with touch screen desks, and state-of-the-art classrooms. I've already spoken with the principal, and she is thrilled to meet you."

John doubted he would love it anywhere other than back at his old school, where his friends and girlfriend were starting the year without him. It was bullshit that they had to move right before his last year in high school.

Who makes their kid start over right before they're done?!

"Yeah, whatever. It'll be fine." He tried not to roll his eyes.

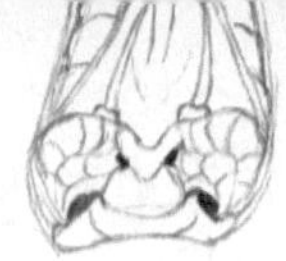

The small campus looked more like a prison than a school as they entered the gates. When his mom parked the car, he realised she was planning to walk him into the building.

"I've got this you know, I'm seventeen not seven. There is no reason for you to come in."

"Are you sure? I can chat with the office ladies and help you get your schedule. I'm still your mom."

"That'd make a great first impression, 'look John's mom still helps him get to class'."

"John, I doubt anyone would even notice. But all right, you can go alone. I'll be here to pick you up after school."

"Thanks, see you then."

He left the car and joined the sea of students entering the front entrance of the only building on the campus.

Where did they hold sports games and athletic classes?

The metal detectors that greeted him were a brilliant touch to the learning experience the website promised.

***

First period was Homeroom. As he entered the class, he noticed that all the students had their eyes glued to their desks.

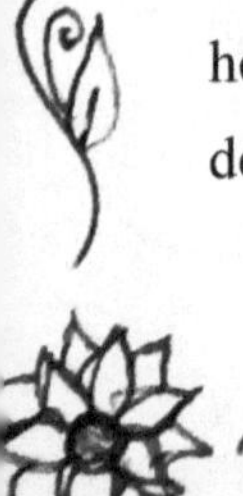

It's 8 am, what could be so engulfing on those touch screens already? There is no way they are letting us use social media...

Once he found an empty seat, he realised the morning announcements were interactive. So he put on the provided headphones and scrolled through the "welcome to the new year" speech that didn't seem to change despite being on a different coast. After the speech, the screen allowed him to fill out his new student paperwork, set up a log in for the desks, and even took his photo for his ID. It amazed him at the advanced technology for it just being a high school.

Look at Pearl Valley living in 2040 while we're stuck in 2020.

After loading the school's app to his phone, he looked around to see what the other students were doing. Each of them seemed to type away at the screen. The eerie silence of the room was making him uncomfortable.

Why are they so quiet?

At his old school, Homeroom was his loudest class, with everyone using it as a socialisation hour.

He decided to interrupt the guy at the desk next to him. Maybe he was missing the next steps for this period.

"Hey."

The guy was entranced by his own screen and didn't

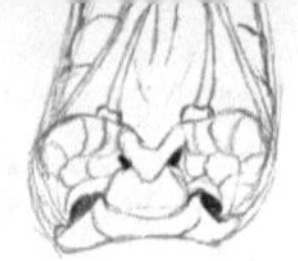

so much as flinch when John spoke. No one seemed to have noticed that he said something out loud.

Strange.

He tapped his shoulder while saying "hey" again, and finally the guy glanced up at him.

"Are we supposed to be doing assignments? I'm new here, I didn't have these touch screens at my old school."

"Oh. Yeah, during Homeroom you're allowed to play the games. Exit out of the announcements and you'll see it on the home screen. The school keeps a running scoreboard, you're going to have a heck of a time catching up."

"Awesome, I'm John by the way." As he said it, he watched the guy change his focus back to the screen and ignore the fact that he had spoken again.

Awesome. This is going to be a marvellous year.

John opened the game app to discover it was brain teasers. He couldn't help but get sucked into beating each level. It was more addictive than Candy Crush, which he was already at level 432, the highest in his friends' group. When the bell finally rang to go to his first class, he barely realised an hour had gone by. He felt drained and uneasy but couldn't explain the feelings.

The halls were as silent as the class had been. It was strange to walk through crowds of teenagers but see no

rough housing or shouting taking place.

This place really is a prison.

It reminded him of the zombie show his mom was obsessed with. Everyone meandering to their destination with indifferent expressions on their faces.

Once he got to his second period, he realised that no teacher would be the norm for his classes; he hadn't noticed that there weren't any teachers listed on his class schedule when he first glanced at it. But it was becoming apparent that the screens did all the teaching. With the desk-provided headphones, he was able to complete his Algebra 2 assignments within the first thirty minutes of class.

After he closed out of the browser, a notification reminded him he was only at level 30, last place for the school scoreboard. He needed to catch up, so it wasn't painfully obvious that he was the new kid. He continued to work through the brain teaser levels with the rest of his class while he waited for the bell.

Why were they even changing rooms if they didn't have teachers?

***

By 3 pm, John was moving at the same pace as his

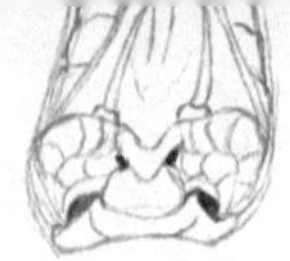

classmates. He couldn't believe how tired he was from barely any work. Most of his classes only had him accept the syllabus and take an assessment test to see where his knowledge base was on the subject at hand. But he felt like he was about to pass out, as if he'd just played a full baseball game with an overtime inning.

He got in his mom's car, told her of his strange day, and how he felt. She assured him it was probably just the stress of an unfamiliar environment. The week would get better. With it being the first day of school, it was normal for everyone to be sluggish.

But over the next few months, it didn't get better. With each passing week, John felt less like himself and more like a drone. He ate less at meals and slept most of his weekends away. His parents tried to bribe him with his favourite foods and activities, but nothing worked. The principal had already assured them twice that with their rigorous AP course work, most students felt drained, and the extra sleep would help their minds process what they learned in class.

By Thanksgiving, John's dad took the matter into his own hands. He contacted a friend back in LA that worked as a part-time private investigator after retiring from the police force.

Charlie answered on the first ring, "Hey, how's the

East Coast treating you guys?"

"It's going good. I don't think we were ready for all this snow." Sean hesitated. "But the reason I'm calling is I've got a favour to ask."

"No kidding, I'm not a fan of snow either. What can I do for you?"

"Is it possible for you to do some checking into John's high school? Something strange is going on up there, we're just not sure what."

"Sure, I can handle that. What kind of strange do you mean? Like criminal strange or alien strange?" Charlie laughed, but caught himself and cleared his throat.

"I guess alien strange?" *It's now or never,* Sean thought as he readied himself to elaborate. "I went to pick up John the other day, and it was something straight out of a zombie movie. The kids were barely shuffling along. It was the creepiest thing I've ever seen."

"After talking to him about it, it seems like the entire school is silent and they use new age touch screen desks for all class work. He said the kids are like a bunch of drones and that he hasn't made a single friend yet. I'm not sure where to even start with it, so I figured I'd ask you first."

"I'll see what I can find out. I've never heard of a high school using touch screen desks before; this damn

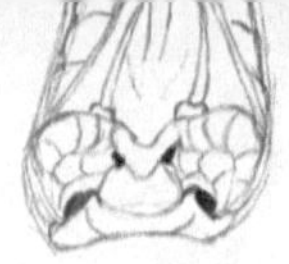

technology will be the death of us all."

"I know what you mean, could be nothing, but I appreciate you looking into it."

***

A week later, Sean sat in his home office finishing up emails from work. Every time he thought he was finished, an urgent one would ping in. This nightly process left him glued to his computer well into the evening. His cell phone rang, startling him out of a deep focus. He saw Charlie's name flash across the screen as he picked it up.

It's about time.

"Hello."

"Hey, I did some digging, and I agree something funny is going on at that school. Did you know they employ zero teachers? They operate all of their classes on the touch screens. To graduate, in the fine print of the graduation plan paperwork, it says each student has to be at least level 800. What the heck is that? Has John mentioned levelling to you guys?"

"Yeah, he said that after he finishes his class work, he gets to play games until the bell rings. He says it helps pass the time and that he is currently in last place on the

school scoreboard."

"That's something else. In my day, they punished us for playing games during class. What kind of school did you get him in?"

"Yeah, I was too, I guess though, it seems to keep the kids busy. John says he hasn't seen a fight break out yet. They were daily occurrences at his last high school."

"You don't say. Huh. Well, honestly, I think you should go check it out. Have you spoken to the principal? That seems to be the only person employed at the campus."

"Yeah, we've talked to her on the phone a few times; she assured us that their curriculum is the best in the state and will help him get into his top pick for college."

"The whole thing is strange if you ask me; something isn't right at that school. Go poke around, let me know what you find out."

"All right, Sharon and I will do it tomorrow, thanks for looking into this for us."

***

When Sean and Sharon drop John off at school the next day, they stayed to investigate the campus for themselves. The silence of the halls gave them chills as

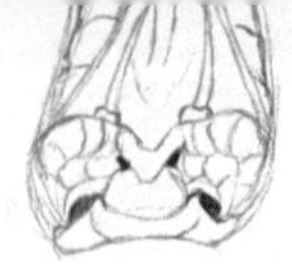

they looked in on classrooms and attempted to find an adult. When the first period bell rang, the walking zombies making their way to the next period overran them.

The longer they stayed in the school, the more disturbed they became at the behaviour of the teens. While they searched the vacant offices, they discovered a door labelled "Employees Only."

After a quick back and forth of the legality on entering the room, they decided it was worth the risk. Sharon lightly opened the door, trying her best not to make any noise. Once inside the room, she attempted to scream or flee, but she remained frozen in place. Sean realised too late that she had stopped and stumbled into her. Once his eyes adjusted to the dim lighting in the room, he realised something was terribly wrong at the school.

They stared in horror at a human-sized cockroach lounging in a chair behind an oak desk. The wall next to the desk looked like something out of an IT hub, with panels of motherboards attached to the wall and cables running from all of them to one central desktop tower sitting on the desk. The desktop had a clear IV cord flowing from it into the cockroach.

Inside the tube, a glistening liquid moved into the

96

roach. It seemed to intoxicate the bug as it hadn't noticed them yet. Sean tried to pull Sharon back out of the room as quietly as possible, but once Sharon snapped out of her stupor, she screamed. The cockroach jumped up, standing on its two bottom legs as if it were a person, and reached for the phone.

Sean yanked his wife out the door and slammed it shut before the roach could make the call. He practically carried her to the car. Too shocked to comprehend what just happened, he drove home in a daze. With his only thought being that he needed to call Charlie as soon as possible.

Before Charlie could say hello, Sean relayed the events of the day to him.

"You aren't going to believe this, I can't even process it. We searched the school and oh my god. There's something wrong in that school. We found the evidence! We've got to get out of here. We need a flight now, I just, I don't even know."

"Calm down, take a deep breath, just tell me what happened. Start from the beginning, so you drop John off at school, then what happened? What did you find?"

Once he finished relaying the story to Charlie, the line was quiet. The pause gave Sean time to breathe and process what they'd seen in the school.

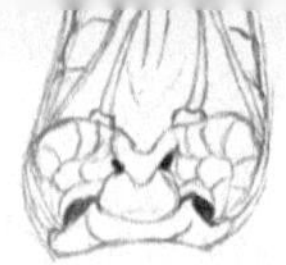

"I think that thing is draining the life out of those kids. That's the only thing that makes sense. The more they play that game, the weaker they get. That roach, being connected to all those motherboards, has to be draining them. He was enjoying that liquid."

"Wow, I just, wow. That's a lot to unpack. Did you guys get John out of there?"

"I know, I'm still in shock; I called you as soon as we got home. Right after we walked in the house, John called and said the school was having an early release day. So Sharon went to pick him up. But you know what the fucked up part is?"

"More fucked up than what you just told me? I guess I'm ready for it, what is it?"

"The entire town acts just like those kids. I didn't make the connection until I was in the sea of kids during one of the period switches, but at my office, and Sharon says at hers too, everyone is quiet and complacent. What if there are giant cockroaches behind all the businesses here?"

"That'd be insane. You guys should get out of there. Pack a bag and get on a plane. Let movers pack your house."

"You're right, when Sharon gets home, we're going to pack and leave. I'll call you tomorrow when we make

it into LAX."

"Sounds good, and Sean, please be safe…"

***

As Charlie paced his office, he decided to give in and call them. It had been forty-eight hours since they last spoke. Either they were at a hotel in LA or something went horribly wrong.

It took two tries before Sean answered his cell phone.

"Hey where are you guys, I never heard from you yesterday."

"What? Oh right, you know, I have no idea what got into me yesterday. When Sharon got home, she found me passed out on the couch. I think it's this damn flu I have. She said I was talking nonsense about bugs and life forces all night. I feel so bad for getting you worked up. This town is wonderful; John and Sharon both love it here."

"What?! What about the cockroaches? Why do you sound so monotone? Since when did you have the flu, you sounded fine yesterday?"

"We're fine, Charlie, I think I was just having fever dreams yesterday; I'm sorry I scared you. I've got to get back to this puzzle I'm working on. I'll call you later."

"Wait, what puzzle?"

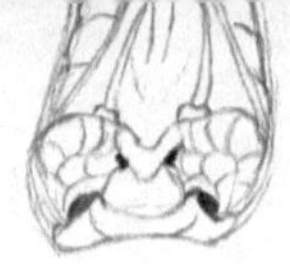

"It's those games from John's school; the principal sent home a copy for our computers, they are so addictive, I need to beat this level. I've got to catch up to John."

"What? Not you too, Sean, snap out of it!"

"Charlie, listen to me. There is nothing to worry about, I'll talk to you later."

"Don't hang up Sean, we need to—" Click. "Fuck."

I'LL BRING YOU MORE

by Chris Bannor

A hundred years ago, they burned the entire school down. They took one brick, in remembrance of the innocents lost, and used it as the keystone of the new building. The flames defeated the horror, but it didn't destroy it.

One brick was all the power it needed to start again. It happened slowly, but time was something they had to spare; a building accident that wouldn't raise suspicions, a bit of blood to christen the ground where they built their new foundation.

Over the years, the call grew stronger. Sacrifices came, little by little until they could manifest anew.

101

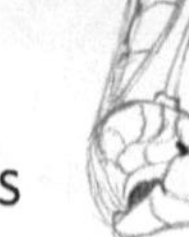

Fifty years ago, they'd held a council and canceled the rest of the school year, telling everyone it was for an early harvest to hide the losses.

Twenty-five years ago, the staff had whispered until the students eyed the halls with unease and traveled in packs. The teachers huddled in their doorways and scanned the corridors, anxiously clutching chalk in hand until a fine dust had carelessly scattered down the front of their clothes. No one walked anywhere alone for fear of some unknown ghost that trailed the hallways.

For all their technology and educational resources, the staff that currently ran the school didn't know a damn thing.

He walked through the building, familiarising himself with the latest classrooms and leaving a trail of temptation across the walls. It would grow and build. And they would feed it.

***

She was the first. He watched her, felt the pull of her loneliness as she tried to make new friends this school year. Rumours spread around her, never quite quiet enough. He watched her cling to her books, hold her head up high, and walk down the halls alone.

102

The boys grew bolder and whispered lewd suggestions as she valiantly marched past. Today, her eyes filled with tears, but they misunderstood. They were not the tears of a scared child. These were the lament of the furious. They were the pent-up frustration of a young woman who had been hurt by too many for too long, and he smiled.

It was time.

He slipped under her skin with just a moment's hesitation from his host. Yesterday he'd been a biology teacher. Today it was English. Now he was her. He was Mackenzie, a girl who'd faced too much in the hands of an ex-boyfriend who spread rumours as quickly as he said she'd spread her legs.

He was a whisper in her heart, a temptation to right the wrongs. In the long years he had waited, there had never been such a powerful surge of potential as there was in the school now. So many young people, hungry for justice in a world that cared little for their opinions or their welfare.

She lured two of them to the basement, demure eyes and a fearful pout making them follow, feeling entitled to some part of her where they had absolutely no right. The door closed heavily behind them; her rage already settled and blood staining the floor when she'd prepared her trap.

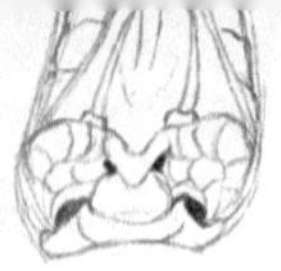

The two smiled nervously at one another—they were going to do this, right?—and she backed herself up against a shelf. The knife waited for her there, carefully placed and ready. She held the knife with the blade along her forearm and with one quick slice, blood streamed down the front of the first boy. His eyes were so wide; she laughed at his guppy face.

The second boy stared at her, uncomprehending, until she switched her grip on the handle. He took a stumbling step backwards and fell, but she leaped on him, straddling him with his arms pinned under her knees. She swung the blade down, blood spreading across his tee-shirt as she continued to plunge the knife in and out. He thrashed under her and knocked her off, and the knife slipped out of red-coloured fingers. He staggered to his knees but fell back down. It was too late.

She pushed herself up to her feet and tripped over to the knife before she dropped it into the circle she had painted earlier. The blood woke his body.

Blood lust stirred in his veins, the hunger and need for that which would sustain him. The blood pooled and ran to the circle, and as it filled, it gained strength. The bodies pulled towards the centre, and a hungry mouth opened, devouring it all. Even the blood on the girl dripped to the floor and slithered to the ravenous beast she

had fed.

When the blood was gone, the girl slipped to her knees and gently patted the edge of the circle. "Tomorrow," she whispered with affection.

"Tomorrow I'll bring you more."

BLACK HARE PRESS

LOCKER 429

by Alistair Crowe

Locker 429 was an empty locker in an empty school. Lockdown had cancelled all academic activities, so the interior halls were dark, even in broad daylight, and silent. This went on for two months until a loud thump followed by a moan disturbed the new routine.

Alexandra Jasmine Harris, known to her friends as Lexa, thought she was sitting up in bed, but fell forward as she was standing. She didn't have far to fall as a metal wall or something similar stopped her journey a few centimetres into it.

"What the hell." Lexa moved to grab her forehead where it had hit.

The last recollection she had was falling asleep at Tallulah Dean's house. She, Tallulah, and Amelie Reed

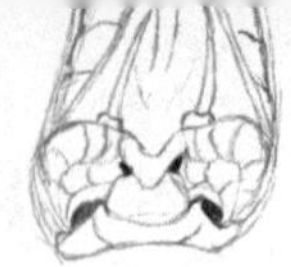

were there. Technically, socialising was verboten and having a sleepover definitely broke the rules, but that virus or whatever was stupid and only for old people, so they did it every week and hung out every day. Just like always. But now she was…somewhere. As she lifted her arms to feel her head, her elbows hit metal within centimetres.

"Shit." She tried to breathe slower. "Where am I?" She moved around hitting every wall, which didn't take much moving at all. They all made a clang. The one in front of her the loudest and it had an echo back. The one behind was more solid sounding. "I'm in a box. A metal box. How, who…fuck."

As she was trying to think, Lexa swung her right foot back and forth, hearing it hit the metal about half her foot length ahead then behind, ahead then behind. The back side made a dull thud and the front an echoing clang with each strike. Leaning her head forward against the metal to relax and think, and as she did, she felt a gentle breeze waft over her cheeks.

"Ok. Air. I'm not gonna suffocate. Ok." Tears forced their way out and down her face as she took a big gulp of air. "Ok. Ok."

The first thing she was aware of thinking and not reacting to was that time had no meaning in here. She

didn't know if five or fifty minutes had gone by since she got here? Woke up in here? It wasn't the most pressing thought, but it took away a sense she didn't know she missed until she couldn't access it. Time. If she knew how long she had been in here, she might work out where she was or how long people had been looking for her. If time could reply to her thoughts, it would say she'd been in there ninety-one minutes so far.

Lexa was getting painfully uncomfortable, so she slouched down and leaned her head against the locker door, her knees bracing her up. It was warm, getting warmer, dark and, despite everything, cosy, so she fell asleep.

Once again she came to and didn't know where she was. And when she remembered, she didn't know how much time had gone by. Then the reality of what was going on hit her full force. She didn't put herself in this box. Someone put her in here. She would have to be quiet, but also get out. Manipulating her arms to a position she could feel around in front of her was an agonising and time-consuming process. There wasn't much room, so by trial and error she found if she angled herself diagonally and put all her weight on her other arm, she could shift it forward a wee bit more. Hours felt like days, maybe weeks. Before she got them fully in front and able to feel around, she got them pinned several times. Once losing feeling in her left arm for a good…amount of time.

Finally, she succeeded and felt her way around the front. Or back. Or maybe side. Wherever she was facing. She started as low as she could and worked her way up, feeling nothing but metal and a frame that extended about the length of a mascara container into the box. About waist height on the side with her right hand, she felt an indention and within it a latch. A laugh or cry escaped her lips as she realised what it was and lifted. Her happiness died within millimetres as she heard a clank from outside, and the latch halted. She lifted it again, and the same thing. Then again, and again, and again. It wasn't a loud noise, so she kept trying, but every time, it would reach about the same height then stop solidly. The last attempt she put all her strength into lifting it to get whatever held it back to let go. She could only fit two fingers into the gap so she lifted with as much leverage as she could, put as much muscle into it as she could, and even stood as much on her toes as she could. She never felt the latch lift any higher, but she felt shock then agony when her fingers slipped and her middle fingernail caught on the latch and subsequently three-quarters of it tore from her finger in a jagged, slightly diagonal direction. She immediately tried to bring her hand to her mouth and banged the finger

against the front barrier. She had avoided screaming through the first moments because of shock, but couldn't help it now. No one came after her from the noises. So that was a wonderful thing.

It wasn't until hour nineteen that Lexa had to go to the bathroom enough that she wet herself. The urine soaking her PINK undies she had been so proud to get from the Victoria's Secret spinoff and her cosy cotton pyjama bottoms. Even her warm sleeping socks got wet, although not soaked. She thought about how she could take off the soaked clothes, but spending hours getting her arms to where she could pull them down wasn't happening. Not after she had worked so hard to get them in front of her. She settled for leaning forward and pressing as hard as she could on her butt to wring out some while sobbing.

Hour forty-seven and she thought she would die in there. Alone, hungry, thirsty—god so thirsty—and why? Why me? Why this? At least she was in a purging phase and didn't have to crap herself. If that happened, she might as well die. Or not. No, she wanted to live. A burst of self-preservation gave her a boost and so she manipulated her body slowly, then violently wrenched herself down to get her arms high enough to explore above her. Damn the scraped skin and carry on. The first

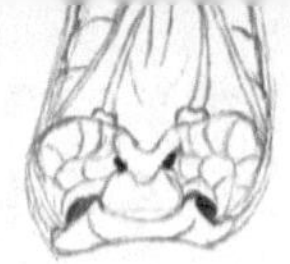

thing she felt were the grates. She explored them with her left hand mostly and found they were some type of vent. Maybe she was in an old furnace or something. Reaching higher, she found three indentions that it took multiple passes to figure out they were numbers. Just before her hands got numb enough that she stopped, she realised it was the number 429. And just like that, she knew where she was.

Locker 429 was where that jerk, that retarded twerp with the loser friends, had tried to get them into trouble. Did his friends do this? They couldn't have. They were spineless. But who else knew. Really knew. There were rumours, and some admin had given them looks, but no one knew except them. Even then it was little boys putting their faith in a dunce. For a while anger replaced fear and gave Lexa the energy she thought she had lost. Eventually fear won back its rightful place at the top.

Her finger hurt, the skin on her arms hurt, the skin on her legs and privates hurt from the rash caused by her urine-soaked clothes. Her stomach hurt from hunger, her mouth and throat from thirst. She hurt, but more than that she was scared because she knew she might, no, probably would, die in here.

Lexa spent her last night, hours 103 to 112, screaming for help, crying and trying to kick the locker

open. Her voice gave out after an hour, much later than the toes on her right foot did. Several of them breaking soon after her fusillade started. Breaking from the repeated kicks as hard as she could muster in such a confined space, the rest breaking later from more, and more, and more, kicks. She couldn't cry anymore as she was suffering from what would eventually, in a few hours, kill her. Dehydration.

***

Lexa awoke sweating and disoriented. As she looked around, she saw Tallulah and Amelie also sitting up.

"Oh my god, I just had the worst nightmare. I'm in something and I couldn't get out. I tried and tried and couldn't." Lexa tried to calm her breathing.

Tallulah lost all colour. "I had the same dream."

"Shit! Me, too," Amelie interjected, "exactly the same. How can we all have had the same dream? It's not possible. It's like some movie or something. And is it me or it is boiling in here and hard to see?"

Just then flames from the fire that had started in the basement dryer vent began flicking under the door.

"Oh my god, get to the window, get to the window…" someone screamed. Maybe even Lexa

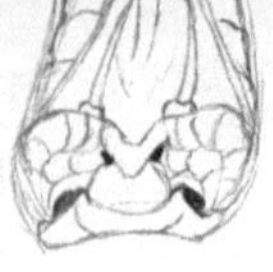

herself.

***

"Are you watching this crap?" Joe shifted his phone slightly.

Marc snorted. "Oh yeah. And crap, my friend, is what it is. A Video Conference Tribute. How 2020. And how utterly undeserved."

"In conclusion," Principal Anderson sighed, "we will all miss Tallulah, Alexandra, and Amelie greatly, but we also know they are in a better place. Thank you all for your attendance today and the entire staff of the Green Valley Independent School District and Rydell High send their condolences once again."

"A better place?" Marc sputtered. "Really? They were THE bullies of our school and maybe our generation. They didn't have a tribute like this to Freddie. Freddie, the guy they stuffed into his locker, twice, once for an entire weekend. Freddie, the guy who was exceptional but had autistic traits, so that sometimes he didn't get jokes and asked them why earnestly when they wanted him to run off and cry. He didn't get honoured because he offed himself. And they don't get punished because their jock boyfriends swore they were with them

114

and couldn't have put him in the locker. Plus the camera that would have caught it was 'accidentally' turned off in the same office Tallulah was a runner for, but it wasn't worth accusing her as her mom is a doctor to the stars. He never got honoured by the school even to just us, but hell, they die in a house fire while breaking quarantine and they get a mandatory service. And I know they are the ones who sent Locker Buddies cards to his parents and us after the funeral. One final stab. Well one last stab for him. They still mock us and everyone else like clockwork. And everyone still thinks they're angels."

Joe hung his head, then almost whispered, "Well yeah. But we got revenge first, don't forget that."

"What? That stupid book my uncle found in Australia? Really? I only brought that out to show you the wicked evil pictures in it. And because you're in Latin Club. Our friend from second grade, dude we knew from second grade on and hung together since then, hung himself because of those bitches and your silver lining is we lit some candles, cut our hands, and chanted some old folk tale called 'Eternal Atonement' and pretended it did anything? I miss Freddie too, man, and I hope they burned and didn't pass out from smoke inhalation like they said, but maybe they are better off. They're not here, and we are, and we will miss Freddie forever. And they didn't pay

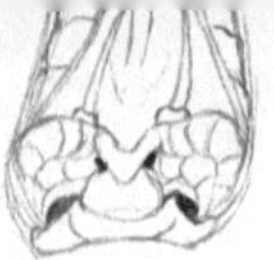

for it at all, man. Not now and definitely not forever like that stupid curse said. Life isn't like that."

***

Alexandra Jasmine Harris, known to her friends as Lexa, thought she was sitting up in bed, but fell forward as she was standing. She didn't have far to fall as a metal wall, or something similar, stopped her journey a few centimetres into it.

"No. No, no, no, no, no." Lexa had landed with her arms in front and up this time. She inched them up, feeling the grates, then extending them enough to once again feel the indented 429. "No. NO!"

DARKNESS OF THE SOUL

by Paula R.C. Readman

"Hey Darren! Wait up!" A lanky lad ran awkwardly, with a messenger bag slung across his chest. The boy ahead of him didn't turn. Instead, he pulled the hood on his jacket down at the front before crossing the busy street. The morning rush hour fought with urban tractors as mothers returned to the daily chore of the school run after the summer break.

Lanky dodged mums with pushchairs and groups of older kids who'd gathered on the street corners to vape. "Darren, wait mate!" Lanky pulled his bag over his head as he ran. Ahead, his friend continued to ignore him until the procession of mothers, children, and teenagers

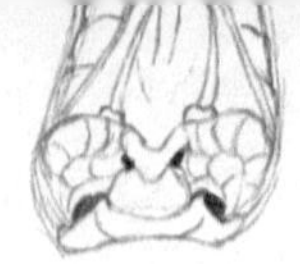

became a bottleneck at the school gate. Lanky touched his friend's shoulder, forcing him to turn.

"What Frankie!" Darren snapped. *Why doesn't he fuck off?* Darren thought, keeping his head down as his stomach lurched as a vision of blood and matted hair slipped through his mind.

"Hey, don't take it out on me, mate!" Frankie scanned the gathering masses. The students were gradually reforming into their usual clicky groups, laughing and chatting while they waited for school to begin. "None of us want this. We all wish the holidays went on forever."

Darren pushed past the chatting mothers and hurried up the steps into the main reception area without looking back. "Wait for me!" Frankie hurried after him. His bag banged against his legs, nearly tripping him up.

For the first time in his life, Darren longed for the sanctity of the classroom, wanting to hear the teacher saying, "No talking, just get on with your work." On reaching his locker, Darren felt in his pockets for the key. He quickly glanced over his shoulder. Frankie making his way through the milling students, acknowledging his friends, with high fives, but keeping his eyes fixed on Darren.

Darren had once been pleased to be part of the scene

, mixing with the geeks and jocks. Computers and sports were his best subjects, but now— he couldn't put into words how he felt now. The tightness around his eyes made his head ache. Darren knew Frankie would want to discuss what had happened. Just the thought of it made him sick. He bit his tongue as he tried to insert the key. His stomach lurched as he recalled saying, *it's going to be a summer to remember.* A pain shot through his chest causing him to hunch his shoulders as his heart raced. His chest stung like hell as though hot needles were entering his skin.

"Are you fucking avoiding me?" Frankie arrived at his side.

Darren took his time in answering. He sorted through his rucksack pulling out the books he needed and piled them on top of the locker. He knew sooner rather than later, he would have to face not just his friend, but the rest of the school. His body convulsed at the very thought of answering to Cassie. While jamming his rucksack in the locker, Darren caught a glimpse of his eyes in the mirror stuck on the back of the locker door. He inhaled sharply, silencing the scream that lingered in his throat. The red pus-filled scratches were real and weren't going to go away.

Last night he'd noticed tiny pink lines below the

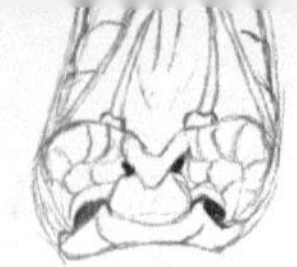
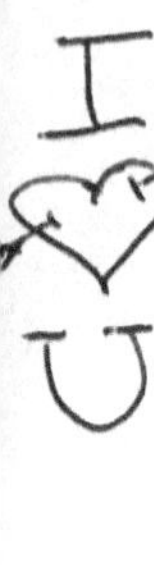

surface of his skin. He thought they were just veins crisscrossing his pale face. On waking, while cleaning his teeth, he became aware something was wrong. His teeth felt loose. On looking down, he saw blood on his brush and in the sink. On closer inspection blood oozed from his gums. Darren snatched up the bottle of mouthwash and took a large gulp. As soon as the antiseptic solution made contact with his gums, his mouth began to burn. He stuck his mouth under the cold tap until the gushing water eased the pain. On straightening, he reached for the towel. "What the fuck!" In the mirror, his once clear skin appeared mottled, with liver spots and purple blotches. The fine pink lines from the night before were red raw now and oozed pus. Darren poured some antiseptic lotion onto a cotton pad and gingerly dabbed the infected areas in an effort to clean them, but all it did was add to his pain. Tightness around his eyes gave him the feeling as though his eyeballs were about to pop out of his head.

The hallway rang to the sound of lockers opening and closing along with a multitude of conversations as everyone waited for the bell to ring. Darren closed his locker door and slipped the key into his pocket before gathering up his books. He pushed back his hood. "Look, I'm sorry, mate, but—"

"Fucking hell! Did the bitch do that to you?"

"Don't call her that!" Darren scanned the hallway. *Dear God help me. Was Frankie trying to invoke her?*

"Look at the state of you! You're a bloody wreck. Why are you ignoring me? I'm your best friend."

"I'm sorry— I need to get to class."

"She's put a curse on you. I told you she's a witch."

"You can see?"

"See what?"

"My eyes, the red marks on my face."

"What's wrong with your eyes?"

"Don't piss me about; I'm not in the mood." Darren pushed by Frankie as the bell rang and joined the throng of kids moving towards their classes.

"Brooke, McCutcheon in my office now!" A voice boomed down the corridor causing all heads to look in their direction. Darren inhaled, wanting it to be over. Frankie looked straight ahead, ignoring everyone. Darren realised the last day of their school holiday had changed their friendship in more ways than one; Frankie was now in control.

"Come on you two, I haven't got all day." The headmaster gestured them into his office. Darren clutched his books to his chest. *Why had he asked for Frankie's help?* After weeks of enjoying the freedom of sunshine, relaxing with his parents and bike rides, a simple spur of

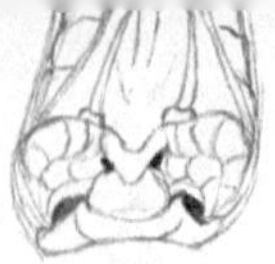

the moment request to someone he thought he knew changed everything.

"Right you two I've had a phone call this morning from Cassie Bickham's father—" The headmaster said, closing the door behind them. At the sound of her name, Darren gasped and dropped his books. Mr Newman focused all his attention on him. "Is there something you want to tell me, McCutcheon?"

Darren dropped to his knees, gathered up his books and clutched them to his chest, the white of his knuckles betraying his fear. What could he say? Frankie's behaviour that day scared him more than what Newman could. "No, Sir."

"Look at me, McCutcheon."

Darren lifted his head and held his breath, the words lodged in his throat. He waited for Mr Newman to see the horror written on his face, the pus-filled scratches, his bulging eyes, and mottled skin with its purple blotches. It screamed his guilt to the world. Beautiful Cassie was gone. Now she haunted him with her horror. A sob escaped his lips as he recalled the quiet girl who always sat at the back of the class, head down, and her nose in a book. She never tried to fit in or hung around with anyone. If it hadn't been for Frankie's offhanded comment, he wouldn't have taken any notice of her.

"I don't think she's got any friends."

"Who?"

"That new girl."

"And?" Darren was trying to put together a description of the First World War trenches using his own words.

"That girl Cassie. I see her most mornings walking to school. She's so old fashioned. Lives out on the old airfield and walks no matter what the weather. Mum reckons she's been home schooled."

"Home schooled?"

"She ain't ever been to—"

"I know want it means." Darren turned in his seat. The sun pouring through the window highlighted the copper strands in Cassie's brown hair as she sat alone. Suddenly, she looked up. Darren smiled. Her eyes widened, and she dropped her gaze. In that moment, Darren sensed something unexplainable had been triggered: a need to know more about her.

"Darren, turn around! You won't learn much staring at the back wall," his class teacher yelled.

After school, Darren waited for her. Sheltering from the rain, he had hidden from Frankie and the giggling girls in the bike shed. While he watched out for her, he reflected on his attitude towards the girls who constantly

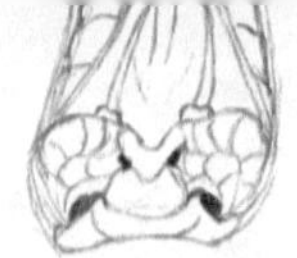

flirted with him. He admitted to himself he enjoyed being the centre of attention during football matches as they cheered him from the side lines, but to win Cassie over was a real challenge. As everyone else dashed to the waiting cars, snatched their bikes from the shed without a second glance in his direction, none lingered. Cassie finally emerged unfazed by the rain. She fastened her thin coat, hugged her bag to her and with no umbrella, head down, she hurried along the road. At a safe distance, Darren followed.

The next day, he tried talking to her, intrigued by her quiet nature. He watched the way she had a habit of walking with her eyes downcast and hugging her bag to her body as though shielding herself from all around. She kept her rich brown hair tied back from her pale face, as she worked, her eyes never leaving the teacher's face as she listened intently.

As Cassie made her way down the busy corridor to the next lesson, Darren fell into step beside her. "Hey Beautiful. Allow me to introduce myself." He stepped in front and she almost collided into him. She pulled back, tears in her startled eyes. "Hey, why the tears, I only wanted to say hello."

She side-stepped him and was gone, her long cotton skirt, a blur of colours. He watched her hurry away. *A shy*

little hare, he thought. *Wouldn't it be something to win her heart? What a challenge, what a laugh!*

The more Darren thought about it, the more he loved the idea. Rumours were abounding about his strange little hare. No one really knew anymore about her other than what Frankie had already told him. Of course, everyone had their opinions. New age travellers who had given up travelling so she could finish her education was one such tale. Darren found there was no escape from Cassie. At night she wandered through his dreams; her glossy hair floated around her heart-shaped face. Her silent smiling presence stared longingly at him, but still she didn't speak. With his lack of progress to get Cassie to speak to him, Darren decided to wait until the holidays. He didn't want anyone to know about his interest in her, though he knew there was one person he could trust.

Frankie slumped onto the park bench next to Darren. "I'm glad you're back. There's only so much Netflix and gaming I can put up with on my own."

"Right," Darren muttered as he focused on a group of youngsters kicking a ball about the playing field in the park. His mind wasn't really on them or Frankie. The summer holidays would soon be over, and he still hadn't plucked up the courage to see Cassie.

"So what shall we do now?"

"Can I tell you something?"

Frankie leant into Darren; the tone in his friend's voice told him it was something serious. "Of course anything. We're good mates, you know you can trust me." Frankie ran his first finger and thumb across his lips.

"Frankie, I don't know the words to say what I want to say." Darren took a deep breath. He saw something in Frankie's eyes and wondered if he had guessed. He was sure he had been careful around his friend.

"Just say it. We've been friends forever. Nothing will change between us." Frankie reached out for Darren's leg, but his friend rose and turned his back.

"I'm in love. Shit, I've said it." He ran his fingers through his hair and turned to face Frankie. "Oh I know I'm a player, but that was just me messing around. You're the only person who really understands me."

Frankie stood. "What made you realise?"

"Oh shit. I just can't get her out of my head. Cassie haunts me."

"Her! She's a fucking witch." Frankie snatched up his bag, as his cheeks burnt.

"A witch—what an odd thing to say. You've been watching too many Netflix *Witcher*, Frankie. That's all fantasy."

"The witch is luring you to your death, it's not love.

I've seen this sort of thing on the Internet."

"Look, Frankie—there's something different about her. The way she moves. That thing she does with her hair when she's thinking—"

"Love! You sound like my sister. She's in and out of love every day. We're too young for that sort of rubbish. Are you telling me you want to get tied down at your age? I thought you wanted to travel and see the world. Remember you talked about us going to America, even Australia."

"Don't get worked up, Frankie. I haven't told her how I feel. I want to go and see her now. Will you come with me?"

Frankie glanced around as his hand caressed his bag before swinging it up onto his shoulder. "You want to talk to Cassie?"

"Yes, if I can get her to listen to me. I really like her."

"Okay, I'll show you the best place to see her." Frankie gave a half smile.

"Thank you. You're a great friend," Darren heard himself saying, but something about Frankie's demeanour unsettled him. Suddenly, their relationship had shifted as Frankie took the lead.

All that remained of the Second World War airfield was an array of derelict buildings. The whole area had

been fenced off for years. Rumours said the site was haunted; this alone attracted the kids, who dared each other to enter. Cassie's father was the caretaker and had to keep the site secure, an impossible task. Most of the land was covered in thick woods, and at its centre, a dangerously deep lake. With care, Frankie led Darren through the ruined buildings, keeping out of sight of Cassie's home.

Once they entered the woods, Darren asked Frankie, "How do you know Cassie will be here?"

"I came looking for otters and saw her swimming here." On reaching the lakeside, Frankie pointed to a clearing in the reeds. "She comes through the trees there—to this bird hide."

Frankie pulled a couple of concrete blocks from a bush and sat on one. He bent forward, lifted the flap on his bag, and began to root around in it. Darren caught a glimpse of its contents, and was puzzled by why his friend was carrying what appeared to be a piece of wood, some nylon rope, and a knife

"Ah, at last, I thought I had two." Frankie offered up a chocolate bar to Darren before checking his phone. "Sit! She won't be along yet."

Darren was just finishing eating his when they heard the crackling sound of twigs and dried leaves under foot.

Before Darren had chance to speak, Frankie leapt up and knocked Cassie off her feet. She landed with a thud on her back. The stunned look on her face winded even Darren.

"Get off her, Frankie!" Darren tugged at his friend's arm, but Frankie pulled it free. With a stinging slap, he hit Cassie across the face. For a moment, she lay still as shocked as what Darren felt. Then with fear in her eyes, in a burst of incoherent grunts, she snarled at him while twisting and turning her body as she kicked out, unable to make contact with him.

"Get off her! Leave her alone!" Darren stood frozen to the spot.

In a burst of energy, Cassie lashed out, pummelling Frankie's chest while trying to scratch his face. Frankie's laughter echoed around them as he swung his fist. As it made contact, a spray of blood covered him as Cassie slumped back, her fight gone.

"What the hell did you do that for?"

"She's a witch! Don't you see? She was chanting magic spells at us." Frankie remained astride of Cassie as he pulled his bag towards him by its strap. He snatched a piece of sharpened wood and a hammer from his bag. Cassie's eyes widened as he placed the stake to her chest. Her mouth opened as he hit it once with the hammer. No sound came, only blood. Darren fell back as it sprayed

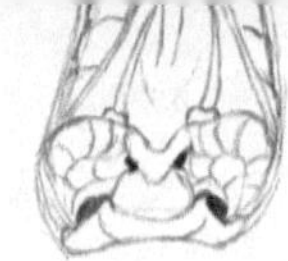

everywhere. Frankie stood, eyes bright with excitement. "I've freed you from her spell."

Darren stared at his beautiful, broken Cassie. He knew his nightmares were only just beginning.

"Come on, witch's magic doesn't work in water." Frankie slipped his hands under Cassie's arms and dragged her to the water's edge. Trance-like, Darren watched as Frankie pulled a boat out of the reeds. After dumping Cassie's body in it, he ran back to grab one of the blocks they had been sitting on and the rope from his bag.

"Push the boat, Darren!"

Darren did as he was told. Stepping back as Frankie rowed to the centre of the lake, he began to retch, bringing up the chocolate.

"Look at me, McCutcheon," said Mr Newman.

Darren lifted his head and wondered, could his headmaster read the guilt written all over his face?

"Cassie Bickham's father is very worried about his daughter. Cassie lost her mother in a nasty car accident three years ago. It took her ability to speak, apart from a few grunting sounds, which made her uncomfortable around others. Mr Bickham told me you had approached her, tried to speak to her. She said you were kind to her—"

SCHOOL'S IN

Darren threw his books at Frankie. "You bastard! You killed her for nothing!"

LOVECRAFT CLUB

by S.O. Green

His homeroom introduction was met with lukewarm peer reviews. Students drifted by with glacial unfriendliness in the corridors. Dom hummed the "First Day Blues" and scuttled to the library. A comfort blanket smelling of sawdust and wood polish, like his last school.

Which had been similarly devoid of friendly faces he knew, but there was something comforting about familiarity. And he was trying not to slide into that passé resentment of his mom that so many teen movie protagonists found themselves wallowing in.

That whole "I know we had to move because we need money to live and you go where the work is, but why

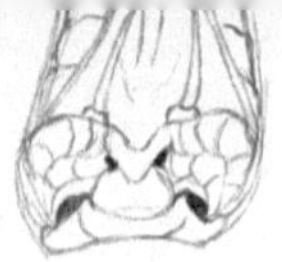

do I have to start a new school" shtick.

He unearthed *The Complete Illustrated Works* of a certain author from his bag and thunked it on the table, earning him the attention of the library's only other occupant.

"Hey, you're into that too?"

Dom nodded. He preferred the company of dead authors, but another living fan was too good to pass up.

"Randall," the stranger said. "I chair the Lovecraft Club."

"There's a Lovecraft Club?"

"Sure is. Four of us so far. You want to join?"

School being akin to the Serengeti, where a lone gazelle was liable to be pulled down and ferociously ridiculed by cackling hyenas, the idea of a herd of four to mingle with had immediate appeal.

So, Dom made his first mistake and said, "sure."

***

"It's really great to have a new member," Randall told him, as he showed him into the library backroom. "Actually, we needed a fifth for tonight's activity."

"You're not going to sacrifice me to Azathoth, right?"

"Azathoth promises only destruction, so that'd be pretty dumb."

Dom laughed at what he hoped was a joke.

"Actually, we're doing our first reading from the Necronomicon."

"*The* Necronomicon? That's a thing?"

"Oh yeah. Someone scanned it and put it online. Joan got us a copy, didn't you, Joan?"

The girl with the glasses, laptop open on her knees, looked up with startled rabbit eyes.

"Huh? Oh! Yeah! Sure did! Not a problem. Thanks, Randall!"

Then she snort-laughed and looked away, cycling through shades of red like a paint swatch. Yeah, socially adroit he was not, but Dom thought he could read that subtext.

"This is Martin. His mom's pagan. That's where we got the black candles and the skull."

Martin nodded. He was spinning the skull on his finger like a basketball. The missing teeth suggested he wasn't very good at it.

"I do it all for the Unspeakable."

Randall rolled his eyes. "First rule of the Lovecraft Club, dude. Don't speak about the Unspeakable."

"Who's that?"

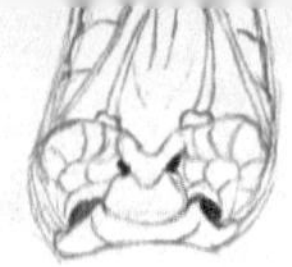

Dom nodded at the girl in the corner wearing the remains of a school uniform. She'd patched the holes with a spiked dog collar, army boots, and fishnet. The faint breeze from the window made her eyebrow piercings jingle like a wind chime.

"That's Kimberly. She's from the Catholic school down the street."

"Devil worship is metal as fuck. But this lame-o school doesn't have any devil worship clubs, so this is the next best thing."

"Right…" Dom had passed second thoughts some time ago. He was up to fifth or sixth by now. "So… What are we doing exactly?"

"We're going to open one of the gates of Yog-Sothoth."

"Why?"

Martin rolled his eyes. "To see if we can?"

There were two kinds of scientists in the world—the ones who theorised probable doom and didn't carry out the experiment and the ones who thought the first kind were quitters.

"The world's in pretty terrible shape, Dom," Randall pointed out. "Our parents are fucking this planet into oblivion. Nobody's listening because nobody cares. Everyone thinks they can fix it after it's already broken

but by then it'll be too late. *Someone* needs to do *something*."

"And you think a Great Old One is the someone we need?"

"Maybe not. But he might be the someone we deserve."

Joan had snapped her laptop shut. Martin was lighting candles. Randall's e-reader was open at Necronomicon.pdf. Kimberly sauntered closer, eyes glittering.

Dom looked at the ritual circle. His last words came to be known as the first true prophecy of the End Times.

"This is such a fucking bad idea."

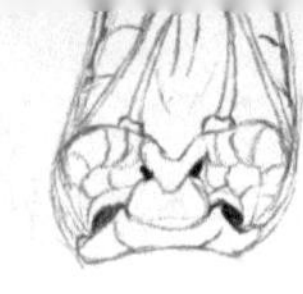

THE HONOURED ONE

by Amber M. Simpson

The freshly polished gymnasium floors squeaked beneath the feet of eager Hellion High students as they filed in for the annual back-to-school pep rally. The bleachers shook as they raced to take their seats, the room buzzing with excited chatter.

Down on the centre of the floor, Vice Principal Sears wore his usual goofy grin, bald head glistening with sweat beneath the bright overhead lights, pudgy hands resting on either side of the podium. Behind him, the cheerleaders stood in a staggered formation, lightly shaking their green

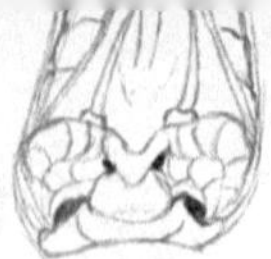

and gold pompoms, their matching midriff-exposing uniforms crisp and clean. As always, their faces were painted to resemble the Hellion High mascot—the dragon-like serpent that decorated the gym walls and floor.

Off to the side, the teachers sat in rows of foldout chairs, chatting amongst themselves. And against the back wall was the Hellion High throne—a jewel-encrusted monstrosity with images of serpents engraved along its golden frame. Lissy Evans, last year's Honour, sat smiling on the throne's plush red seat, the coveted Hellion High crown atop her head. The principal, Ms Naga, stood at her side, whispering into her ear.

"Watch it, freak!" spat senior Devlin Thompson, shoving sophomore Jeremy Ridder from behind as they entered the gym. With a startled cry, Jeremy fell to his hands and knees, his glasses flying from his face and sliding several yards across the smooth floor. Devlin's jock friends snickered as they all jostled past, leaving Jeremy humiliated and half-blind on the floor.

Mumbling to himself, Jeremy got to his feet, searching through blurry eyes for his missing glasses. Hearing the fast click-clack of heels, he squinted to make out Principal Naga approaching.

"Here you go, sweetie," she said, gently placing his

glasses on his face, a smile on her plump red lips. Jeremy swallowed hard, shoving the glasses up the bridge of his nose. One lens was cracked, but he could still clearly see the exotic beauty of Ms Naga's face—the fantasy of every Hellion High School boy's wet dream. She had been principal for as long as anyone could remember, yet her looks never seemed to age or become any less beautiful with time.

"Th—thank you," Jeremy mumbled, embarrassed that she may have seen Devlin pushing him and calling him a nerd, even if it would mean trouble for Devlin.

"Don't you worry," Ms Naga said softly, her tongue darting out quickly to wet her lips. "Children like that never make it very far."

"Y—yes, ma'am." Jeremy hurried off into the bleachers, the feel of Ms Naga's eyes hot on his back. Taking the steps two at a time, he found a seat halfway up beside his only friend in school, Barry Wilkes. Almost immediately, they were assaulted by a barrage of spit balls raining down on them from a few rows up—Devlin and his jerk-jock friends, laughing hysterically.

"I really hate that guy," Jeremy seethed between gritted teeth. "If I were the Honoured One, I know exactly what I'd do."

Barry rolled his eyes with a snort. "Don't hold your

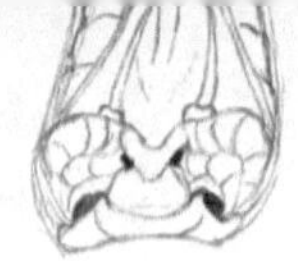

breath. Guys like us never get chosen. Besides, the Honoured One has been a senior the past three years. I think it's rigged."

Jeremy knew what Barry said was true; the chance of him being chosen as this year's "Hellion High Honour" was slim to none. But as his eyes found Ms Naga on the gym floor and she gave him a wink, he couldn't help but allow himself a little hope. And as another spit ball landed on the back of his neck, he zoned out and went to his happy place—a place where he *was* the Honoured One, complete with crown and throne, the most popular and beloved kid at Hellion High for ensuring another successful school year. Even better, he imagined the look on Devlin Thompson's face when he realised the kid he'd been bullying for over a year was the one with all the power.

"Good morning, Hellion High!" Jeremy was pulled reluctantly from his happy place by the voice of Vice Principal Sears booming through the podium's microphone down on the gym floor. "Now, I know we're all excited for our special tradition of choosing a new Hellion High Honour." The students clapped and cheered enthusiastically. "But before we get into that, there are a few things we need to cover first."

He talked for a few minutes about classes and student

expectations, then had Coach Meyer come up to discuss the football season. Devlin and his buddies jumped up and pumped their fists in the air, the cheerleaders doing flips and splits on the floor. Jeremy and Barry rolled their eyes at one another.

A few other teachers came up to the podium to speak but Jeremy hardly listened. His focus was intent on Ms Naga, his stomach in knots as he awaited her turn. Finally, it came. As she click-clacked in her heels to replace Mr Sears at the podium, the room went wild. It was the moment they had all been waiting for. *This* was what the annual back-to-school pep rally was all about. This was where the magic happened. Jeremy clapped louder than anyone.

"Good morning, everyone, it's so nice to see all of you again, fresh faced and ready for another fantastic school year!" Ms Naga paused as the students applauded and whistled, smiling around at all of them. "Before we begin this year's choosing, let's show our respect once more for last year's Hellion High Honour, Lissy Evans!" Lissy bounded up to the podium amidst the hooting and hollering, the large gem-encrusted crown slipping down one side of her head.

"Thanks, everyone!" she cried with a beaming smile. "It was so amazing being Hellion High's Honour last

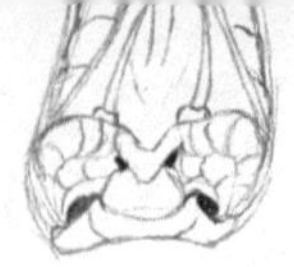

year, but the time has come for someone else to wear the crown. I'm looking forward to passing it off to the next Honoured One, who I'm sure will make it the best year yet!"

Ms Naga hugged Lissy then resumed her place at the podium while Lissy stepped to the side, adjusting the heavy crown. Jeremy's heart ached with jealousy. What he would give to wear that crown! With it came instant popularity along with instant fame. The Honoured One each year became a local celebrity, forever immortalised in the school's (and the town's) annals of history. It was what every child aspired to be, yet very few ever were.

"And now," said Ms Naga, her voice washing over the cheers of six hundred excited students. "Let the choosing of this year's 'Hellion High Honour' begin!" The applause was so loud, Jeremy's eardrums felt close to bursting until Ms Naga put a finger to her lips and all was silent. The entire room watched, breathless, as Ms Naga performed her first trick, and it was still just as amazing as Jeremy remembered it. She tugged at her hair, her long curly locks transforming into writhing snakes that slithered down her body and onto the floor, heading straight for the students in the bleachers.

Though he knew it was part of the tradition of choosing, it still made Jeremy a little nervous to have

snakes nipping at his shoelaces and wriggling over his feet. At his first pep rally last year, he had nearly pissed himself when one had borne its fangs at him and hissed, but this year he felt better prepared. Aside from the occasional gasp as a snake lingered here or there, the bleachers remained silent as they slithered through—tongues darting in and out as if tasting the students' auras. After about five minutes, Ms Naga snapped her fingers…and the snakes swarmed together around a shocked and gaping mouthed Jeremy. He sat, frozen, as the snakes enveloped him, twisting around his ankles and creeping up his legs, looping around his arms and draping about his neck. He wondered if he was dreaming.

"Holy shit!" Barry cried, his eyes nearly popping out of their sockets. "You're it!"

"Our Honour has been chosen!" Ms Naga cried and the hissing of the snakes in Jeremy's ears was drowned out as the room erupted in earth-shattering applause. He could hardly breathe. Was he really the chosen one? Him?

On shaking legs, he stood and descended the bleachers, kids reaching out to touch or high five him as he passed them by. Everyone wanted to touch the Honoured One, as if his luck might somehow rub off onto them.

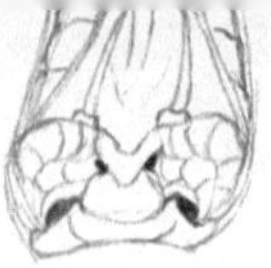

As he joined Ms Naga and Lissy Evans on the floor, the snakes slid down and off his body, returning to Ms Naga's head as normal hair once more. She swept him up in a warm squeeze and kissed his cheek, her lips slightly touching the corner of his mouth. Though still stunned, he flushed red, a big goofy grin on his face.

"Congratulations!" Lissy gushed, removing the crown from her own head and placing it on his with a flourish. He turned and looked out at the sea of cheering students in the bleachers, now stomping and calling his name.

"Jer-e-my!"

"Jer-e-my!"

Several cheerleaders crowded around him and ushered him to the throne, planting kisses all over his head and face. They pushed him onto the plush, red-velveted seat, their beaming faces shining down on him like bright rays of the sun. His body moved as if on autopilot, his brain still trying to comprehend his good luck.

"And now, to complete the initiation of this year's Hellion High Honour, Mr Jeremy Ridder, it is time for our chosen one…to choose!" The bleachers broke out in a fresh wave of excitement as Ms Naga click-clacked over to Jeremy and pushed the microphone to his mouth. It was the second most important part of the tradition—next to

the actual choosing of Hellion High Honour—and it was taken very seriously. Jeremy's first responsibility was to choose a fellow classmate as sacrifice—the only way to ensure a successful year. His eyes slid out to the bleachers and landed on Devlin, his face red and horrified. Jeremy couldn't help but grin.

"Devlin Thompson," he said, his voice loud and clear through the mic.

Ms Naga patted Jeremy's cheek as she brought the mic back to her lips, then turned to face the other students. "And so it shall be."

The room lapsed back into silence as every last eye was glued on Ms Naga. The hair snakes were nothing compared to what they were all waiting for her to do next. With a small jerk of the head, her face slowly morphed, transforming into the face of the dragon-like serpent for which the school was dedicated. It stretched outwards to create the creature's long snout, razor-sharp teeth protruding from the elongated mouth. Her hair withdrew into her skull as her flesh hardened into thick green scales.

It was a horrific sight to see Ms Naga's womanly body before him, her head such a monstrous visage. But Jeremy knew the only person in the room with something to fear was Devlin, whose jeans were at that moment darkening as he pissed himself.

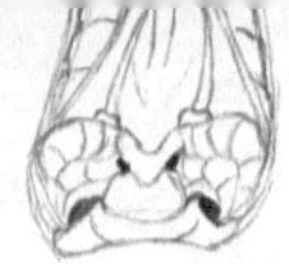

With a loud dragon-like roar that shook the building, Ms Naga's neck stretched hellishly long as it wound its way up into the bleachers. It didn't stop until it reached the choice of the Honoured One, hovering above Devlin like a showerhead. Everyone near shrank quickly away, leaving a wide berth of space around him. Ms Naga snorted, thick smoke billowing from her gaping nostrils, enveloping Devlin in a hazy grey cloud.

"Puh—please," Devlin stuttered, shaking, his teeth clacking together. "D—don't."

Ignoring his pleas, Ms Naga opened her enormous jaws wide, Devlin hunched and cowered on his seat. A jet of bright red flame shot out of her mouth and engulfed his body, burning him to a crisp on the spot. With a loud chomp, she bit him in two, the upper half of his body disappearing in her mouth. Her neck slowly retracted, growing shorter as she brought her head back towards her body, a bit of his entrails dangling from her teeth. Yellow eyes sparkling, she swivelled her head towards Jeremy and presented him with the meat. Lifting his arms, Jeremy plucked an intestine from Ms Naga's teeth, wet and sticky with blood.

The gym was so quiet, Jeremy's ears rang as everyone waited to see what he would do. The fate of the entire school year was literally in his hands. The bit of

intestine made his stomach turn, and for a moment, he didn't think he could do it. But then he remembered all the shitty things Devlin had done to him the year before as a freshman, all the abuse Devlin had put him through. Shoving him into lockers, pulling his pants down in front of the girls. All the name calling, the embarrassment, the absolute humiliation.

No. Screw Devlin. Jeremy deserved this moment, this happiness…this honour.

He shoved the meat in his mouth and chewed, suddenly ravenous, hot blood spurting out and dribbling down his chin like the juices of an apple. The gym erupted once more in a cheer, the bleachers shaking with heavy foot stomping.

A bright flash went off in Jeremy's face, blinding him momentarily—a camera, taking his picture for the high school yearbook, as well as the local paper. He grinned—bits of viscera stuck in his teeth—imagining his face splashed all across the papers and school walls. He was Hellion High Honour! Hero of the Year! It was all he had ever dreamed of.

Beside him, Ms Naga's face returned to normal and she wiped at her mouth delicately with French manicured fingers. "Well done," she said with a smile, and Jeremy's heart soared. It was going to be an incredible school

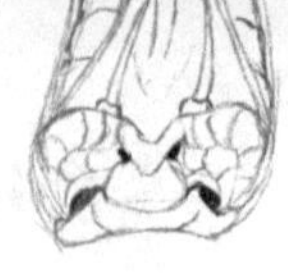

year—the best year of his life.

MY BABY SHOT ME DOWN

by Archit Joshi

Eleven-year-old Aryan Gulati had been spending the last day of his vacation redoing most of his project work. The darn pencil writing had worn off over the course of summer hols. No big deal, it happened to most of them. Just one year more and they would finally shift to pens, which were more permanent. But Aryan was bittersweet about it. Bitter—because it irked him that even the scribbles in his notebook had faded, but the shame he'd faced over the break had lasted so long. Sweet—because the messy jumble in his mind had suddenly sorted itself

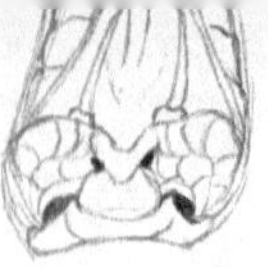

out into one final decision. Just like the choice of a darker HB pencil, Aryan realised he could change the course of things by deliberate choice alone. It had all started out as a coincidence, then become tragic due to an impulsive decision, but now Aryan realised he couldn't leave it at that.

For most of the break, Aryan had felt trapped in an invisible room, the walls closing in on him. Every time he replayed the incident in his mind, his panicked lungs would scream for more oxygen and his hands would ravage the snacks cabinet for whatever food they could find. He would then stuff it in his mouth, most of it spilling on his clothes and the floor. Even the release of new *Detective Conan* episodes every Thursday was not enough incentive to be excited. Of course, you don't share such humiliation with your parents. Why would you? They blame everything on too much TV. So, he had trudged ahead, forgetting to enjoy the break, confused, lonely, and hurt. But today, he felt miraculously clear-headed, a plan forming in his head. He completed page upon page of his project work, feeling as if he'd chugged down several swigs of *Felix Felicis*. By the time he was done, a resolve had dug into his flesh with talons.

He threw the notebooks in his bag with a burst of nervous energy. Tomorrow, his life would change.

***

Vishakha Talreja awoke to find butterflies playing a game of catch in her stomach. First day after the break always mattered. How you show up sets the tone for the coming year. Her uniform had to be creased just enough to show the teachers she didn't follow any of their rules, but not so much that it looked battered. Her hairdo had to look unkempt enough to have that careless sexiness to it, and yet combed enough not to make her look like an uncivilised B. When you're thirteen and on your way to becoming the most popular girl in school, you have the world's eye turned on you. The entire school looked up to her. She wouldn't let them down.

Vishakha took over forty-five minutes to get prepared—God, when will I get enough time to get properly ready?!—and then ate her usual breakfast of two dried raisins and one seedless date. Then she put on her uniform and admired herself in front of a full-length mirror. For a second, she thought about stuffing a little padding into her slip, but decided against it. The chances for a public faux pas were too many. God, why do the fat ones already have full breasts?! Screw it. The sport studs didn't ogle the fat girls, they ogled her.

The familiar triple honk announced the arrival of the

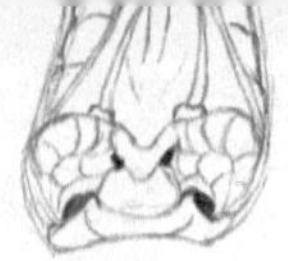

school bus. She squirted a few sprays of perfume into the air in front of her and walked through it. Blowing kisses at her parents, she walked to the bus and was instantly greeted with a chaotic chorus of "Hi Vish!" and "Vish, missed ya baby!" and "Looking hot, babe!" (This from the captain of the under-14 basketball team, which she pointedly ignored. Let them grovel.)

Time to rock the first day.

***

Samkit Gulati returned home after dropping his son off at school, his mood foul. Aryan refused to opt for the school bus, said he was too shy. On entering the premises, he had tucked his head down and made straight for the class, diffident as a mouse. He had no friends and Samkit suspected the bullies gave him a hard time. All his attempts to toughen his son up had failed. Aryan wasted his days reading thick books, and of course too much television, his bulging sack of a body not thanking him for it. The kid needed to play some rough sports, clean up his act. Otherwise, the ugly world was going to devour him whole.

"Sushma, your coddling is destroying Aryan's life," Samkit declared loudly, peeking into this and that room to search for his wife. "You should see how he behaves at

school…" He finally found his wife and instantly regretted his tone. She knelt before an overturned dustbin in the rear balcony, where they stored all the waste till the weekly garbage truck visit cleared it out.

"Mister, how many times have I told you we need to enclose this balcony? Cat's been at it again."

"We live on the ground floor, Sushma. These things are bound to happen." Samkit decided to postpone the rants about his son to a later time. "Why's that dratted cat nosing around in the garbage anyway? I threw my razor in there today. Maybe the cat will choke on it. Problem solved!"

His wife shot him one of her patented ugly glares.

"You don't do anything around the house and you expect me to look into all of it and also look after our son. You don't allow me to hire a maid because you 'don't like strangers knowing so much about the house'. Why don't you at least do the things I tell you to do? As man of the house, it is your duty…"

Samkit's brain had already supplied him with his happy place melody, and he hummed it in his head, his wife's nagging already a background chatter. *Should've taken a longer route coming home.*

***

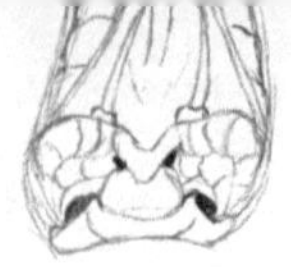

"Oh em jee, that fatso?!"

The school bus had all but exploded with all the noise and excitement inside. But the loudest voice was coming from one Milakshi Garewal ("It's Milo, okay?!").

"Umm hmm!" Half of Vish's attention was down at her lap. The thigh gap! Narrowing every day. Time to cut down on meals.

"You *have* to tell me everything!" Half of Milo's attention was towards the others. *Look! I'm friends with Vishakha Talreja.*

"Not much to tell, babe. I was at the superstore to buy, you know…about to head out. He was there in the— surprise, surprise—biscuit aisle, confused over which kinda sugar he should buy to fatten up his butt more."

"Hahaha! Fat ass!"

"Anyway, he saw me—God why?!—and waddled up to me like the ugly duckling. Had this creepy smile on his face. Anyway, he comes up to me, puffing and sweating, balancing who knows how many packets of biscuits in his arms."

"Lol, prob'ly a hundred."

"He gets down on a knee, all hundred kilos of him juggling and flapping. Some old croons at the checkout line actually 'awwwwd' ya know! Clutching at their saggy hearts and all."

"He must've dropped all the biscuits in his hand, the clumsy idiot!"

"Yeah! How'd you know?"

"The guy's a noun. My li'l bro studies in his grade. Every time someone stumbles down the stairs or trips on their laces, they call it pulling a Gulati."

"El oh el! So anyway, that was about as far as I could take it. I like shouted 'Eww gross!' so loud, the lovestruck grannies could've had an attack. You know what he did next?"

"I dee kay. Cried?"

"Worse! He farted."

Milo gave out a part-guffaw, part-snort. "Stupid shouldn't have gotten into something his nervous little bum couldn't handle. What was he thinking? Asking out Vishakha Talreja. LMAO!"

All conversation died out as they saw the usual signal crossing speeding at them. If timings matched, on the other side, another school bus would arrive at the same time. If they were lucky, both signals would be red, resulting in a classic face-off. On green, both drivers would dash as crazily as they could, without putting lives in danger, in a mad scramble to reach the school gate first. Today they were in luck.

"Hang on kids," Sopan, the driver, shouted. "It's about

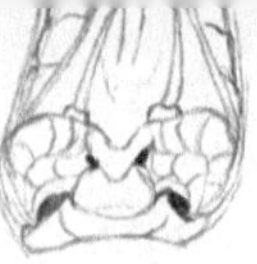

to go wild!"

Gossip turned into loud gasps and yells as Sopan deftly guided the bus through narrow gaps and rough turns. First day was already off to a great start. Anticipations soared high. Neither driver seemed ready to back down. The traffic was light at this hour of the morning, giving them both some leeway to throttle their engines a bit more.

In a matter of minutes, the final slope which led down to the school gate came into view. Vish's bus erupted into chants in the name of Sopan. The other bus retaliated almost instantly. Vish looked at Milo and rolled her eyes.

"I go to school with a bunch of kids," she muttered. Milo pursed her lips and grimaced in agreement. But one of her fists was deep into her pockets, clenched in excitement, rooting for their bus to win.

When the swerve came, it was as unexpected as homework on the first day. Excited chants turned into bewildered shouts as Sopan skidded in a wide arc, narrowly missing a large gathering at the gate, and came to a shuddery stop inches from the school wall.

"I'm hurt!" a shout rose near the driver's seat.

"What's going on?" another helpless voice asked.

The other bus squealed to a halt smack in the middle of the road, inviting angry blares and some shouting. In the bus, worried murmurs replaced the cheer. Milo had leapt into

Vish's arms, her eyes wide and eerily focused at a point nobody could see.

"You're getting your hot breath all over my uniform, idiot!"

Milo straightened herself, dazed, and dusted off Vish's uniform, who in turn gazed out the window. Something was up. The entire staff had collected by the door. Principal Akkalkothkar was standing with her back ramrod straight, wiping her brow with a napkin. A few feet away, the early nerds huddled together. Something about their lack of enthusiasm for the first day unsettled her.

One by one, the students piled out from both buses. Some of those who'd been hurt were taken aside by the PE coach and given a quick check-up. Sopan apologised profusely to the offboarding children, genuinely concerned. Vish brushed off his worried hand with a nonchalant wave. As soon as she stepped outside, with Milo at her heels, all twenty-seven staff members turned around in unison to stare at her.

What's happening?

***

He had read the quote by accident one dreamy Saturday afternoon, back when life was a bed of roses. He

had been searching for a different Michelangelo. One that lived in a gutter and learned from a rat. His chubby fingers had flown over the keyboard of his stocky old-fashioned desktop computer, looking to download a picture of his favourite ninja turtle so he could print it out and stick it on his cupboard. The Internet of course had thrown at him its own result, more precisely, a saying by a great sculptor.

Every block of stone has a statue inside it and it is the task of the sculptor to discover it.

Yesterday, giddy from an epiphany, he had just an empty conviction. No idea how he was going to pull through. But then, the millions of thoughts hurricaning through his mind must have collided and brought up an old memory of having read the quote. From then on, it all became a matter of simple planning.

Once at school, he'd gone straight to a bathroom. Eyes pointed at his polished shoes. He'd hugged himself to keep his shivering hands from showing. If anyone had stopped to take a good hard look at him, the game would've been up. He couldn't keep his eyes from reflecting the terror he felt for what he was about to do. But for once in his life, he felt thankful that nobody ever paid him any attention.

In the bathroom, he'd pretended to take a leak until

another student was done washing his hands. Once he was alone, he took off his backpack and threw it in a yellowed, stained urinal. He struggled to keep his fingers steady as he unbuttoned his uniform. Aryan stood half-naked in front of the dirtied mirror in the bathroom and winced. *Unlovable.* He stood a good way away from the washbasin, and yet, he felt its cold enamel against the skin of his protruding belly. *Why would she ever have said yes? You're a monstrosity.* Well, not for long.

He thrust his hands into his pocket and brought out the make-shift parcel of loose paper. Unwrapping the folds, he discarded the paper and held onto his father's razor. Ab routines weren't the only way to get rid of belly fat. He got to work.

***

Lokesh Gadre had been sweeping the fifth floor near the science lab when he heard distant, chaotic bursts of screams and shouts coming from students. He turned to see a kid running towards the lab. He was shirtless and had an alarming, crazed look in his eyes.

"This won't do!" he kept repeating. "Need a scalpel, need a scalpel." He left a trail of dripping blood in his wake, cuts lining his rotund stomach. Lokesh tried to grab

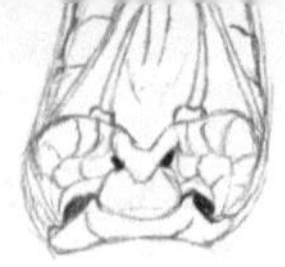

the student but he dodged and went around.

"Don't you dare come between me and my Vishakha," the student shouted and brandished a blade in his hand. "I just need a scalpel!" He continued his dash towards the laboratory.

Relying purely on instinct, Lokesh ran the opposite way, down to the first floor, towards Principal Pallavi Akkalkothkar's cabin.

***

He was covered in blood, loose fat, and sweat. A morose painting of red and buttery yellow. His hands were trembling, his vision tunnelling. The hacked-off tissue slithered down his stomach to the sand. Bad decision, taking it to the school ground. Sunlight stabbed at his cuts. Prickles everywhere, unabashed. Right at breaking point, he saw her. With the principal close and Ameen's older sister by her side. Behind, a procession of worried teachers and other students trickled inside. His brain shot all kinds of crazy signals to his body. *It's just your body bettering itself. You're not fat anymore.* His audience drew closer. Vishakha's jaw had dropped. *She's proud of me.* His hands worked the scalpel in frenzy and cut away at the fatty pus and flaccid skin clinging to his

stomach. A bit more and he'd get rid of all the flab.

"Stop it, Aryan!" Akkalkothkar pleaded, the crisp edge absent from her voice for once. "Vishakha has told me everything. She's…she's agreed to become your…your girlfriend." She spewed nonsense about his parents being on their way.

Aryan wobbled towards Vishakha. His knees buckled, and he fell, just a few feet from his god-sent angel. He crawled towards her wondrously perfect legs, looked up, and smiled. Vishakha momentarily gawked at him and then vomited, right onto his upturned face.

"Thank…thank you, Love." He managed to croak feebly, before his mind shut down.

***

Aryan awoke in a hospital ward. He shuffled towards the attached bathroom to splash water on his face. His torso was swathed in stitches and they stung as the hospital gown brushed against them. In a mirror above the tap, he saw a lipstick mark on his forehead.

Strange, he thought, turning on the tap. *Mom doesn't wear this shade.*

Wiping his face down with a nearby towel, he staggered back to his bed. He found a buzzer by his bed,

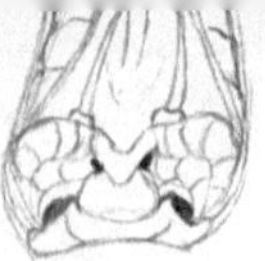

probably to call for a nurse or waiting parents. Before he could press it, his eye caught a few items on a bedside table. Mom had packed him his favourite desiccated coconut delicacy. Dad had left behind his Pokeball. Aryan smiled. Below these two items was a piece of paper. Plopping down on the bed, he began reading it.

Hey Aryan,

It was vry brave wht u did ystrday. All 4 a girl's attention? Othrs mite think its reckless but i thot it was vry passion8.

God, had it worked? He hurriedly read ahead.

Wht u did wasn't dramatic or radical at all. TBH, i envy ur courage. i know what its like 2 live under smbdy's shadow. How it feels never 2 be noticed.

That didn't sound like Vish at all. Aryan skimmed through the rest of the letter to the signature.

i dnt want u 2 becm the skul's freak. Letters rly arnt my thing. Once u get well, lets get 2 knw each othr better in prsn.

Kisses,

M.

M? Who could it be?

***

They had taken a stroll together and were approaching a bus stop. Vishakha walked aimlessly, grim-faced and detached. Milo, for once, didn't care for fawning. Vish had called her up, said she needed a friendly face. School had shutdown, and it was tough not to spiral.

"No remorse?" Milo asked at length, tersely.

"Dude, the fuck did I do?" Vish lashed out. "Everything's on him."

What a bitch. Milo lapsed back into angry silence. *Poor Gulati.*

A bus sped towards the stop. Milo placed a comforting hand on her friend's back. "It's going to get better you know." She let her hand linger as Vishakha mumbled a thanks. They were so…prosaic—two girls at a bus stop—that no one paid them any heed. There were neither passengers wanting to board the oncoming bus nor those looking to disembark. The driver didn't slow down his speed.

Milo gave a sudden shove to Vishakha's back as the bus was inches away.

"Oops." Milo turned back and disappeared amidst shrieks and wails, cutting past the scared crowd hurrying

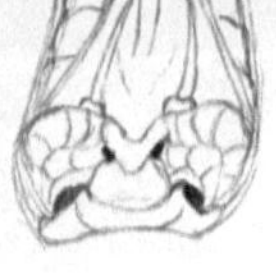

towards the screeching bus.

She didn't deserve you, Aryan.

MONSTER

by Catherine Kenwell

"We're going *where*?" Ryan asked, an incredulous grin slicing his face in two. "No way! You've got to be kidding me!"

"Yeah," answered Brandon. "They have to move us into the old Lakeview School for the rest of the year. It's gonna be unbelievable. Like messed up, man. Unbelievably cool."

It had been eight days since a shop class fire at Eastland Secondary School accelerated into a five-alarm blaze and rendered the institution unusable.

That was on January 21. After emergency meetings and deliberations, the school board agreed they could get a skeleton site ready to go by the end of February. The catch? They'd be moving into Lakeview School, the ancient behemoth on the hilltop overlooking the town and Lake

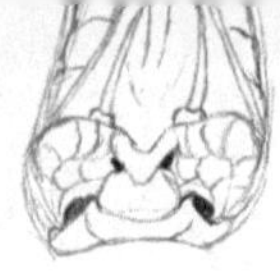

Michigan.

Lakeview School was built in 1902 as an umbrella institution to house both elementary and secondary grades in one half and a locked-down sanitorium on the other half. The sanitorium was itself separated into two parts—one, a lunatic asylum, and the other, for tuberculosis patients.

While it was upgraded several times over the 1950s and 60s, it eventually fell into disrepair. The school closed in 1965 when the town's population expanded, and students moved to more suburban institutions.

When tuberculosis faded into history and the last patients died, the sanitorium became the region's mental health hospital. From the 1940s on, the once-barbaric institution experimented with new forms of mental health therapies—lobotomies gave way to insulin and shock therapies and experimental drugs.

By the mid-1970s, only the most severely ill patients were still institutionalised at Lakeview. New types of medication and therapies offered hope for a cure to persistent psychiatric symptoms; therefore, patients were more likely to remain in the community.

In 1982, the entire facility was closed. It sat untouched on Mortimer Hill, which itself was a battleground conquered by the British in the War of 1812. Considered a heritage site, the school was maintained well enough to keep it from

falling apart, but peeling paint and boarded up windows gave it a decidedly spooky air. Its prominent architecture and creepy aura had proven perfect for a couple of big-budget Hollywood horror movies over the decades, and locals relished repeating the rumours of supposed haunts and tragedies associated with the place.

Ryan and Brandon could hardly contain themselves. For years, they'd talked about breaking into the old building and checking it out. They were horror fans: slasher movies, high school horrors, Halloween, Carrie, Prom Night—they had seen them all. The movies that were filmed at the old school? They analysed them line by line and couldn't wait to witness for themselves whether some of the rumoured odd happenings during filming were actually true.

"Holy shit, if I'd known they'd put us there, I would've burned Eastland long before now!" Brandon exclaimed. Not like Brandon had set the fire at Eastland. Surely not.

Ryan's mind started reeling. "Imagine all the things we can do in there," he mused. "We can scare the crap outta everyone. It's like we already know what to do. A few well-placed tricks, and they'll all believe the place is really haunted!"

***

The end of February couldn't come fast enough for

169

the duo. Meanwhile, the time away from classes meant that they could get into a different kind of mischief: they were developing their plan to "haunt" their new school, to disrupt classes, and prank the way they'd never been able to before.

The two started to prepare. They collected Halloween masks—three of Mike Myers and one each of Freddy Kruger and Jason Voorhees—and stockpiled matches, accelerant, hammers, paint, fake blood, and a remote-controlled machine that played a series of spooky sound effects. They'd spook the classrooms, dump fake blood in the gymnasium, and even troll the boiler room, just like in *Nightmare on Elm Street*. If Lakeview wasn't already haunted, they'd be responsible for making both the administration and their fellow students believe it was.

***

As usual, construction and upgrades to the temporary learning institution took longer than anticipated. Wiring had to be torn out and replaced, contractors had to install class computers and Internet, and washrooms and common areas needed to be brought up to twenty-first century standards.

The mammoth boiler still worked fine, and even

some of the furniture was still usable. Physical clean-up was minimal—enough to keep the teens safe but no interior decorating was in the budget. With media, camera crews, and school administrators present, the school principal and the mayor cut the grand opening ribbon on March 15.

The school's 950 students swarmed the building, hurrying not only to find their classrooms but also to gaze with awe at the old fixtures, high ceilings, and barred windows. Shouting and chattering, they ran in, greeting friends they hadn't seen in a while and super excited about being let loose in the creepy old landmark. Almost a thousand people were about to inhabit a legendary spook-filled building for at least the remainder of the school year.

Brandon and Ryan stood and watched, waiting until the rush slowed and then sauntering in, taking in the somewhat familiar scenery.

As they pushed open the heavy steel door, they high-fived each other. This was going to be their year.

***

The first few weeks were rife with problems one might expect with an old building: the lights flickered, breakers were blown, and rusty iron-laden water flowed from the washroom faucets.

171

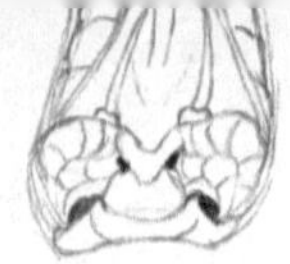

The boys laid low and monitored the not-so-strange happenings; they would use the building's deficits to their advantage when they began their "haunting" campaign.

Classes continued as well as they could, but cell phones and wi-fi connections were almost useless. A simple text from one student often took several hours to show up in another's. School had been in for almost a month and the "new normal" was starting to become routine.

Brandon slammed his lunch tray on the banged-up metal cafeteria table. "This is wild," he said to Ryan as he folded himself onto the attached bench. "Imagine if these tables could talk. I mean, look at the dents and scratches on them… It's like they were built to withstand knives and hammers and weapons-crazy psychopaths might get their hands on."

"Yeah, and did you see the back wall in Room 17?" Ryan exclaimed. "I know they tried to fix things before we moved in, but I swear it looks like there are scrawled words underneath the paint on the back wall."

"Gonna file that under 'creeptastic'," Brandon noted. "That's something we can use to our advantage. So…when do we start?"

"How 'bout tonight? After everyone leaves?"
"Sounds good. Let's start with Room 17."

***

Despite the building's bright new purpose, the rumours lingered. Janitors didn't want to work in the school after dark, and extracurricular activities ran immediately after classes and were over by dinner time. The boys knew that if they bided their time, the school would be empty before sunset. They'd discovered a broken ground-floor window at the unused back of the building. That would be their entry point.

Equipped with paint that had been stashed in Brandon's locker, they made their way to Room 17. They stood in front of the back wall, trying to determine what the faded scrawls revealed.

"D…IE!" Brandon exclaimed. "Die? Oh shit, that's too good to be true! What's the rest, can you make it out?"

"Looks to me like…N…O…N…NON…STR? NONSTR?" Ryan guessed. "No, that doesn't make sense!"

"No, it's an M! MON…STER! MONSTER!" Brandon yelled. "Oh my god, it says 'DIE MONSTER'!"

"I'm gonna piss myself." Ryan laughed. "DIE MONSTER. It couldn't be better than this. Seriously, let's get to it!"

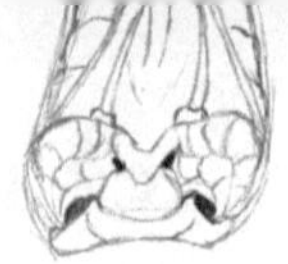

Ryan opened the can of red paint and Brandon dipped the brush. "Make it messy," Ryan directed. "Creepy, like it's written in blood. This is gonna be hilarious! I can't wait to see everyone's reactions tomorrow morning."

The red paint itself did one better; it dripped and rolled at the end of each letter, making the words DIE MONSTER appear even more horrific. They stood back and admired their creation.

"We're in here first thing tomorrow, right, Homeroom," Ryan said. "Let's get out of here. Hoo-ee, the sparks are gonna fly in the morning!"

Ensuring their tracks were covered, and after cleaning up meticulously, the boys left for home. They were so excited, neither one slept a wink.

***

The next morning, Brandon and Ryan met at the front steps of the school. They were giddy with anticipation.

"Ready, monster?" Ryan laughed. "Let's go to Asylum Room 17!"

In the corridor, students were buzzing with excitement—there was something going on. Mrs Patchett

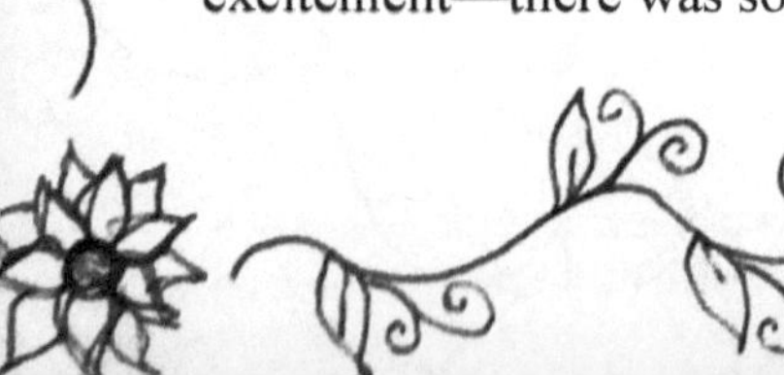

174

exited from Room 17, wringing her hands and crying. Two ghostly pale, blonde-haired girls ran after her, all the way to the front door.

Their little plan was working, they thought. Everything was happening as it should. The boys grinned with satisfaction.

"Nonchalant, man…" Brandon whispered. "Like nothing's going on, just a little curious, that's it. Nobody saw. No one will know it was us."

Ryan pulled open the classroom door. Several students were milling in front of the back wall, looking shocked and terrified, with whispers and gasps all around.

Brandon and Ryan chuckled. "First one down, how many more to go?" Brandon sighed. "It's just gonna get better and better!"

Displaying what they considered to be an appropriate level of interest, the boys walked towards the scene of last night's artwork. They froze.

"YOU WILL DIE. I AM A MONSTER," it now read.

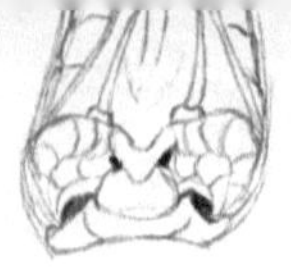

BLACK HARE PRESS

MAKING THE GRADE

by David Green

Principal Philips gazed up at the teenagers kicking their feet, gasping for air. Several swayed this way and that, necks broken.

Benjamin Todd, the principal thought, looking up at the boy's purple face. The whites of his eyes turning red, *as nasty a child I've ever come across.*

The dead and dying hanging from the stage lights in the auditorium were those deemed, after their first term, as too aggressive, too ordinary, or not having the correct fit.

Principal Philips turned to leave, satisfied his school's high standards would keep for another year.

 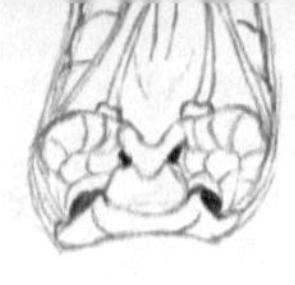

He'd burn the bodies in the morning.

SCHOOL DAZE

by Dawn DeBraal

No one liked Mrs Lorby. We didn't think she was a missus, only that she used the title in front of her name to pretend someone found her deserving of love. Billy Mueller and I were best friends. We sat across the aisle from one another in the sixth grade. We used to draw pictures and poke fun of Mrs Lorby. She would turn around and try to find out why we were snickering, but we would be as still as church mice. She would then turn back to the blackboard and start writing, and in Mrs Lorby's fashion, she would spin around and try to catch us again, but we were on to her and knew she would do this little trick. We never fell for it and, so far, had avoided her wrath.

At lunch break, Billy and I headed for the lunchroom

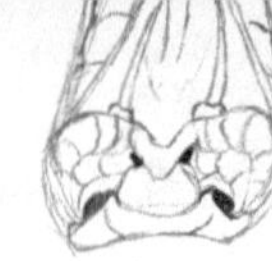

after we put some thumbtacks on her chair. We glued them upside down, just a couple of them to watch her reaction. We didn't want to hurt Mrs Lorby, only to aggravate her. I don't know why she brought out the worst in us, maybe because she didn't seem to like any of the boys in her class; she favoured the girls, and we all knew that.

After lunch and recess, we returned to the classroom. Billy and I waited for what seemed like forever. Then Mrs Lorby pulled her chair out and sat at the desk. When she sat down, nothing happened.

How could that be? We wondered. Did she find the tacks and somehow get them off? But she had playground duty, so the entire time we were out there, she was outside.

Did she not have a nerve in her bottom? Billy drew a picture with the word "nerve" with a line through it. Meaning the woman had no nerves. My shoulder huffed a couple of times. Mrs Lorby's head jerked up. She might not have any nerves in her bottom, but she had the best hearing of anyone I knew, especially for a woman her age. We knew if we went to look at the chair after class, we'd be giving ourselves away. So, we remained aloof.

The next day, Billy hit me on the shoulder. He had Mrs Lorby's yardstick stretched out in the aisle between

us. I shook my head mouthing the word "no" at him. Billy just laughed at me. Mrs Lorby spun around and began walking down between our chairs, looking to see if anyone had a note. She wasn't paying attention to the yardstick stretched between the chairs and fell over, grabbing her leg in great pain when she hit the floor. Billy pulled out the yardstick, putting it back in the corner as he ran down the hallway to get help. He came back with Miss Denning, the principal who already had an ambulance on the way. The EMTs took Mrs Lorby out on a gurney. They said she had a compound fracture. That didn't sound good. Either way, Miss Denning asked us all what happened. God love them; my fellow students did not give us away.

"She tripped. One minute she was standing and the next she was on the floor holding her ankle and moaning," Billy reported. Then Beth Ann started to cry. Miss Denning took her out in the hallway to calm her down. I told Billy we had to stop. This rankling was getting a little too carried away. He rolled his eyes and then looked at me, like warning me I'd better not say a word. He had me on the thumbtacks, I went along with that, but breaking Mrs Lorby's ankle, no. I wasn't a part of that, and if questioned by anyone of authority, I would sing like a canary. Billy knew that.

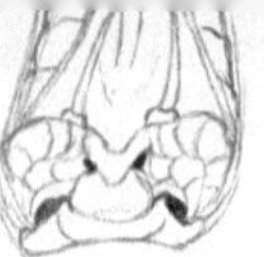

With Mrs Lorby out for a few weeks, Billy started picking on some of the other kids. They were the weaker ones—frail, shy, emotional cripples. It did something for Billy to see them cry. Madison Reilly was the worse. She had juvenile diabetes and could jump rope better and longer than anyone in the class. Billy was mad when she beat him in gym glass. He was red-faced lying on the floor, while Madison kept jumping like a bunny. Hop, hop, hop. He said something like "I'm gonna kill that Madison." I laughed knowing (hoping) he was kidding. Madison was small for her age. She looked like a fourth grader. I made some mean joke: Madison was a pygmy and that was why she could jump so long because she didn't have the body weight that Billy had. That seemed to take the edge off his anger.

I had known Billy all my life. He was always pushing, but lately, he was mean even by Billy's standards. I asked him if something was wrong at home? Billy gave my wrist a snake bite twist and told me to mind my own business. He was crazy, and everyone around him knew this about Billy Mueller.

He leaned on Madison at lunch, pushing her off the end of the lunch table bench and onto the floor. Madison was brave; she got off the floor and sat down next to Billy, shouting at him to his face. I think Billy was surprised

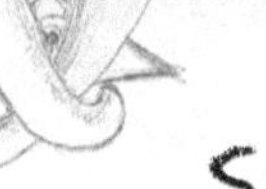

Madison could be that fierce. Billy pushed her off again.

Madison promptly got up, sat down, and opened her Jetson lunch box pulling out a syringe. She wasn't supposed to have one in her lunch box, but she did; she jabbed Billy Mueller in the leg with it, pushing the plunger.

"Ouch! What did you do to me?" Billy hollered. Madison smiled sweetly in return.

"You need a little sweetness." Madison left us at the lunch table; the fight was over. Billy and I went out into the playground; a few minutes later, Billy broke out in sweats leaving the basketball game.

"I gotta sit this one out." Billy went over to the chain-link fence and sat down. I asked him what was wrong? Billy wasn't making any sense. He said, "Mmm jusss tired."

I could see his eyes were rolling back in his head. I told the playground monitor. She rushed to Billy. Next thing, Billy was on his back, jerking around on the ground. The playground monitor told everyone to go back inside; an ambulance took Billy away.

Later that day, I saw Billy; he was sitting in his seat across the aisle from me. I shook my head and rubbed my eyes. How could that be? Billy looked at me with a thumbs-up, and then when I looked again, he wasn't there.

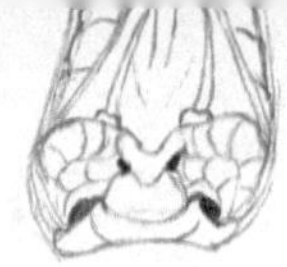

I knew he didn't make it.

Did I tell Miss Denning that it was Madison Reilly who stabbed Billy with her diabetic shot thing? Could that be the reason Billy was dead?

Before we left for the day, the Miss Denning's voice came over the intercom, informing us that Billy Mueller didn't make it. The whole class gasped in shock. I trudged home with tears flowing down my face. Somehow, I knew Billy wasn't meant to live a long life. I understood this about him. He would have probably done death by cop suicide or overdose on something. Billy was just a loose wire.

I had a creepy feeling. I turned to see that Billy Mueller was following me home. Or at least the Billy thing was. Something told me to get going. I picked up my pace, trying not to look behind me too much. I suddenly didn't feel safe going back home to an empty apartment. I ducked into an alley and ran back to school. The building was still open. I walked around, looking for an adult. I couldn't control my life. I wanted to be a kid again with adult protection. Mr Rankin, the janitor, asked me why I was in the building. I told him I forgot my book. He nodded his head in the direction of my room. I walked in and there she sat with her foot up on a chair, Mrs Lorby. She glared at me, and I knew she thought I was part of the

tripping. I could have warned her; I was guilty of that. Did Mrs Lorby know that Billy was dead? He did get punished, didn't he?

"Nick?" she said it more of a statement than a question.

"Mrs Lorby, you're back!" I stammered.

"I am here doing some lesson planning for the substitute. Why are you here?"

"Mrs Lorby, Billy died today. I saw him sitting in his chair. Then I saw him following me home from school a few minutes ago. I'm afraid to go home." She said nothing to me, looked over her glasses with that Mrs Lorby scowl.

"You see the dead," she whispered.

"What?"

"You are a seer of the dead. Once you see one, you can never unsee them. Billy has chosen you to be his connection here on Earth."

"I don't want to see Billy. He's dead. I don't want to see him anywhere. What can I do?" Mrs Lorby rubbed her leg and gingerly put the cast to the floor. She stood up, hopping on one leg to get the crutches under her.

"I can walk you home; you only live a block or so from here. We will have to find out how to stop Billy from seeking you out. I will need to do some research." She limped out of the room, and I tried to keep up with her. I

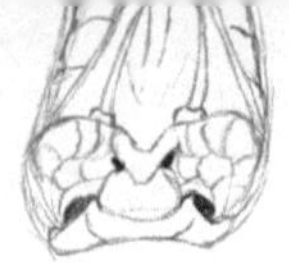

was surprised how quickly Mrs Lorby could motor along on those crutches; it had only been a couple of days since she had broken her leg. I was even more surprised that she knew where I lived. I guess she had access to my school records.

She stood outside my door and waved me in. I asked her if she wanted to come in, she said no. By the time I turned around to shut the door, Mrs Lorby was out of sight. I did see Billy Mueller standing out on the sidewalk waving to me, I slammed the door.

I had trouble sleeping that night, feeling guilty. Maybe I should tell Mrs Lorby how sorry I was not to warn her about the yardstick between the chairs. Billy had become uncontrollable, and I went with his plan out of fear. He would have done to me what he was doing to the others. Billy was a bully, but he was also my friend. I knew I had to keep him my friend; otherwise, I would be the object of his disdain.

I dreamed that night of Mrs Lorby telling me to be careful, that I should watch my back. When I left for school the next morning, I dressed in my Boy Scout uniform. It was funny how my life was falling apart, and yet I was still doing the normal things I would do, trying to make some sense out of a life that seemed to be spiralling out of my control. Putting on my scouting cap,

I looked both ways before I left the house. There was no Billy; I ran as fast as I could to school, bumping into Madison Reilly, accidently knocking her to the ground.

"Watch it!" she shouted at me. I knew all about the medicine she takes. I looked it up in the encyclopaedia when I got home last night. The kind that she stabbed Billy with after he pushed her to the floor for the second time. I didn't blame her for defending herself, but Madison had to know she was a murderer.

"You gave him your medicine," I simply said. Her face registered shock.

"You don't know what you're talking about, Fat Boy." She had to add that part, the old tag name I had before I started to hang with Billy Mueller. He beat up anyone who called me that, and the name disappeared. If Madison had slapped me, I couldn't have been more stung. I suddenly felt terrible about Billy. It was registering in me how much Billy had protected me, and now I would be relegated back to Fat Boy lane. And then, I was angry. Billy not only was haunting me, but he also had left me high and dry.

"You shut your little yap. I know what you did, and I will tell everyone. You killed Billy with your medicine. You call me Fat Boy again, and I will make sure you don't call anyone that name *ever*." For good measure, I leaned

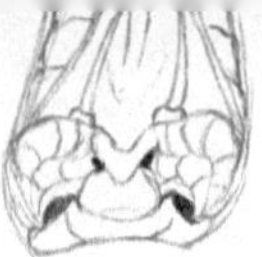

in and pushed her up against the hall wall. Madison shrunk, and I laughed. It was just the reaction I'd hoped. Madison was now scared of me. As long as she was afraid, she wouldn't say anything.

Two teachers stood in the hall, whispering. The looks on their faces were one of shock and concern. They stopped talking when I walked by them. I saw Mrs Lorby standing on her crutches in the nook of the coatroom.

"Mrs Lorby?"

"Here, Nick. I think this will help you keep Billy at bay." She put a little doll made out of a nail in my hand. "Carry it on you always. It will keep him away. It's got strong mojo. Good luck." She hobbled down the hall and out the door. The nail had hair and material wrapped around it. I wondered if it were Billy's hair and how Mrs Lorby got it. I put it in my pocket. The first bell rang. I didn't want to be late for class. I hurried from my locker with my books.

The substitute teacher took attendance. I could feel the nail sticking into my thigh, so I reached in my pocket to rearrange it. The intercom sputtered to life.

"This is Miss Denning. I am sorry to report the death of Mrs Lorby. I will have further information on the funerals for Billy Mueller and for Mrs Lorby for anyone wanting to attend."

188

I couldn't catch my breath. I ran out of the room. The substitute teacher didn't know my name. I ran down to Miss Denning's office.

"Nick!" Miss Denning was surprised when I burst through her office door.

"When did Mrs Lorby die?" I pleaded with her.

"Well, I think she died yesterday morning. Her daughter only called me to let me know. Complications from the surgery, I think."

"Yesterday morning!" I'd seen Mrs Lorby myself yesterday afternoon. She was in the classroom. She walked me home. I saw her this morning. She gave me the talisman. How could that be?

Her words came back to me. "You see the dead." I ran out of the office down the hallway. Mr Rankin, the janitor, stood with an axe coming out of his head.

"Nick, you need to get back to class." Blood oozed down the side of his face. I screamed and ran for the front door of the building, hitting Billy Mueller square in the chest. I smelled the smoke.

"What's happening?"

"The school's on fire," Billy chuckled.

"Pull the alarm," I screamed. Billy held the alarm pull in his hand, dangling it in my face. The kids were locked in the classrooms. I could hear them shouting for

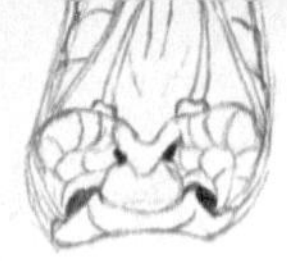

help, pounding on the doors.

"Break open the glass. There's an axe in a box down the hall." Mr Rankin pointed to his head, laughing at me. I could hear the screams of everyone locked in their rooms as the fire spread around the old school. I pulled out the nail doll and held it towards Billy, who backed up and allowed me to pass, running through the front door. The fire engines were pulling up.

"Get out of the way!" the firemen shouted as they pulled the hoses off the truck. The old school, built in the early 1900s, now engulfed in flames. I stood there watching, and suddenly there were many kids around me, their faces burned off, their clothes still smoking.

I am the seer of the dead. They can talk to me. They will follow me around every day. Madison Reilly appears next to me. Her long beautiful hair burned in the fire as well as her eyelids and part of her nose; she is missing an ear. Madison's hand moves out to hold mine. I shriek. I refuse to hold her hand. I see Mrs Lorby motioning to me. She has guided me so far through this nightmare, I now trust her implicitly. I follow her to the sidewalk. She is standing on her crutches.

"Nick, I know you are having trouble with this. I can help you end it."

"Please, Mrs Lorby, I don't want to see them

anymore." Mrs Lorby threw down her crutches and was able to hobble.

"Come, be a good Boy Scout. Help me cross the street." I took Mrs Lorby's arm and helped her to the middle of the busy street in front of the school. A loud vehicle horn blasted. I found myself under the wheels of the ambulance. Looking to the side, I saw Mrs Lorby's outstretched hand, and I took it. Mrs Lorby led me back to the other children who stood in a large circle, watching the school burn down. I wasn't afraid anymore, I was among friends. Billy Mueller walked up to me, clapping his hand on my shoulder.

"At last, you made it, Fat Boy." Only Billy could get away with calling me that. Together we watched the roof tumble in on the old school. The children clapped at the beautiful fireworks display of sparks that blew up into the sky.

 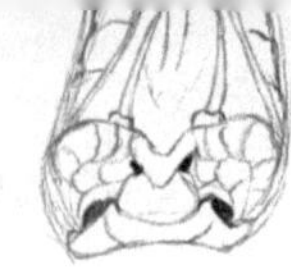

BLACK HARE PRESS

CORRIDOR

by Denver Grenell

Jamie's father bellowed through the thin plywood wall of her bedroom, his voice like a hateful foghorn. "Come on girl, get the fuck out of bed! I don't want to tell you again!"

"I'm up!" Jamie McKay sat on the edge of the bed, staring at the floor, clutching her worn copy of *Edgar Allan Poe's Complete Works*. She had gotten dressed ten minutes ago but had yet to summon the strength to leave her room. One more year, she thought. One more year of that prick.

The bedroom door swung open. Her father's puffy, bearded face glared around the doorframe.

"Well, at least you're dressed. Come and eat something if you're hungry. I'm leaving in five." She

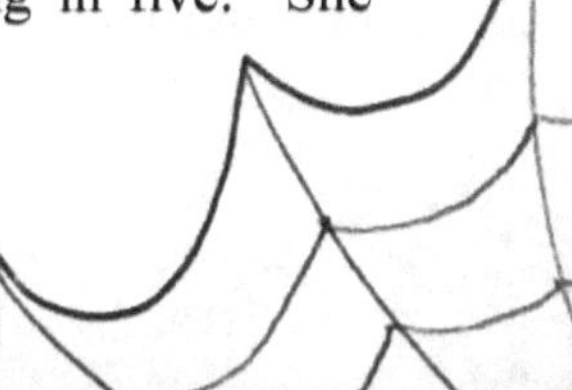

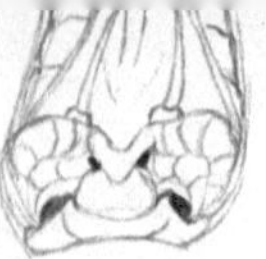

opened her mouth to speak, but he was already gone. "Otherwise, you can walk," he yelled back down the hallway. Jamie slowly rose from the bed, looking for the strength to "appear normal" for another day. Tucking her book into her school bag, she rose and took a last look at herself in the mirror. Tired eyes peered back at her from a pale face surrounded by long auburn hair. She exhaled and left the comfortable darkness of her room and stepped out into "his house."

Dave stood at the kitchen bench, gulping down the last of his morning coffee. His eyes glanced disapprovingly across Jamie's body as she entered the room.

"When are you going to get yourself a longer skirt, girl?" he grimaced at his daughter. The last thing Jamie needed now was a fight with her dad on an already challenging day, but this was an ongoing debate and one from which she refused to back down.

"I told you, it's regulation, and besides, no one at school has any problem with it."

"I bet they don't," he spat, "the boys least of all."

"Well, Mum helped me pick it out, so take it up with her if you're not happy," she said defiantly. His eyes widened, and his cheeks flushed red with anger, his default setting.

"Oh, I will, believe me, little missy. And I'm leaving right now, so it looks like you missed your ride, smartass!" He snatched his keys off the kitchen bench and stormed out of the kitchen.

Relief washed over Jamie. The thought of a drive to school with him made her feel anxious. She would have to walk quickly to make the eight forty-five bell, but she'd jog if she had to. She grabbed an apple from the fruit bowl on the bench and stood by the front door and waited. Outside her father's truck roared to life. Once it had pulled out of the driveway, she exited the house into a pleasingly overcast autumn day. Just as she was glad to be spared any more time with her father, the lack of sun brought a sense of peace. Jamie breathed in the cool air and ambled along the footpath with a smile on her face.

***

Spencer Collins stood at the edge of his bed, staring fixedly at the large Bleeding Skullz poster on the far wall. A white graffiti-styled skull returned the gaze from hollowed sockets. The black void of the skull's eyes invited him into the darkness. It promised him salvation.

Spencer's eyes went to the cheap digital clock on his bedside table. The red display blinked 8:30 am. He was

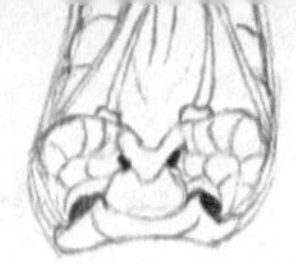

going to be late for school, but that didn't matter. It was better if he was late. *Everyone would be there. The more, the merrier,* he thought. He gazed lovingly at his "toys" on the bed. Spencer reached down and felt the coolness of their bodies, marvelled at the intricacies of their design, the power they held within their small frames. *Soon,* he thought. An electric charge ran up his spine. He tried to pinpoint what it was—excitement. He never thought that he might feel excited about today. Nervous perhaps. Energised. But not excited. He smiled. Good. A sign that he was on the right path.

He carefully placed his toys into the deep pockets of his black bomber jacket, concealing them safely inside. He turned to the full-length mirror that hung on the back of his bedroom door. Yesterday when he looked in this mirror, he saw a weak and scared little boy. Today, a man stared back—tall, confident, strong. Under the bomber, he wore his black Bleeding Skullz tee shirt—the spitting image of the poster—as well as his tapered black jeans and brown laced boots. It's what he wore most days, but today it was a uniform to be worn into battle. He pulled a grey beanie over his straggly blond hair, further enhancing the militaristic look he desired. "Righteous," his reflection spoke back to him.

SCHOOL'S IN

Jamie usually listened to music on her way to school, but today she was content with the soundtrack of the outside world to accompany her journey. Dry leaves crunched underfoot. Warbled birdsong meshed with the hum of traffic. A skateboard rattled down the opposite footpath. The shrill voices of a mother and her two young children bubbled away behind her. She looked at her watch, instinctively quickening her pace—8:35 am, ten minutes till the bell.

English class was first this morning, and today they were talking about the works of one Edgar Allan Poe. Her teacher, Miss Jamieson, had only assigned the class one story and poem to read, but Jamie had devoured the Complete Works over the weekend and even found time to re-read "The Raven" and "The Tell-Tale Heart" in preparation for today's lesson. She had closed the book at 2 am which explained the dark rings around her eyes, but wasn't Poe's gothic prose meant to be devoured in the witching hour? Certainly not under the fluorescent lighting of the classroom by yawning, disinterested students.

Jamie turned left onto Centrepoint Road. Only another few minutes to school if she hurried. Ahead of her

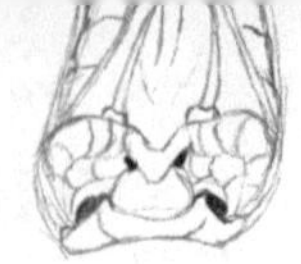

sauntered a familiar figure dressed all in black, tall, slim, and hunched over. Spencer Collins. They had fooled around once at a party a year or so ago, but she had put the pin in that budding relationship when it became evident that he wasn't exactly a nice guy. Jamie slowed her pace. She'd rather be late to English than have to suffer a cripplingly awkward conversation with Spencer Collins.

***

The grey pall of the overcast day brought a similar sense of calm to Spencer as he approached Whitecliffs High School for what he was certain would be the last time. The excitement that had surprised him before in the bedroom returned as the school loomed closer. There were a few stragglers in the carpark racing into the main building, but it was apparent the bell had rung for first period. Everyone would be in their classrooms. Good, he thought coolly—less commotion in the hallway. With everyone hunkered down in the classes, he would have much easier access to his targets. His hands sunk into the pockets of his jacket, encircling the cold steel within. Another shiver of excitement rippled through his nervous system.

SCHOOL'S IN

A cool breeze swept down the road, kicking up a swirl of rust-coloured leaves into the air. Spencer stopped for a second and stared at the leaves that had settled onto the footpath. He was stunned by what he saw spread out before him. How had he not noticed this before? Spencer didn't see an array of maple leaves before him. Instead, there was an intricate tableau of death—beautiful explosions of blood, blooming before him like a flower unfurling its petals. Exit wounds. A further sign he was on the right path. A serene smile crossed his face, and he strode across the road with a renewed purpose. Spencer looked up as he passed under the large Whitecliffs High School sign that sat atop the main gates. *Crossing the threshold,* he thought. Today, he made history. He may not be around to hear his name spoken or to see the articles or news reports. The obligatory parade of think pieces and political debates. The soul searching. It didn't matter. He'd seen it all before. And he wasn't in it for the infamy. Or to be remembered. He was doing what was demanded of him by the thick black tar of pure hatred that flowed through his veins. This poisoned blood that had always been inside him had finally curdled to the point that it had demanded a tribute from the body that contained it. The blackness had shown him its truth. It had come to him in the night and whispered the secrets of the

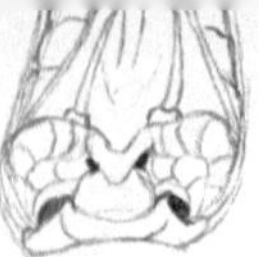

dark into his ear. When he awoke though, he wasn't lying in a pool of sweat, screaming. He was cool and invigorated, with a raw power flowing through him like an electrical current. Guiding him here. Today his tribute would be paid, and the transfer of power would be complete.

***

Jamie waited until Spencer had entered the school before she started moving again. Thank God he hadn't seen her. But now, she was late. She broke into a light jog and flitted across the empty road. Moving through the carpark towards the main building, she looked towards the doors and stopped suddenly. Standing before the entranceway was Spencer. He was hunched over, bobbing up and down like a boxer getting ready for a title fight. What the hell was he doing?

Then Jamie saw the guns. One grey pistol in each hand. They looked like the plastic guns she had used at Laser Strike when she was a kid.

"Oh shit," she whispered. Ahead of her, Spencer bounced one last time, then he started walking up the steps. Jamie pulled out her phone. She dialled the police number, but they wouldn't get here in time. He was going

inside now.

***

Spencer entered the warm corridor of the main school block. One of his pistols clipped the door as it swung closed. The metallic sound it made was pleasing to his ears. He stopped and surveyed the corridor before him. There were four classrooms in this block, all filled with students and their teachers, like a bunch of lambs in a holding pen waiting for the killing bolt to shoot through their dim skulls. He checked the Glock G19s. Safety off. Clips loaded. He'd double-checked them before leaving home, but now he was on the cusp of realising his dark dream, he rechecked them to be sure. He breathed deeply, willing himself to do what had to be done. He took a step towards the nearest classroom. It was Year 12 English class with Miss Jamieson, that snooty bitch who had long since given up trying to get Spencer to read the assigned books or hand in work.

Instead, she ignored him and happily wrote F in red pen on all his grade forms. Not that he cared. He had long since stopped caring about anything except what he was here to do today.

Spencer put the pistol in his right hand back in his

jacket pocket and grasped the door handle. Inside he could see Miss Jamieson addressing the class. Her high-pitched voice always sounded like a dismissive whine to his ears. He could hear it floating across the room and through the wood and glass of the door, goading him on, daring him to enter. His left hand tightened around the other Glock. "Now," he said affirmatively to himself. Spencer started to open the door when a hand reached over from behind and gripped his shoulder firmly. Startled, he turned around, raising his left arm, bringing the pistol up to face level, right in line with Jamie McKay's pale forehead. "What the fuck?" His finger quivered nervously on the trigger.

"Spencer. Don't do this. Please." Jamie's voice wavered. There was fear in her voice, but something else as well that made Spencer pause. *Do it. She's the first. Do it. Achieve greatness,* the dark blood whispered as it pumped through his veins. But something held him back. It was her voice. Beneath the fear, there was love.

"Spencer. Please. Talk to me."

"No," the black blood spoke through him. It was in control now. His left index finger twitched.

"Spencer. You must be hurting. I could…I could help you." Jamie slowly raised her right hand and placed it between the barrel and her forehead.

"You don't understand," Spencer's voice forced through clenched teeth. "I'm not hurting. This is who I am. What I am...for." Jamie's hand lowered the barrel—slowly, slowly.

"Don't. Don't. Don't."

Spencer's eyes closed. The dark blood roiled within him trying to force its way to the top, threatening to spill out of his ears, eyes, and nose and run freely down his body in an unstoppable flood.

"Don't. Don't. Don't." A whisper now. Softer. Softer.

The black blood strove to choke his thoughts from his head and replace them with its own. Jamie put her arms around Spencer and drew him in close. Her warmth cut through his thick jacket, seeped into his skin, entered his veins, and met the cold blackness that pulsed there. His eyes closed.

"Don't. Don't. Don't." Barely audible now. Spencer wasn't sure if it was him whispering or Jamie. The black blood screamed in his ears. Sweat ran down his temple. The warmth from Jamie's body engulfed him in invisible flames, seeking to burn the cold hell within him. From him.

The handgun shook as it rose back up towards Jamie. Her head was resting on his chest, her eyes closed.

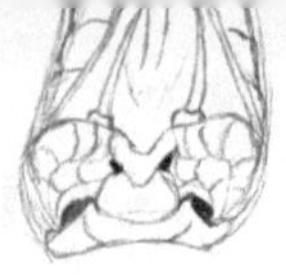

"Don't. Don't. Don't."

***

"Now, before we get into the stories with any depth, I'd like to go around the room and hear what you thought of them. What did they make you—"

A thunder crack exploded in the air.

Screams. Pupils dove to the floor. Miss Jamieson gasped. The large Poe book dropped from her hands. Crying. Whimpering.

The classroom door slowly opened. More gasps. Jamie McKay entered the classroom, a distant look on her face. Covered in red paint? No. Not paint. Blood. Dark and fresh. More screams. Miss Jamieson snapped out of her initial shock.

"Jamie. My god! Are you—are you okay?" Jamie nodded. She slowly crossed the classroom, passing the students cowering and whimpering beneath their desks. Jamie found her seat and slumped down into it. The teacher rushed over to her, placing a hand on her bloodstained forehead.

"Jamie, dear, where are you hurt?"

Jamie slowly looked up at her teacher and smiled sadly.

204

"No. Not me. Spencer." A bloody hand pointed to the corridor. Beyond the open door, out in the hallway, surrounded by an expanding pool of crimson, lay the still body of Spencer Collins. The darkness seeped out of him into the corridor. His open eyes looked upwards to the ceiling.

Jamie had opened her own eyes and seen Spencer. He'd looked peaceful. The gun pointed to his temple. He had smiled at her and said, "Thank you." And then he'd pulled the trigger.

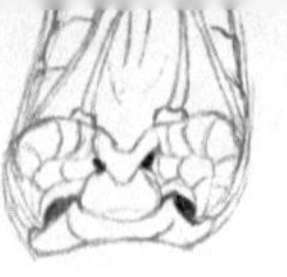

BLACK HARE PRESS

THE CUTEST COUPLE

by Gregg Cunningham

They all want him, and it is no secret to the bitches in the cheerleading team, that I am just as hot for Eddie as they are. Only, if he was going to choose between those skinny skanks and me, I am going make sure he sees exactly what I have to offer him this summer, *before* we got back to school.

Eddie Vegas doesn't stand a chance; this year we *will* be King and Queen, cutest couple for sure.

He's been watching me for years, from the moment he put on that helmet in junior league in fact, all the way up to him now being the school's number one quarterback. So, I reckon that bulge in his pants is ready to pop those tight

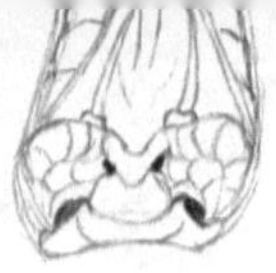

shorts of his.

Eddie with his tight butt and his slick-back hair. Eddie with his daddy's money and his own flat. Eddie with his skanky fan club. Yes, it is only a matter of time before I have him begging for mercy under my own tight cheeks as they bounce his balls black and blue. I've spent enough time on this body down the gym; its time this girl got herself some reward, and we *are* going to be cutest couple this year, even if I have to kill someone to get that damn crown.

So, when I heard he was having an end of summer party tonight with some of his mates, I thought it was about time for me to step up and show him just what he is missing.

But I have to be quick. *Mika the Squeaka* is already prowling and threatening to take my captaincy; I don't want her taking the number one quarterback from me as well.

"Hey Stacey, I hear Eddie is having a party down his place tonight, you hooking up with Barry again?" Mika giggled as we stood on the by-line watching the boys' practice.

"I hear you'll make cutest couple this year!" I roll my eyes and sigh. Barry had been a drunken mistake and a total immature jerk who couldn't even get it up at Michelle's

party the week before, and I had sworn Chelle to secrecy.

Michelle, the sneaky hoe, let that out of the bag by posting a group chat photo of me and him on all fours. But I'll get her back.

"No, I thought I'd give Eddie my full attention tonight. How about you? Another night in with your dildo?"

"Hell no, Eddie asked if I wanted to join them tonight; didn't you get an invite?" She smiles.

"Bitch, I don't need an invite!" Touché, that should shut the hoe up for a while, give me a chance to show Eddie what I got as I follow them off the pitch and into the boys dressing rooms.

I have to show him some skin to get him going, so I admit to giving him just a little more cleavage than normal, and a bit blonder attitude thrown in for good measure, eyelashes giving it full Betty Boo.

And boy, does he fall for it.

Eddie looks like he is ready to jump me here and now, and if it wasn't for the coaches in the locker room corridor, I'd have him.

So, with that image planted deep into his head, I head home to prepare for a long overdue hook up with the school's hottest rookie quarterback. I'd just have to make sure Mika doesn't steal my thunder.

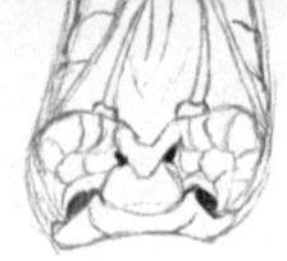

Bitch is always cock blocking me.

But I know how to put her off her game, I have an ace up my sleeve that I *know* will piss her off.

She hates the Ouija board. In fact, if I remember, the last time I broke out the spirit board, she burst into tears and up and left the party without so much as a dry hump from her target that night.

Mika was going to get the full queen bitch Stacey Wallbecker treatment tonight.

***

I decided to go for slutty, but nice slutty, figure; I'll let him see a bit of leg before I pounce. I just need to knock the competition from her perch first though.

I know the usual crew will be there; Barry and Jack will smoke anything that is on offer tonight, while Dan, the ventriloquist, and Michelle will be making out before it gets dark, his hand so far up her skirt she'll be making all the right noises without moving her lips. I swear that pair have no filter. So that leaves Eddie and the twister mat for me. I just need to get Mika all hysterical and make sure she wants to leave the party early. Once the Ouija board is set up, we should see her true colours. The last time I moved the glass, she fainted.

210

It only takes me ten minutes to make the journey in my car to Eddie's new place, and I see that Michelle's car is already parked in the driveway. I recap the mantra, naked twister, Ouija board, pounce on Eddie. Easy.

"Hey Stacey, wow, you look great!" he says as he stands in his doorway in nothing but his boxers, and I like what I'm seeing.

"Hey Eddie, started the orgy without me?" I Betty Boo him again with my eyelashes as he blushes.

"No, we just got the twister going. Want a drink?" He closes the door, getting an eyeful, but I just smile and catwalk my way over to the Kama Sutra lesson on the floor.

"Left hand, red!" Barry laughs as Mika slides on the mat, and I sit down next to Eddie, Michelle looking on with distaste.

Jealous much?

"Who's winning?" I ask taking a can from Eddie and handing him my Ouija board.

"Something for later!" I wink.

The boys get loud and naked, the girls get loose and giggly—it's the way the night always go. But I keep my eye on the prize; Eddie sees that.

The more we flirt, the more skin I show him, and it's only a matter of time before I have him. Phones are out, Snapchats are going left and right, while Mika livestreams

every nipple slip and cock flop on the twister mat. She's going to be a tough opponent tonight, but after a while Dan gets the cones out and we ease up with a joint, I suggest it's Ouija time.

Mika seems up for it this time, but I'll change that with a few scares. Bitch almost has a panic attack when I make out the glass moving on the board is possessed and she's the one it wants to haunt!

We drink, we eat our Uber eats, we joke and yes, haunted glasses are smashed, and well…it all gets a bit messy. The Ouija board is a mistake; I'm called all the bitchy names under the sun, so I have to back off while Mika gets the attention. And boy, does she lap it up.

This chases Barry and Jack away to finish their joints down the park in peace, while Dan and Michelle quickly say their goodbyes. Michelle warns me to ease up with a glare, and yes, I hold my hands up and declare a truce. Jesus, what a total bitch she is tonight.

Mika wins, halleluiah!

But instead of winning, she wants to share Eddie. The three of us. Together on his futon.

Now I'm a girl of the twenties, and more than happy to give this a go, I just don't want to have a go with Mika the drama queen. She squeals as he rides her like an inflatable orca pool toy, all *oohs* and *ahhhs* and carpet

burns, rolling her way around the floor like she is shooting a freshman porno, fish pouty faces and leg spreads for Eddie, who I might add is loving every position he is bending her into.

"Do us, do us both, Eddie!" she screams.

This is not what I want. I'm not here to be second fiddle to *Mika the Squeaka*. I feel like I'm just here to hold the tequila bottle and cut the lime. I slap her ass, kissing Eddie and pouring a mouthful of tequila into his mouth.

"Move over, skank!"

This bitch has got to go, so I elbow her in the ribs just as she's wailing away another fake Hollywood orgasm. This knocks her off her game and sends her tumbling from the futon, legs pointing to three and nine on the clock. Eddie is laughing as his dick flaps in the breeze. Jesus, he is totally spaced, and I doubt the poor guy will remember any of this in the morning.

"Okay Eddie, let's see how you like it on *your* back!" The poor guy is completely stoned, but he sure is up for the challenge and shrugs, "Sure Stacey, whatever you want!"

So, I throw him to the bed and straddle him like the warrior goddess I am, riding him like he is my trusty stallion. Mika takes out Eddie's phone from his lumberjack shirt and starts streaming again, but I'm wearing the stirrups now; it's my turn to ride that bull, and although I

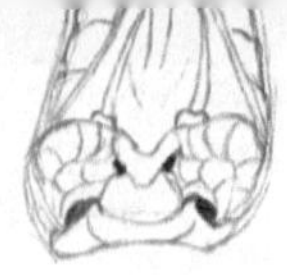

tell her to back off, she just shrugs and knocks back the tequila, cutting up the lime into wedges while she records, waiting for what's left of an exhausted Eddie.

"Hey Chelle, pick up your phone, you gotta see this bitch in action!" She's laughing now while she films me on top of Eddie and that's when I sort of lose my cool and grab the kitchen knife.

***

I'm first awake and I turn around to see the knife in Mika's chest. Eddie is lying sparked out next to her and the bottle of tequila lying on its side, spilling what's left onto the floor. My head is pounding and my hair feels like someone has shoved it inside a candy flossing machine and is stuck to my face.

Gross!

She's dead of course, *Mika the Squeaka.* Lying there with the knife in her chest like she's the sword in the stone prop for Excalibur, and I can't believe I actually done it. Eddie's phone is lying there buzzing away, and I see Mika has used it to send two sex videos to Michelle.

That's a worry, and I stop to think how I can get out of this one as I read the text.

Eddie, Michelle needs a lift to come get her stuff—she

214

lost her phone.

Well that's a relief, for now, and I grab Eddie's phone and throw the duvet over them both; he'll have to deal with that mucky little issue when he wakes up.

Damn, it smells of sex in here.

Now I have a problem with Michelle and that video Mika sent, so I send Danny a text back suggesting I pick her up on my way to work to look for her bag as Mika and Eddie are sleeping one off.

I leave the two lovebirds entwined on the futon and dress quickly, making my way through last night's party carnage, standing on something that squeaks under my heels as I step through the mess looking for Michelle's bag. Hopefully, I find her bag before she does or that vid will go viral.

When I look down, I see poor Archie, Eddie's hamster, and let out a squeak myself. His back was broken and he is squished against the floor, guts spilled. Least I can do is pick him up and try to flush him down the garbage disposal; dry retching a little, I decide to leave his little feet poking from the plug hole.

The more important issue is Michelle and the sexy snuff video Mika had unwittingly filmed. I need to get to her lost phone before Michelle sees it.

Her bag is not hard to find, lying there on the floor.

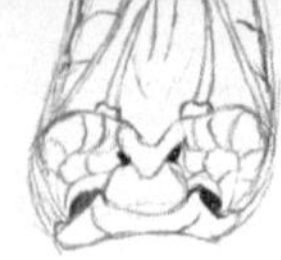

But her phone is locked, and if I hide it, she will come up and start snooping, maybe even find Mika.

I have a better plan though and pick the bag up. I've decided to burn this place to the ground with them all inside, if I can.

***

"I think I left it on the table after I paid for the curry?" Michelle says as we drive along Johnson way back to Eddie's house, but I'm already working out how I'm going to get out of this situation as we pass the gas station.

"How was last night?" She smiles, but she hates being inside with me, I can tell.

"Oh, you know, pretty lame, Eddie and Mika ended up going for it next door, leaving me to feel like a third wheel!" I stroke the metal bar tucked down the seat.

"Really? I thought you three looked pretty well on your way to, you know…skanksville." She winked.

Bitch!

"Yeh, na!" I reply, already planning her downfall.

"Oh, I totally forgot, I found your bag," I say matter of fact as we turn onto the gravel, "it's in the trunk!"

She scowls at me as I park behind her car and pop the trunk, waiting until she has her phone in her hand before I

216

join her and swing the tyre iron against her head with a crack, watching as she falls inside the trunk.

Next!

It doesn't take long to find and delete the sex videos on Michelle's phone, before I make my own video of Chelle bleeding out in the trunk of my car with Eddie's phone, blowing him a kiss.

Comfy?

I have the perfect setup now and just need to return all phones back to their owners. Michelle's Gucci bag is dumped in the curry tray, Eddie's phone is put back into his lumberjack shirt that's wrapped around the stiffening Mika, and all I have to do now is drive down the garage and fill my gas can up and burn his flat to the ground.

Easy-peasy!

Well it would have been had Eddie not showed up in the gas station to screw things up. I thought he'd be out for another few hours after the tequila shots we had him sink last night.

What's he doing outside anyway? Surely, he must have found Mika stiff as a board lying next to him, with his kitchen knife stuck deep in her chest?

I have to think fast, catch him out to see if he knows I did it.

"Hey Eddie, I was just heading back to cook you a fry

up, and my stupid car died" I lie, Betty Boo time again.

"Didn't you get my note? I've been ringing you, but they went straight to messages."

"Er yeh Stacey, I was just making sure you were okay, you've been ages!"

Now I know he's lying, because I left no note and he looks shady as all hell.

"Great, well you can take me to my car then and help me fill her up!"

I show him the gas can and tell him where I'm parked. Obviously, I don't tell him I'm parked outside the gas station because I still have Michelle in the trunk. I need some time to think and get him as far away from my car as possible.

Eddie is sweating; I can see it on his brow when we get inside his car, and he keeps glancing back for some reason. Maybe he saw my car and knows what I'm up too? But I think it's something else too.

"Where did you break down?" he asks nervously and I make some nonsense up while playing with the curls of my hair.

Has he got Mika in the car with him?

Is he trying to call *my* bluff here?

I take out my own phone and try an experiment, scrolling down and hitting his phone number while he

watches the road.

I hear the ringing from his trunk and can't believe he is actually doing the same thing I'm doing with Michelle's body.

"Is that your phone, Eddie?"

He blanks out; I see the panic in his eyes.

"Eddie, why is your phone in the trunk of your car?"

Eddie stops the car and I curse at him to open it up before I kick his ass, and the poor guy sounds like he is having a mental breakdown. He's actually mumbling away to himself behind the wheel.

Inside the boot of Michelle's car, like I thought, is Mika.

This is classic, he's trying to get rid of Mika's body. He's wrapped her up neatly in a blanket and I actually feel sorry for him. Should I tell him I know what happened, then we can sort this out together and still be the school's cutest couple.

It's all going to be wonderful. Eddie's the perfect boyfriend for a psycho bitch like me. We can even clean up together.

"Someone's been a busy little beaver!" I smile, sticking my head in the window and pulling my phone out to show him last night's snuff movie with Mika.

We could be the next Bonnie and Clyde, the next

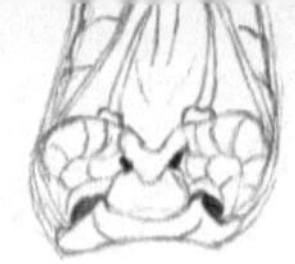

Romeo and Juliet, I imagine. The cutest couple to terrorise the streets of Wantham.

He flinches, I see the tears in his staring, panicked eyes as he denies everything, his fists clenched tight as he punches out in panic.

"I'm sorry, I'm so sorry, Stacey!" he begs and I suddenly feel the sharp knife in my neck as he thrusts it in deep while I stumble back wide eyed, clutching at the blood oozing from my gaping wound.

"Eddie, no!" I gurgle, trying to show him what I had done for him, trying to tell him it's all okay, we are going to be great together, the cutest couple!

From somewhere above, a haunting voice laughs.

Do us, do us both, Eddie!

Then all I feel is the coldness creeping up my bare, tanned thighs.

ZOMBIE BOARDING SCHOOL

by Henry Herz

The noisome cafeteria in which the zombies meandered was a large stone hall, with a copper cauldron at one end, out of which a hulking ogre cafeteria monitor, dressed in leather armour for the purpose of defeating overly famished zombie bites, ladled the clotted brain broth at mealtimes; of which composition each zombie had one porringer and no more—except on Samhain and then each had two bowls and a half-ulna besides.

Zombie boarding school never let out for summer and the bowls never wanted washing. The zombies

221

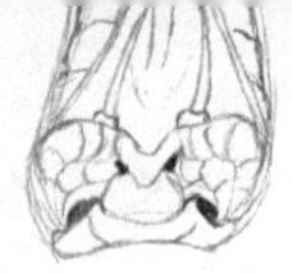

polished them with their rotting tongues till they shone again. And when they had performed this operation, which never took very long, their mouths being nearly as large as the bowls, they would resume their aimless shamble, staring at the copper with such ravenous eyes as if they could devour the very metal of which it was composed; employing themselves meanwhile in sucking their fingers most assiduously, with the view of catching up any stray splashes of blood that might have been cast thereon. Some in their zeal severed and devoured their own digits.

Zombies have generally excellent appetites. Oliver Twisted and his undead companions suffered the tortures of slow starvation for their first three months at summer school; finally, they got so voracious and wild with hunger that one zombie leered darkly at his companions, making clear without words that unless he had another basin of brain broth per diem, he should some night eat the zombie who rested next to him. He had but one crazed, hungry eye, and the others implicitly believed him.

An impromptu council of moaning zombies was held, the conversation meagre given their limited capacity for thought, a few lacking tongues or lips, though still capable of nodding their decaying heads in silent agreement. Lots were cast on who should shamble up to

the ogre after supper that evening and ask for more; and it fell to Oliver Twisted.

***

The evening arrived. The zombies took their places; the ogre in his flea-ridden leather armour stationed himself at the copper. The brain broth was served out, and the ogre mumbled a long mocking grace over the short commons, though the zombies dug in without pause. The crimson gruel disappeared, and the zombies moaned and stared at Oliver, while his neighbours nudged him. Smallish as he was, he was desperate with hunger and reckless with misery. He rose from the cold cafeteria bench, and shuffling, bowl in hand, to the ogre, uttered, somewhat amazed at his ability to form words at all— "More brains…"

The ogre was a fat, ruddy-skinned specimen, but it turned very pale. It gazed in stupefied astonishment at the small rebel, clinging for support to the copper.

The zombies stood paralysed with fear mixed with hope; the latter soon dashed forever.

The ogre shrieked aloud, pinioned Oliver with one arm, and with the other delivered a mighty blow with the ladle to Oliver's head, striking it clean off.

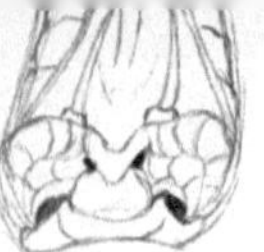

Oliver's corpse collapsed to the floor. The others resumed licking their bowls.

MASTER OF THE HUNT

by John Clewarth

On the night that I first encountered Edward Massingham, the air was gripped by freezing temperatures. Snow helter-skeltered in frenzied flurries, creating miniature snowdrifts around the corners of my window.

I had long since consigned the boys to their beds, under order of silence until their alarm call at 7.30 the following morning. I was sitting in "the Housemaster's hovel"—the bedroom-cum-study allocated for my comfort and convenience by the Headmaster of Rashville Preparatory School—slashing the immature scripts of thirteen-year-olds with bloody red ink.

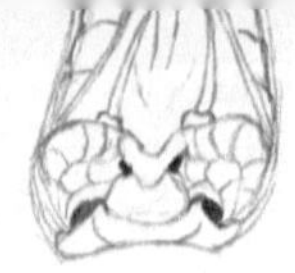

When I say I "encountered" Mr Massingham, I didn't actually *see* him. I *heard* him. Heavy footfalls on hard, bare wood. Footsteps on the ascent. Climbing a short flight of steps. Overhead.

The only room above mine was the attic space of the school. I had been up once only. And once had been enough. Here was stored the collected junk and memorabilia of a hundred years of schooling; rusted cups and shields, flaking portraits of long-dead masters, broken tennis racquets, badly painted stage scenery, and the like. Incongruous amongst all this was the stuffed fox, whose glass eyes glimmered with an eeriness all their own.

Yes, once had been enough.

But now someone was climbing the short set of wooden steps and, of course, I was obliged to investigate. It had to be one of the boys. Apart from myself, they were the only living souls in the building. I put down my pen and capped the bottle of ink. As I went to the door, my eyes fell upon the curved-handled cane reclining against the wall, my thoughts determining that the young reprobate's rear-end would be stinging from it before the night was out.

Upon leaving my room, however, and walking the few feet along the corridor to the small door that led to the steps, I experienced a creeping sense of malaise and

uncertainty. Whether this was connected to the phantom-like shadows that my candle cast in animation around the walls and ceiling, or something still more sinister, I did not know. Nor did I want to.

As I opened the door, the sight was one of complete blackness, barely pierced by my flickering flame. But more unnerving than that, as I began my clambering, was the sudden and quite noticeable plummet in the already freezing temperatures. As I reached the top of the steps though, there was nothing different to be seen. The usual bric-à-brac. And the fox with its menacing dead stare. This defied all reason. I had clearly not imagined the footsteps on the stairs; I am not one given readily to flights of fancy. Yet here I stood in the only entrance to the attic. And the only exit.

Shivering, not solely from the sepulchral temperatures, I descended the steps and returned to my room. I did no further marking that night, rather I consumed three parts of a bottle of brandy; the fervid bite of the alcohol did little to relieve the chill which seemed to reach to the very core of my being.

*****

The second time I encountered Edward Massingham had been the last. He had been the Housemaster in post before me, so I had been well acquainted with the story of his untimely death. Rashville being a school for the sons of the gentry, it was traditional for the Housemaster to be invited onto the local hunts. Massingham had joined them with relish; accompanying them long and often after his first blooding. His ardent practising of the blood sport had proved to be his undoing.

On the May Day hunt last year, he had been thrown from his mount and might well have survived had he not been impaled upon the lethal point of a wooden fence post.

After his death at the hunt it had been considered tasteless to keep his prize trophy in its case in the library, so the stuffed fox had been removed to the upper limit of the school—the attic.

I am more compassionate than superstitious, and it had not been long before I had all but forgotten the ethereal footsteps on the attic stairs. It was also my compassion that prevented me from partaking of a pastime that sought nothing more than the exhaustion and tearing apart of one of God's creatures. Or as Wilde put it, "the unspeakable in pursuit of the uneatable".

And so it was that I accompanied a number of boys and masters on the following May Day, one year after Massingham's demise, to pay respects at his graveside;

well away from the planned hunt. Even in this early summer month, the air was chill and cheerless. Silence smothered the churchyard like a shroud. The smell of dead things was in the atmosphere. We stood around his grave, heads bowed, like a bed of dying blooms.

That feeling infiltrated me once more. The unnatural coldness that penetrated my very soul. And still the silence persisted, though it was now being stabbed by the distant sounds of horn, hoof and hound.

With what seemed alarming swiftness, the impinging sounds grew ever louder, coming closer and closer. When I raised my head, my companions had gone. Could I have lost track of time so greatly? The baying grew closer; hooves thundered on. Yet I saw nothing. The horn sounded once more. Ear-splitting.

And then it appeared. The gasping, sweating fox burst through the gates to the cemetery and skittered towards me. Closer. Closer. Straight at me. Good God, the creature was going to run right into me! But it never made contact. It *dived* head-first into the ground that was Edward Massingham's grave. Yes—*into* the grave. Somehow it disappeared beneath the turf, six feet below which lay Massingham's coffin.

The hounds bolted around the corner and through the same gate used by the fox only seconds before. A

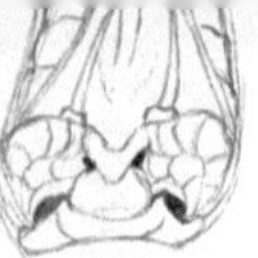

heartbeat later they were jumping, spinning, yelping and squealing with vicious intent around the headstone. Their noise was hellish and deafening. The huntsmen stood in grim fascination with their steeds, just outside the graveyard, as if not daring to enter.

The hounds snarled and snapped, fangs bared, muzzles spitting saliva, eyes crazed.

Then they started to dig. They frantically worked their front paws at the ground, making frightening headway into the tomb, sending soil spraying up in dirty gouts. Soon, all that was visible were their hind legs, as I heard the soul-tearing noise of claws on a coffin lid. The sound of splitting wood. Then the resounding crunch of powerful jaws on long-dead tissue and bone.

The last thing I remember about the gruesome scene was the hounds emerging from the newly dug pit, dragging the ravaged, partially decomposed corpse of Edward Massingham out with them, into the deathly cold May air.

***

Now they keep me here. In this room. With the soft walls.

They don't believe me.

They say that the policeman who found me was physically sick at the sight of me, half in and half out of Edward Massingham's grave, hands soiled, nails encrusted with earth, gnawing at his mouldering cadaver.

Yet, I know what really occurred on that dreadful May Day.

So why do they lie?

I can still hear them when I'm alone. The horn blaring, the hooves hammering, the hounds crying madly. And I see those eyes. The dead glass eyes of the fox.

Watching me in the dark...

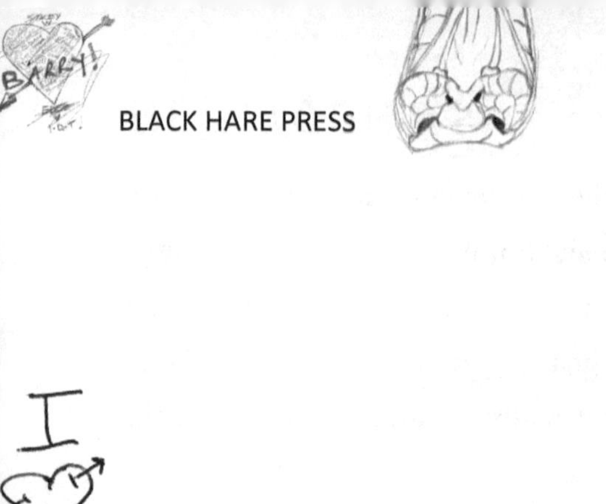

BLACK HARE PRESS

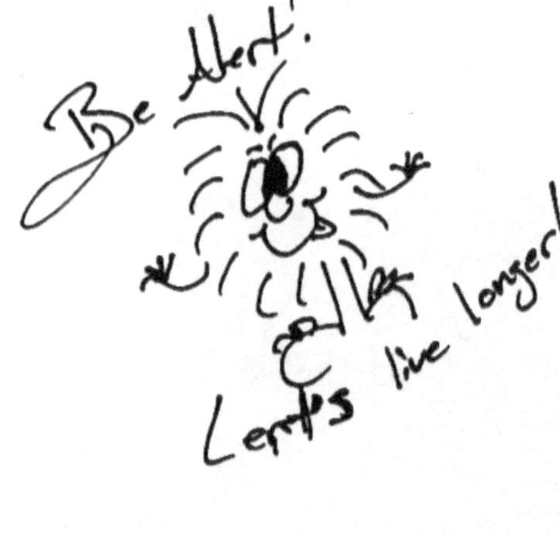

MISS LILY

by Kimberly Rei

Lily had been telling herself all summer that she loved kids. Of course she did. That's why she was a teacher. If she didn't like children, why would she do this job?

She stood at the Victorian-styled standalone mirror and sighed. The mirror was a knock-off, like everything else in her life. Teaching didn't pay well. You did it for the love of the work, she was told. For the children. Who will think of the children?

Every year, she thought of the little bastards as the hot, lazy days slid by and the threat of autumn loomed closer. Every year, as she bought supplies her school wouldn't fund and her parents couldn't afford, she thought of them. Every year, as she watched her meagre

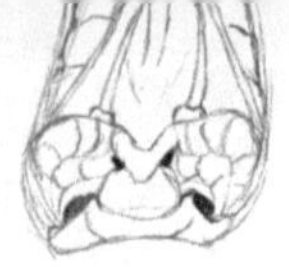

savings dip that much lower and knew the dream of a little house with a bloody white picket fucking fence was fading away, she thought of them.

And she thought of them now, standing at the mirror, making sure her First Day of School outfit was just so. Professional, yes. But also warm and inviting. Comfortable. Mustn't scare the kids or offend the parents.

Lily's cat watched her from the bed, tail idly swishing back and forth. Vlad was black as ink and mean. He'd started out with a cute name Lily could no longer recall. After a month of claws sinking into flesh, she changed his name, in honour of The Impaler himself. She loved Vlad dearly. He was practically her soulmate. But she also rarely turned her back on him.

He liked licking at the blood he drew a little too much.

She turned from the mirror and dipped into a sarcastic curtsy. "Behave yourself, evil spawn. No more dead mice in the kitchen, you hear me? You kill it, you eat it."

***

Lily was waiting by the door to her classroom when her new students started streaming in. The school

234

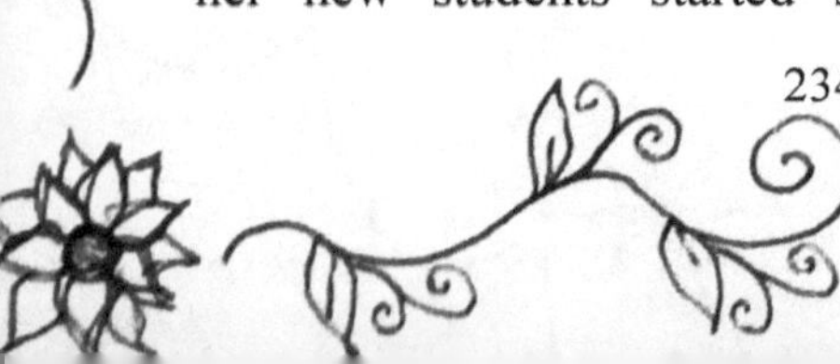

encouraged parents to drop their children at the playground, but there were always four or five who were natural helicopters and just had to see their precious baby safe and settled.

She smiled at each one, introduced herself, let them linger. It was critical that they like her and see her as the consummate professional.

The first hour of the day passed before she managed to herd anyone over the age of five on their merry way. By then, the class was in complete disarray. She returned to her desk and stood in front of it, hands folded before her. It was the first test every year. Some students noticed and found their seats. Others ignored her entirely, too caught up in their freedom. And then there were the few who looked directly at her and carried on with their devilry.

She clapped her hands sharp. "Seats, please! Take your seats!"

Two dared further defiance, but she simply waited. She wasn't about to get into a battle with a child. That was a lesson learned many years ago. She may look like she was fresh out of college, but Lily had been at this for a very, very…very…long time.

Eventually, everyone was perched on their chairs, eyes locked on her. She broadened her smile from Polite

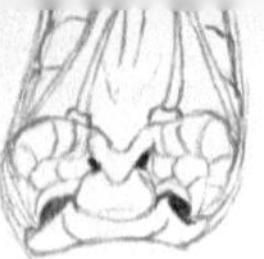

Parent Interaction to First Adult Best Friend and was rewarded with returned grins from most of her students.

"Let's get started! All of your names are on your desks. We'll take a break a little later today and you can all get to know each other. I'm Miss Lily. I know you won't all be friends, but the first rule in my class is to at least be friendly. We must be kind to each other. Right?"

Twenty-one heads bobbled. One boy glared at another across the room. He was going to be a problem.

"Good! I think we're going to have a lot of fun this year. We'll learn, we'll explore, and we'll laugh a lot."

She paused, letting her posture and face convey the seriousness of her next statement before she gave it voice. She was not disappointed. The class went perfectly still, waiting on a razor's edge. She kept them there, making eye contact with each child before settling on one.

"Michael R. Please step to the front of the class."

He wasn't one of the troublemakers. In fact, he was shy and impeccably behaved. He blinked and fear flashed through wide brown eyes, but he obeyed. Slowly. His chair screeched as he pushed it back and shuffled to stand at her side.

Lily moved him in front of her and laid a hand on each shoulder. She squeezed reassuringly and felt him relax under her touch.

236

"I need you to pay close attention, children. There will be more rules as we go but this one you must keep close to your heart. It is important. You all understand what that means? Good. The rule is…"

She kept them on that edge for another moment, then tenderly slid her hands up to Michael's cheeks. One hand shifted to his chin, the other to the back of his head. Before he could question or panic, she twisted her arms sharp.

The crack of his neck breaking hung in the shocked silence. She let his limp body drop to the floor and folded her hands in front of her again.

"The rule is never ever make me angry. Never defy me. Never argue with me. Are we clear?"

Tears filled the eyes of several students, but none dared let them fall. Everyone was in a state of shock. Miss Lily's nose wrinkled as a particular scent drifted her way. Well, that was to be expected. At least one little brat pissed themselves every year. That was why she kept clean clothes in a cabinet.

She waved a hand over the small, crumpled body. "Michael, return to your seat please. Thank you for your help."

The boy wobbled to his feet, looking dazed. He turned his head from side to side and all the children

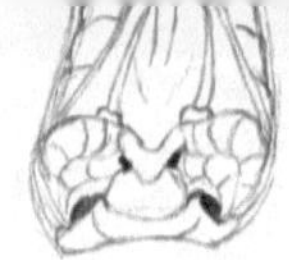

winced at the crackling sound. In moments, he was back at his desk, still slightly out of it but not really any worse for his ordeal.

Miss Lily smiled. "Shall we begin our first lesson, class?"

***

Principal Samuels led the young couple and their fragile, but adorable, girl on a tour of the school. They'd covered the gym, the cafeteria, the playground, and were now making their way around the classrooms.

The principal pulled herself up proudly. "This is Miss Lily's room. She's been with us for six years and every student under her care has been successful. We set a high bar here, and Miss Lily's students always surpass expectations. No failures, no demerits, no lost privileges."

The couple looked sceptical. "There haven't been any problems? None at all?"

Principal Samuels swayed slightly, memories licking at the edge of her thoughts. *There was that one year…so many students…so many, many accidents…*

She looked through the window and Miss Lily's gaze caught hers. Ms Samuels tugged at her collar, overly warm and suddenly eager to finish the tour. As she looked

away, her thoughts drifted into a soft, peaceful blur and she smiled at the parents.

"Not one! I wish we had more like her. She's pure magic, she is."

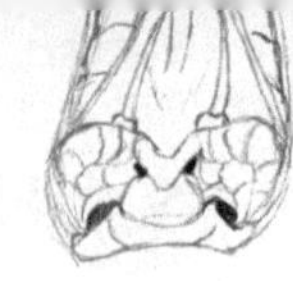

I WAS ASLEEP

by Sarah Jane Justice

Annabel's eyes snapped open at the buzz of her message tone. Struggling under the groggy weight of sleep, she fought to open her eyes enough to make out the words.

Are you watching? The countdown is almost over!

Annabel sighed, shaking her fingers awake as she tapped out her reply.

Chill, I'm here!

With a deep yawn, she slapped her cheeks, knowing that she would never live it down if she missed the music

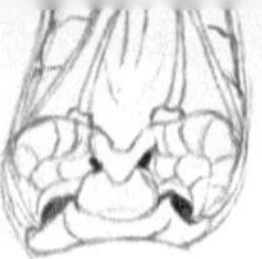

event of the year. Stifling a groan as she rubbed her eyes, she reminded herself that this would be worth the effort.

It was a struggle to focus on the small phone screen, but she pushed through sleep to continue watching. The numbers were ticking down in front of her bleary eyes, rapidly approaching zero. With her head propped up on her hands, she watched the clock hit midnight. Immediately, the video flickered to life.

"Hey everyone," a lithe, blonde woman chirped into the camera, waving her hand in a delicate motion. She was decked out from head to toe in shimmering glitter, grinning with the self-satisfied look of a woman who knows exactly how famous she is.

"Mira here," she giggled. "But I guess you already know that."

Mira took a moment to adjust her outfit, a gesture that was undoubtedly planned to make her seem more relatable, while conveniently showing off her least relatable body parts.

"Thank you all so much for tuning in. It means the world to me." Mira clapped her hands. "I'm so, so happy to be able to share this with you. The most special of special events. The online world premiere exclusive. My new song, the long anticipated…"

***

In the social aftermath of falling asleep right before Mira's midnight premiere, Annabel had never felt such a strong desire to see the end of lunch. Her friends raved on about the new track, pausing only to laugh at the circumstances of Annabel missing it.

"It's actually kinda funny." Jacqui grinned across the table. "You missed a song called 'I Was Asleep' because you fell asleep."

"That's not kinda funny, Jacqui." Elise laughed along. "It's very funny. So funny."

Annabel nodded along, hoping she looked like she was laughing at herself more than anyone. The truth was that she felt the hit of every word but knew her best option was to swallow the jokes and wait for her friends to get over it.

"Yeah," she replied, picking up her backpack. "So funny. Hey, I have to go to the bathroom before lunch ends. I'll see you guys in science."

"Ok." Jacqui waved a brightly manicured hand back at her. "Don't fall asleep again."

While her friends burst into a new round of laughter, Annabel forced a smile that faded as soon as her back was turned.

***

"I was asleep, but now I see," the off-key singing echoed over the bathroom walls, "I was asleep, but now I hear."

Annabel tried to focus on her reflection in the mirror while the singing girl dried her hands. Eve was top of the class in an impressive number of subjects, but music was not one of them. Seeming completely oblivious to Annabel's foul mood, Eve paused her crooning to grin broadly at the other girl.

"Did you watch it?" she beamed.

"Missed it," Annabel grimaced back. "Hating myself for it."

She forced a laugh to accompany the statement but knew exactly how insincere it sounded. Eve looked back at Annabel with a smug expression, before pulling out her phone.

"Here," she smirked. "I recorded it."

Annabel frowned, looking at the device without trying to hide her scepticism.

"I thought they were preventing people from doing that," she muttered.

"Please." Eve laughed, pushing the right combination of buttons before thrusting the phone into Annabel's hand.

244

With a characteristic flounce, Eve turned back to the mirror, leaving Annabel to watch the recording. She felt her face burn red at the second viewing of the words that had led her to fall asleep, but Eve was thankfully too focused on her hair to notice. Despite her embarrassment, Annabel couldn't help but feel a speeding rush of excitement as the opening bars began to play.

I was asleep, but now I see…

Annabel glanced up again to see Eve miming along to the recording as she fished a lipstick out of her bag.

I was asleep, but now I hear…

Out of nowhere, the tune was interrupted by the crash of a heavy bag dropping to the floor. Annabel looked up at the sound, expecting to see her classmate cursing her own clumsiness. Instead, she saw Eve staring back at her with a steely, blank expression, completely ignoring the bag at her feet.

"Eve," Annabel muttered. "Are you—"

Her question was abruptly cut off as Eve's hands shot out towards Annabel's throat with an unnerving strength. Managing to duck just in time, Annabel darted towards the door, struggling to figure out what was happening. Without explanation, Eve aimed a powerful kick at the door of one of the bathroom stalls, splintering the wood under her boot. Still staring at Annabel with empty eyes,

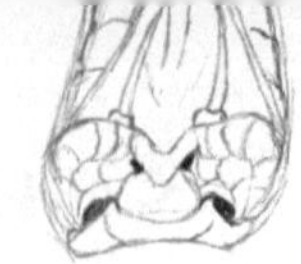

she cracked one of the sharp wood splinters out of the debris and lunged forward with a movement that suggested rage.

Annabel darted out of the way just in time, feeling her heart pounding. With fear surging through her veins, she ran out of the door, questioning her judgement for every PE class she'd ever skipped. Without stopping to figure out what had happened, she poured her focus into sprinting down the hall as fast as her legs would carry her.

I was asleep, but now I see…

The drifting lyrics made it clear that Eve wasn't the only one who had managed to get a recording of Mira's broadcast. A few metres short of making it back to her lunch table, the impact of gritty shock stopped Annabel in her tracks.

With the same steely expression as Eve, Elise knocked the small Bluetooth speaker to the floor to grab Jacqui by the throat. After a high-pitched scream and a brief moment of flailing struggle, an invisible presence seemed to hit Jacqui with sudden force. Her expression fell blank and she moved with the same rigid strength as the other students. Rising from the floor, she kicked Elise off her and slashed a manicured hand across the other girl's face. As Jacqui's sharp nails carved through her classmate's skin, dragging blood from flesh, Elise didn't even flinch at the pain.

With a sick feeling rising in her throat, Annabel picked up her feet and ran into the nearest classroom. As soon as she slammed the door behind her, she realised with a sinking feeling that she had been trapped by her own instinct. The only windows in the room were tiny, opening to a second floor drop that made escape seem unrealistic at best.

I was asleep, but now I see...

Shaking with panic, Annabel pulled herself under a corner desk in an attempt to hide. Her mind was flooding with worst case scenarios, but she forced herself to hope that she could wait out the situation without being found.

I was asleep, but now I hear...

Trying to make herself as small as she could, Annabel felt a cold surge of fear sweep through her as the door burst open. Her skin prickled as she saw one of her classmates slam another girl onto the desk closest to the door. As the assailant swivelled around in search of a weapon, the girl on the desk jumped back up without warning. Grabbing a stray pen, she lurched forward and stabbed it into her attacker's arm.

Without any sign of emotion, the movement of recoiling seemed hauntingly empty, but Annabel kept watching. A powerful kick from the would-be victim sent

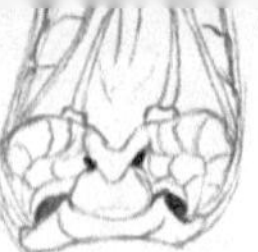

the other girl flying back into the hall, faced with a door that was immediately slammed shut and barricaded with a heavy chair.

Annabel held her breath and tried to stay silent in the wake of being locked in with someone who might be dangerous. She watched the other student's every movement, not sure what she was hoping to see. With a deep breath, she felt her panic subside as she noticed that the girl's face still held emotion. Far from the dead-eyed stare that Annabel had seen in all her other classmates, this girl looked terrified, shaking like a leaf as she jammed the door with more and more furniture. Counting down from ten to help her gather courage, Annabel pulled herself out of hiding.

"Hey," she ventured, failing to find any other words.

The other girl spun around at lightning speed, taking on a defensive stance as she looked Annabel up and down. Annabel held her hands above her head in a gesture of surrender, leading the other girl to let down her guard, along with the release of a tightly held breath.

"God," she huffed. "You scared the shit out of me."

"Fair." Annabel nodded. "I have no idea what's going on out there, but I'm not a fan."

"To put it mildly." The other girl shook her head,

finally stepping forward to breach the space between them. "I'm Lisette."

"Annabel." She nodded back.

In the haze of shock, the distinctive name took a minute to spin through her head before Annabel realised why it was so familiar.

"Oh!" she exclaimed. "The school martial arts champion?"

"Yeah." Lisette shook her head, eyes fixed on the barricaded door. "Guess I forgot to wear the medals today."

"Yeah, wow," Annabel muttered. "Pretty useful skillset to have on a day like this."

"No shit," Lisette replied. "I'll have to make sure to get a recording for next time my parents want to lecture me about valid career options."

I was asleep, but now I see…

With the reference to recording, Annabel felt her mind jolt into action.

"That song," she muttered, "from Mira's midnight stream."

"The most vapid and pointless major event of the year." Lisette rolled her eyes.

"I take it you didn't watch it either?"

Lisette snarled for a moment, before a visible look of

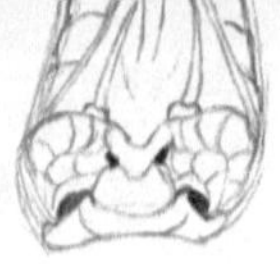

realisation snapped onto her face.

I was asleep, but now I hear…

The drifting repetition of the chorus was punctuated by a surge of violent shouts and crashes echoing through the building. With trembling hands, Annabel pulled out her phone and started typing.

"What are you doing?" Lisette stared at her, an incredulous look plastered across her face.

"Mira's website," Annabel managed to stutter out.

"Oh right," Lisette snapped. "I forgot that she followed up the livestream with a handy tutorial for switching her brainwashed drones back to normal."

"Do you have a better idea?" Annabel snarled.

Lisette responded with bare silence, which Annabel took as an indication to keep reading. Mira had put an intense amount of PR money into promoting her live midnight broadcast as a once-off special event. Everyone knew how important it was to tune in, knowing that the pop star was planning to remove it from all channels immediately. It was the ultimate exclusive, a premiere that piqued the interest of even her harshest detractors. With that in mind, Annabel was surprised to find the recording of "I Was Asleep" being splattered with pride across every one of her channels. Annabel gulped as she saw that the number of views was already well into the

thousands, ticking up higher every second.

"Well?!" Lisette urged.

"Give me a minute," Annabel stuttered.

Scrolling hurriedly through every part of the page, she desperately hoped for something to jump out at her. Outside the door, a blood-curdling scream was snapped into an eerie silence. As a splash of deep red splattered across the door's tiny window, Annabel poured her focus into Mira's website. She scrolled with a heavy tremor of fear in her hand, a pressure that led her to unintentionally highlight a section of text. Stopping in her tracks, she gasped as she noticed that the highlighted text had been buried against the page's background in a matching colour.

"Hold up," she muttered, feeling her hands shake even harder.

I was asleep, but now I see...

Lisette breathed over Annabel's shoulder in silence while the two girls attempted to focus over the sounds of violence that were growing louder by the second.

"There's a link." Annabel jumped at the realisation, rushing to paste it into a browser window.

"Oh shit," Lisette muttered as the page loaded. "Is that another song?"

"It is," Annabel breathed, her finger hovering over

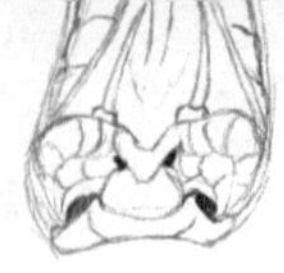

the play button.

"Wait," Lisette burst out. "Will this stop them? Or…"

She trailed off, jumping to her feet as a bloody fist began pounding on the window of the door.

I was asleep, but now I hear…

"Only one way to find out." Annabel gulped, her finger still hovering in frightened reluctance.

As the glass window broke, the girl on the other side didn't seem to notice the blood pouring from her arm while she continued to beat against the door. Without stopping to think about it, Annabel pushed past her fear to hit play on the clip.

Despite the undeniable quality of Mira's singing, the new song felt jarring as it blared out against the lyrics that were already drifting through the halls.

Free, at last, I'll make you cry…

As the girl at the door finally managed to bust it open, a sense of presence fell over her eyes. Dropping the weapon in her hand, she blinked, looking around with visible confusion.

Free, at last, you'll always wonder why…

"What—" the girl coughed. "What's going—"

Lisette sprang to her aid as the girl began to stumble, blood still dripping from the cuts on her hands.

"Shit," Lisette swore, looking around for anything she could use as a bandage. "If only we could get that song over the PA system."

"Bold of you to assume we can't," Annabel burst into cackles of sheer relief. "The admin staff have started trying to figure out Bluetooth, but they seem to be struggling with it. They haven't realised yet that pretty much anyone can connect to their network."

Her hands were still shaking, but Annabel was struck with sudden optimism as she fumbled through settings on her phone. With a triumphant gesture, she hit play as soon as she saw it connect.

Immediately, the song began blaring through the halls at full volume. The shouting stopped as students felt their minds return to them in a haze. Suddenly feeling the pain in their wounds, they stopped attacking each other and blinked at their surroundings as if they'd just looked straight into the sun.

"Christ almighty." Lisette laughed. "Never thought I'd find myself enjoying the sound of Mira's voice."

Annabel laughed, feeling exhaustion hit her as the fear subsided. Before letting herself relax, she copied the link to the video and began pasting it anywhere she possibly could.

Free at last, you'll never see me…

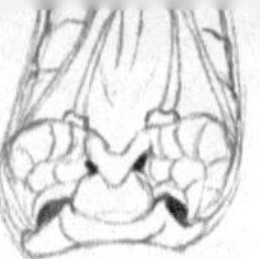

Staring at her phone with hands that had yet to stop shaking, Annabel watched as others saw her message and began sharing it along. Within minutes, she could see the link making waves across the world.

Finally feeling like she could breathe, Annabel closed her eyes for a moment before clicking back to Mira's website. A sharp pang of ominous confusion hit her in the stomach when she discovered that the page seemed to have been deleted. Looking up, she heard the last lyrics of the song as they drifted through the halls.

Free, you'll never know what I could be…

A GAME AT THE NURSE'S OFFICE

by Luis Manuel Torres

Leona Raven was walking past the nurse's office when she spotted something in the corner of her eye. She entered the waiting room. "Nate."

He looked up at his older sister. "Oh, hey Leona."

She sat next to him. "What's wrong? Are you sick?"

"No, I'm fine. Just needed to get away."

"The bullies?" asked Leona.

"I don't want to talk about it."

"Alright, would you like to play the phobia game?"

"Guess their phobia," said Nate as he smiled. "Sure."

255

A young man entered the room and went over to the nurse's office. Brother and sister watched as he knocked on the door. Leona observed the man carefully.

"What do you think?" she asked. "Arachnophobia? He gives me the impression of someone who'd be afraid of spiders."

"A lot of people are afraid of spiders," said Nate. "Whatever problem he has, I doubt it's spiders."

"You're probably right, but I'm getting the game started. If not arachnophobia, what would you guess?"

Nate pulled out his cell phone and went on Google. "I'll guess he's afraid of germs." He googled the phobia as Leona peeked at his phone. "Verminophobia."

"That's not a bad guess," said Leona as she returned her attention to the young man. "He is very well dressed, and look at that napkin sticking out of his shirt pocket. He does look like a neat freak. You've gotten good at this."

"I'm always playing," said Nate. He watched as the young man took a seat across from them. "Now is a good time to use your powers."

Leona chanted something under her breath as she stared at the young man. He had no idea what was being done to him when a toad appeared at his feet. He hadn't seen it yet as two more appeared. The young man was on his phone when another toad jumped onto his lap. He

leaped out of his chair and his cell phone flew across the room due to the fright. He was surrounded by toads and frozen in place.

Leona and Nate were giggling as the young man found the courage to jump over the amphibians, dashing out of the room. Leona and Nate weren't able to contain their laughter any longer and their voices filled the empty room.

"A fear of frogs," said Nate.

"Of toads actually," said Leona.

"How could you tell they were toads?"

"You know my twin is an animal nut," said Leona. "Her zoology lessons have apparently sunk in."

The nurse poked her head out of her office. "Richard?" she called out.

"He left in a bit of a hurry," Leona told the nurse.

"Oh," she said. "That's strange. Do you need anything?"

"Nope," she answered. "Just visiting my little brother."

"Alright," she said before returning inside.

Nate and Leona laughed again. "You don't change," said Nate.

"I don't know about that," said Leona as she turned her attention towards the entrance. "Here comes another."

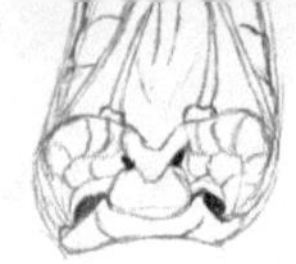

A younger white man entered the waiting room. He wore a hoodie as he made his way up to the nurse's door. He kept his head down as he waited for the nurse.

"He kind of reminds me of you," said Leona. "You both have a similar style."

"What do you think his phobia is?" asked Nate.

"Could be many things, but I'd rather you go first with this one."

"Do you really find us so similar, you'd want me to take the first guess?"

"Something like that."

The nurse returned and the young man shyly approached. The woman seemed to have to repeat herself a couple of times before sending him to take a seat.

"I have a guess," said Nate as he looked at his sister, a smirk on his face. "Don't think this is a reflection on myself by the way."

"You're guess is based on that interaction?"

"It is. I'm going to say he's afraid of women."

Leona returned her attention to the hooded man. "He's shy but I'm not sure I would have gone with fear of women. I'm going to say he's afraid of crowds."

"I'd like to see your power create a crowd in here. You'll probably scare off the nurse as well."

"I guess I better hurry before she returns."

SCHOOL'S IN

Leona chanted something under her breath and a priest appeared in front of the hooded man. He was startled as he fell back on his seat. He had his eyes locked on the priest, who brought out his bible.

"A clergy phobia," said Leona with a slight laugh.

Nate gave her a light tap with his elbow. "Don't laugh at that."

The priest began to read his bible. The man shrank in his seat as the priest continued his sermon. His body went rigid and his face was covered under his hood.

"That's enough sis. He's scared stiff."

Leona let out a deep breath and the priest dispersed like a mirage in the desert. When the young man could no longer hear the priest, he gained enough courage to look up. They could see the relief in his face as he stood up and made his way to the door. The nurse returned just in time to see him leave.

"Wayne," she called out, but he was already out the door. "That's strange. He's the second person to leave today." She returned to her office.

"That was messed up," said Nate to his sister.

"What do you mean? What makes this one different from the others?"

"He was afraid of a priest. You heard those stories about priests with children?"

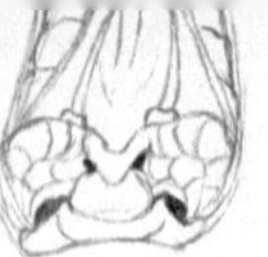

"Oh, I understand. You don't need to worry about that. I don't think his fear of the priest had anything to do with that."

"What makes you so sure?"

"It's the way my illusions work. If his fear of the priest was because of something physical, the priest would have been approaching him, not giving him a sermon."

"I see what you're saying," said Nate as he went through his phone. "Maybe what he had was homilophobia, a fear of sermons."

Leona laughed. "Sounds about right. Who gets the point for that one? I said crowds and you said girls. Who was closer?"

"Who got the point for the first one?"

"Well for the first one, you guessed germs and I guessed spiders. His phobia was toads and I would say spider was closer than germs. First point to me."

"Sounds fair. Crowd is the complete opposite of a priest. Girl would've been closer."

"How so?"

"Girls like to give out sermons, in a manner of speaking."

"Funny. I'll give you the point. One point for you, one point for me," said Leona. "Now the next person will

260

be our tie breaker." Just as she said those words, another person entered. "Speak of the devil."

The person to walk in was of Arab descent and looked like an adult. He must have been a senior. He didn't seem to be as nervous as the others, walking up to the nurse's door with more confidence. Nate and Leona observed him closely as the nurse came out to meet him.

They watched as the Arab student and the nurse had a friendly conversation. He took a seat and she returned to her office.

"This one isn't afraid of women," said Nate.

"Definitely not," said Leona. "He has no visible faults. He's going to be hard to guess."

"He's here so there must be something wrong with him."

"Everyone is scared of something." Leona observed the student carefully, looking for any sort of fault. He got on his phone as he got comfortable in his chair. "You have any guesses?"

"I don't know. He seems to be of Middle Eastern descent. I bet whatever phobia he suffers from, it has something to do with his culture."

"You think he's from the Middle East?"

"I think it's possible. Shit, his phobias might be something serious. Maybe we shouldn't do this."

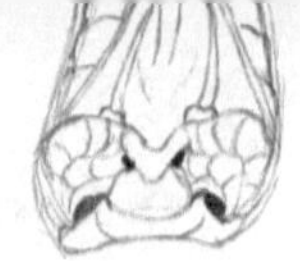

"Nah, don't worry about that," said Leona. "Look at the way he's dressed. Skinny jeans, designer shirt, and his hat matches his shoes. He has fuck boy written all over him. I bet you his underwear matches his socks, too."

Nate laughed, causing the boy to look in their direction. He gave them a dirty look before returning his attention to his phone.

"He didn't like that," said Nate.

"I saw. Not sure it helps in figuring out what his phobia is exactly."

"That look was of disgust, not fear."

"I have a guess," said Leona. "I'm going to say he is afraid of the police."

Nate leaned back in his chair. "That's a good one. I'm going to guess." Nate stopped to give it a good thought. "He's afraid of work."

"Work? Really?"

"It's a thing. It's called ergophobia." He showed Leona his phone which had a page opened on Google with the word *ergophobia*.

"There's a phobia for everything nowadays. I can't help but feel that one is made up by people who want to avoid work."

"I believe that and I think he is one who supposedly suffers from it," said Nate as he pointed at the fuck boy.

"Alright, we've made our decision, time to use my powers," she said before starting her chant.

The boy was on his cell phone when a pair of red high heels came into view. He looked up from his phone to find a beautiful woman standing in front of him. "How are you doing?" he said as he stood up.

"What's your opinion on our current administration?" asked the woman.

He had a bit of a weird reaction to her question. "Sorry, I'm not really into politics."

"What are you into?"

"More into sports and video games."

"Me too!"

"Really?"

"Yes, in my opinion, football is one of the greatest sports in the world."

He had a slight flinch at her words. "Which football? American or the other one?"

"Soccer of course. There's a reason why it's the most popular sport in the world."

"I can't say I'm a fan."

"What's your favourite sport?"

"Boxing."

"In my opinion, it takes more skill to do mixed martial arts."

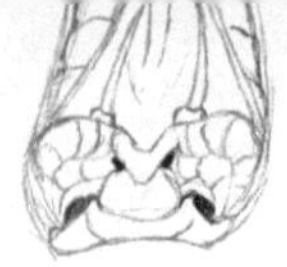

He flinched again. "Oh."

"Think about it. In boxing, you only have to master one type of fighting style. In my opinion," she said and he flinched again. "It takes a lot more skill to master different types of fighting styles, like karate, or judo for example."

He had his head down as he tried to look away. "Yeah, but do they really master those styles or are they just okay?"

"Maybe, but in my opinion…"

"It was nice to meet you, but I have to go," he said, cutting her off and walking away.

"But I didn't get to finish giving you my opinion," said the woman as her image dispersed and he went out the door.

"That was a strange one," said Nate. "I'm not even sure what had him so messed up. I know her opinions were kind of annoying but still."

Leona rolled her eyes. "Maybe his phobia was an opinionated woman."

"Is that a phobia?" asked Nate as he went through his phone.

"Didn't we already establish there's a phobia for everything?"

"Yes, but I'm not finding a phobia for opinionated women. I did find a phobia for fear of opinions," he said

with a laugh. "It's called allodoxaphobia."

"That's probably it. He flinched every single time she said 'in my opinion'."

"So allodoxaphobia it is."

"I said his fear was the police and you said work. Opinionated woman is closer to an authority figure than to work. I was closer. I win."

"That's arguable, but I'll give it to you. Congratulations," said Nate. "I'm surprised you're so good at this."

"I watch people when I'm bored."

The nurse returned. "What happened to Tarek?" asked the nurse. "That's the third person to leave."

The nurse approached Nate and Leona. "How do you feel Nate?"

"I'm fine," he answered as he stood up. "I think it's time I get going."

The nurse put out her hands to stop Nate from leaving. "Wait a second. I need to talk to you."

"What about?"

"The real reason you're hiding out in my waiting room."

Nate offered his hand and the nurse took it. Nate whispered something under his breath, casting a spell, and his hand began to glow. Leona sat back as she observed

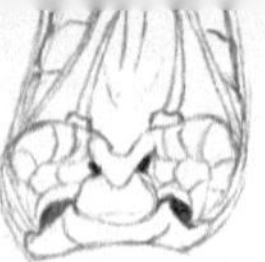

her brother use his magic. Nate held the nurse's hand for almost ten seconds before releasing it. "That won't be necessary. You're doing a great job. Thank you."

Her face seemed to get a little more relaxed. She had a big smile on her face. "You have no idea how happy I am to hear that."

"I have to get going," said Nate. "Thanks again."

"Take care of yourself," said the nurse as Nate and Leona left.

***

Leona and Nate were out in the halls and on their way to their next class. "What did you do back there?" asked Leona. "You used your power, right?"

"I did," answered Nate. "I made her feel good."

"Eww."

Nate laughed. "Not like that. I gave her a sort of a feeling of accomplishment. She deserved it."

"Wait, did you actually use your power or did you just tell her the truth?"

"Both. My power is empathy. I can transfer any type of feeling I want into someone. For example, the feeling of accomplishment."

"Yup, I still don't really understand it. I'll take my

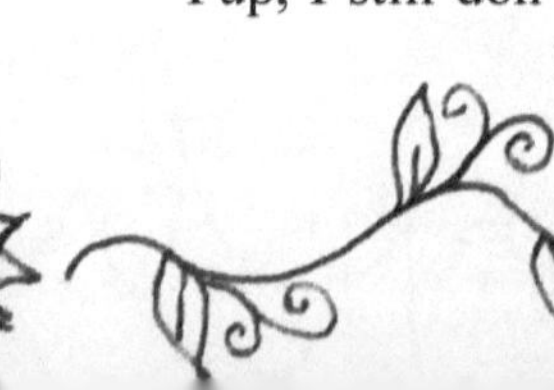

power over yours any day. It's fun making people see their greatest fears."

Nate stopped and grabbed Leona's arm. "That's one of the bullies."

"Why don't you try using your power against him?" asked Leona. "If you can make people feel better, you can make them feel like shit."

"I've never done that before."

"Give it a try."

Nate approached the bully as he cast his spell and his hand glowed.

The bully saw him coming and turned to face him. "Look who we got here, little ol' Natie."

Nate grabbed the bully's wrist. There was anger in Nate's eyes. "You are worthless. You are good for nothing and stupid."

The bully's expression seemed to change. "I am stupid and good for nothing."

Nate looked back at his sister and smiled. "It's working."

Leona pointed behind Nate and he turned around to see more of his bullies coming their way.

Nate looked into his bully's eyes. "Your friends! It's your friends' fault you're so stupid. You should make them pay." When Nate saw a look of acknowledgement

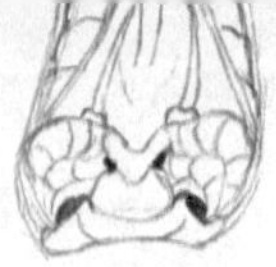

from the bully, he released his wrist.

The bully made his way to his friends, who seemed happy to see him, when he struck one of them. Nate and Leona watched from down the hall as the bully fought his friends.

"Seems like it worked," said Leona.

"Yeah," said Nate.

The bully was on top of his friend, beating him to death as everyone watched in horror.

"I think it worked a little too well," said Leona with a smirk on her face, while Nate had his hands on his head, not knowing what to do.

THE PRINCIPAL IS MISSING

by Lynne Phillips

The office light flickered once before it went out. Sitting alone in the dark, Meredith Anderson cursed under her breath. She fumbled around her desk until her fingers found her phone. Switching on the torch, she muttered, "Thank God for mobiles."

The torch helped her find the switch in the hallway outside her office. She flicked the switch, but the hall remained dark. *Maybe it's a blown fuse or a blackout.*

The raucous sound of an animal startled her, its mournful cry making the hairs on her arms stand on end

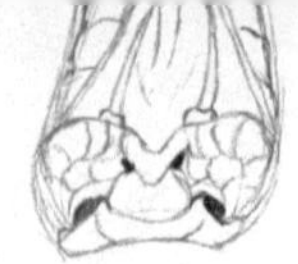

before her brain registered *fox*. She picked up her handbag, searching for her keys. A branch scratched against the window and her heart raced. She took a deep breath. *Why are schools so different at night?* During the day, the happy sounds of children echo around the buildings and the hustle and bustle of students moving from room to room give schools a special vibrancy. At night, they become spookily hollow, where every sound is exaggerated.

Meredith had experienced the uneasiness before at her last school when she had worked late. She tried to shake off the memory of how frightening it had been as she shoved the staff profiles into her briefcase. She would read them back in her hotel room, a temporary accommodation until she found something more permanent.

Come on Meredith, just pack up and get out of here.

The other staff members had scurried out the gate within half an hour of the bell, in a hurry to get home or to the pub. They all wanted to relax, perhaps have a glass of wine or Friday night fish and chips.

As the newly appointed Principal of Waddington Primary School, Meredith felt obligated to clear her in-tray before she signed off for the weekend. Somehow she had become so engrossed in the task, she lost track of the

time. She hadn't realised it was so late. She meant to be gone by six, but her watch said eight.

Her appointment, as Principal, was at short notice, mid-term. The previous principal, John Morgan, had disappeared. One day he didn't come to school. The Senior Clerical Assistant reported him missing after unsuccessfully trying to locate him. A police search of his home revealed nothing. No clothes were missing. His passport was in his safe and his bank accounts were untouched. His phone was unresponsive. Unofficially there were rumours that he had absconded with a woman. Others said he had large gambling debts and was avoiding the loan sharks. Officially he was listed as a missing person, case open.

The school board accepted the official version and appointed Meredith to the position.

At the first staff meeting, Meredith met the teachers and clerical staff. They were all friendly except for Douglas Harris, the Deputy Principal. He'd been Relieving Principal since John Morgan's disappearance.

"I should be the principal," he challenged Meredith. "They didn't need to appoint someone else, and a female to boot," he almost spat at her. Meredith knew whatever she said would only make things worse so she excused herself and went to meet the janitor and gardener before

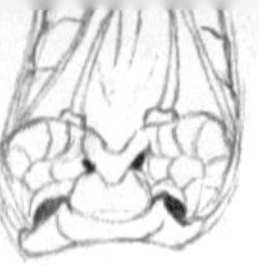

they finished for the day.

"Hello luv," the janitor said. "Nice to 'ave a lady principal. Just call me Perkins."

The groundsman was raking autumn leaves. He limped over. Meredith knew Jack, aged seventy-five, had been the gardener at Waddington School for fifty years and was proud of the gardens.

"Mr Frost, the grounds are looking good."

"Yeh, autumn is a pretty time, but it plays up with my arthritis, winter's worse," he said smiling, pleased that she had noticed his handiwork.

"What have you planned for there?" Meredith pointed to a freshly dug garden.

"Lilies, once the ground settles. Get your own place, Miss, and I'll give you some bulbs."

"I'll hold you to that, Mr Frost. Hopefully, I'll have my own place before you retire."

"You've got plenty of time; no need to talk about retirement. I've got years in me yet."

With the profiles in her case, Meredith moved towards the door. She smiled as she remembered the two old men. Staff management was always the hardest part of being a principal and the more she knew about the staff the easier it would be.

The clock above the door ticked loudly, the sound

echoing in her head.

"Why are clocks louder at night?" she muttered as she moved across to pull down the blinds.

As she reached up for the cord, *tap, tap,* someone rapped on the window. Her heart thumped faster, and she stepped back groping for the letter opener she was using earlier.

A face, highlighted by a torch beam, appeared at the window. "Police, Miss," a male voice boomed.

Meredith sighed, trying to steady her heart. Using her mobile, she walked to the front door. A red-faced police officer stood there looking serious.

"Sorry to startle you, Miss. Someone reported a light on at the school. We don't usually see lights here at night. Thought there might be an intruder. We were just checking." A bright torch beam filled the hallway as he stepped in followed by a small policewoman.

"I suppose you're the new principal. Why are you here alone in the dark, Miss?"

"Meredith Anderson. I was just trying to catch up on some paperwork when the light went out. I was packing up to leave. I didn't realise it was so late."

"Not a good idea to be here alone at night, Ms Anderson. Would you like an escort to the carpark?"

"Thank you. That would be great. I'll just have to

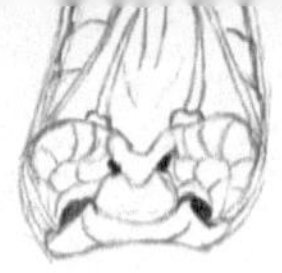

lock up and set the alarm."

A row of tall, dark classrooms loomed ominously, silhouetted against the skyline, as Meredith followed the police officers to the carpark. The familiar buildings seemed so threatening at night. Overhanging bushes, needing to be cut back, clutched at their clothes as they moved along the path. A colony of flying foxes took flight from the rainforest adjacent to the carpark, a screeching seething throng, off to scavenge for food. Their black mass completely filled the sky, temporarily blocking out any light. Their distinctive musk scent and raucous shrieking assailed Meredith's senses. "Creepy things, they make me think of vampires."

"They're only fruit bats; they're not going to bite you," the policeman said, shining his torch on Meredith's car.

"It was nice to meet you, Ms Anderson. You take care now."

As she watched the police car drove off, Meredith decided she wouldn't work on her own at night again; it was too stressful.

The next week passed quickly. Douglas Harris continued to treat her with disdain, but the school ran smoothly. Several students were suspended for smoking in the toilets.

"You'll be sorry you suspended me, Miss. My dad is on the school board," Mickey O'Callaghan said, slouching in the corner.

"Are you threatening me, Mickey?"

"Take it how you like; I'm just saying you'll be sorry."

As a principal, Meredith was used to young people mouthing off when they were in trouble. It was just bravado, trying to be tough, not losing face.

"Here's your dad now," Meredith said smiling at Mr O'Callaghan.

"Apologise for your behaviour, young man, and go to the car. Sorry, Meredith, I'll talk to him," Trevor O'Callaghan said.

Mickey shuffled his feet and mumbled an apology.

After school, the banter in the staffroom was friendly. One by one everyone left for the day until there was only Meredith and Douglas.

"I know you expected to get the principal position, but the School Board appointed me and I'd like to work with you for the good of the school if possible," Meredith proffered.

Douglas sneered, "You think you'll last here. This school needs someone to sort it out, just like I sorted out John Morgan."

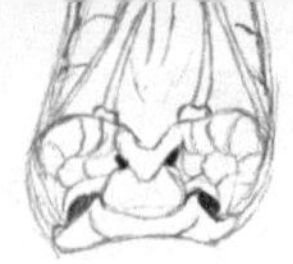

"Are you inferring you had something to do with his disappearance?"

Douglas looked flustered at the suggestion. "No, nothing like that, he just didn't know what was going on. I told him so several times, but he wouldn't listen."

"My door is open anytime you want to enlighten me," Meredith said as she left the staffroom.

Douglas's car rocked as he kicked the tyres. *Probably out of frustration,* Meredith thought as she turned from the window before he drove away. Determined to be gone before dark, she placed work in her briefcase and left as the sun was setting.

"Shit, four flat tyres," she exclaimed. "Douglas, that's just petty."

"Road Service, what is your problem?" a nasally voice enquired.

"I'm at Waddington School. I have four flat tyres.'

"Sounds like a student playing a joke if all four are flat."

"Probably, but not funny. How long do I have to wait?"

"At least an hour, sorry, we're busy."

Meredith sat in her car and scrolled through her phone before pacing outside impatiently. The flying foxes screeched and chattered as they left on their nightly vigil.

She shivered. The hair on the back of her neck bristled; she felt someone was watching her but saw no one. The school was dark and foreboding. The glow of a cigarette somewhere in the gloom appeared and quickly disappeared. She thought she heard someone whistling.

A horn tooted. Meredith was relieved to see the Roadside Assistance man drive in.

"Someone doesn't like you, Miss, four slashed tyres. You won't be driving anywhere tonight."

"Slashed? I only thought they were flat."

"Definitely slashed, lock your car and I'll give you a lift."

Four new tyres had to be ordered so Meredith hired a small sedan. She bought sandwiches and coffee at the deli on the corner.

She worked at her desk until late into the afternoon. A single sheet of paper appeared under the door. Intrigued, Meredith opened it. A typed message said, *"You aren't wanted at this school, leave."*

"This is getting ridiculous," Meredith said. "First Douglas making innuendos, the slashed tires, someone watching me, and now this note, I guess it's time to report to the police."

The same red-faced policeman was on duty.

"Not having a good welcome to Waddington, Miss,"

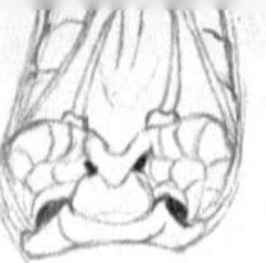

he said seriously as he took down the details. She mentioned Douglas and Mickey, but she expressed her reservations.

"We'll look into it, Miss."

School ran smoothly for a week, no suspensions. Even Douglas was almost civil.

She was just packing up to leave when she was startled by a knock at her door.

"Excuse me, Miss." Perkins stood in the doorway nervously turning his cap in his hand. "I don't wish to disturb you but its old Jack. He keeps muttering to himself about not going to be forced to retire and he is digging over gardens that he has just planted. I think he's getting dementia; I'm really worrit about 'im."

Meredith noticed Perkins's speech deteriorated when he was nervous.

"Thank you, Perkins, I'll speak to him. It might soon be time for him to step down."

Jack Frost was digging a new garden bed. Meredith wasn't sure how to broach Perkins's concerns.

"Hello Jack. The dahlias are looking pretty. How are your joints?"

"Stiff but won't stop me from doing my job."

"Would you mind doing some pruning along all the pathways? They are getting a bit overgrown. I could hire

someone to help you if it's too much for you."

"I can do the job. I suppose you want me to retire. Get someone in to help and next thing I'm being replaced."

"No, I could hire someone for the heavy work, maybe one day a week."

Meredith knew she hadn't handled that well as she walked away. Jack Frost glared after her, muttering under his breath, before resuming digging.

As Meredith walked to her car, the scent of roses filled the air until it was replaced by a more intense smell, the smell of something dead or decaying.

Compost? No, a dead bandicoot or lizard. The overpowering smell churned her stomach and she dry retched as she passed the empty garden bed Jack Frost had reserved for lilies.

I'll check with him tomorrow, she thought as she drove away.

After dinner, she couldn't get that decaying smell out of her mind. The receptionist was busy on the phone. Meredith waited patiently. The girl gave her a vague look when Meredith asked if she could borrow a shovel and a torch. She rummaged under the counter and produced a large torch.

"It's not very reliable, but it's the only one we have.

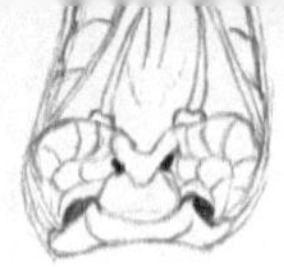

I guess you could look out the back for a shovel.”

No moon shone and a brisk autumn wind buffered the car as Meredith drove into the car park. Perkins's little Volkswagen stood forlornly in one corner.

That's strange; Perkins should have left hours ago.

The gate creaked in protest. The sound amplified in the cool night air and she jumped in fright. The torch pierced the dark, disturbing a lone flying fox feasting in the date palm. As it released its musky scent, its wings lightly touched her hair.

“Shit, filthy things.”

She took a few steps forward and the hairs on her arms stood on end. A shiver ran through her body. *I should go back to the hotel.* A nagging idea in the back of her mind wouldn't let her turn around. *Perhaps I should have told the police my suspicions, but I don't want to look like a hysterical woman.*

She decided she would just dig up the bed, find out what was causing the smell to put her mind at rest, and go back to the hotel.

The smell of rotting flesh was more intense in the damp night air. Her stomach heaved. The torch flickered and went out. Shaking it hard, she managed to get it going again, but not before she tripped over something large and soft sprawled across the path. The beam revealed Perkins.

The side of his head was caved in. Terrified, Meredith screamed and started to run only to be hit in the side of her head with a heavy shovel. Blood trickled down her face. The shovel hit her again, connecting with her legs, bringing her to her knees. She tried to crawl away.

"You are just like John Morgan, you want me to retire," Jack Frost's rant rang out of the dark.

Meredith fought the dizziness. *So, my suspicions are right, John Morgan is buried here.*

"No, Jack, you've got that wrong. I was going to hire someone to help you with the heavy stuff."

"Perkins said I was an old fool and you were going to get rid of me. I would have to leave the gardens. He wouldn't shut up about it."

Meredith shone the torch on Jack's face. She could see he was too far gone to listen to reason. He hit her again with the shovel, this time slicing her cheek.

Bleeding profusely, her head throbbing, Meredith switched the torch off and crawled away from the old man, hoping to hide in the dark. Wriggling along the ground, she managed to cover several metres, but her head felt like it was about to explode. Blood ran into her eyes and trickled out of her left ear.

"She is too clever. She knows my secret. I can't let her live," Jack muttered. "I just wanted to work here until

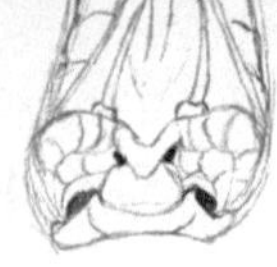

I died."

Meredith reached the end of the garden bed. Her phone was in the pocket of her jeans. Fumbling, she dialled the emergency number. *Perhaps I have a chance.*

"What service please," the operator said. Meredith whispered, "Police."

"What's your location?"

Before she could answer, Jack loomed out of the dark, swinging the shovel knocking her unconscious.

"What's your location please?" the voice on the phone repeated.

Jack picked up the torch and turned it on. He stomped on the phone, crushing it. He looked sadly at Perkins and Meredith before shuffling over to the garden bed and began digging.

Engrossed in the task, he didn't notice Meredith rally. She kept her eyes closed pretending to be dead. Jack whistled as he dug.

He really has lost it.

Meredith lapsed in and out of consciousness.

The first rays of light filled the sky before Jack was satisfied the holes were deep enough. The whistling stopped. Meredith could hear Jack dragging Perkins's body, heaving and puffing with exertion, the sound of a shovel tamping down the dirt and then nothing. She

282

lapsed unconscious again.

"Your turn next, pretty lady," Jack's voice crooned as he dragged her to the hole and dropped her in. Large clods of dirt showered down on her face rousing her. Realising she was being buried alive, Meredith grabbed the sides of the hole and frantically tried to claw her way out, but she was weak from loss of blood and the hole was deep. The rich soil rained down faster than she could push it away. She sobbed and fought uselessly trying to get to her knees. Jack saw that she was still alive. He hit her over and over again. Her limp body collapsed back into the hole and he continued to fill the hole. The rich soil quickly covered her completely. He tamped down the dirt with his boots and looked at his shovel all caked with blood, gore, and dirt.

"How did that get there?" he grumbled. "I better clean that straight away. A good gardener looks after his tools."

He stepped back and looked at the empty garden. "Lilies? No, I think I'll plant more roses." He smiled. "A pretty woman would prefer roses."

He picked up his shovel, lit a cigarette, and walked down to his garden shed, whistling his favourite tune.

 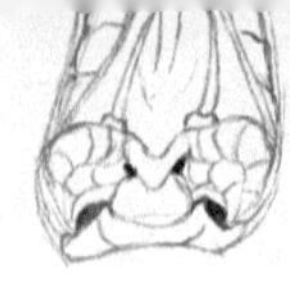

BITE OF THE BUG

by Matthew Wilson

After murdering his lab partner, Henry Thompson knew that he would miss him but hoped the police wouldn't. James Bradley's research was worth millions, but Henry didn't like sharing or putting the work in. Groaning at manual labour, he dragged his oldest friend's body across the cold tiled floor and switched on the machine.

In a few seconds, the transportation device would hurtle James's body across the stars, with any luck he wouldn't be found for millions of years till someone's twentieth grandson invented a high-grade telescope to find his grave in Alpha Centauri.

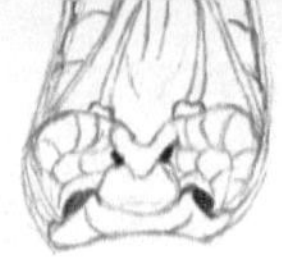

Henry wished that he'd listened more to James's nerdy small talk instead of thinking of murder. Shrugging, Henry pushed a switch and then another one.

He considered himself a smart man, certainly clever enough to get away with murder. Working on some lab project would be a piece of cake but Henry still jumped when the air throbbed with red static that burned his eyebrows.

The portal opened and Henry smiled when a surge sucked James's body through the rip in space between the machine's safety barriers.

Perfect, now all he had to do was to get some bleach and clean—

Henry stopped thinking when he realised he was floating. His feet left the floor and he realised with horror that he was being pulled towards the portal.

"No, no," he yelled uselessly.

There was a scream, a burst of scarlet light and when the transportation machine switched itself off, there was no sign of life, save a ladybird fluttering its wings, annoyed that it had been diverted from its journey on the other side of the room.

Twice, a red jolt of lightning travelled down the bug's body and then hungry, it took off, fluttering through the window, snapping its jaws, towards the laughter of

children.

Outside the little bug rode the breeze and headed towards the next building.

Redgate School.

***

Richard Kingdon told himself that he wasn't scared; it was just another day at school. With a knife tucked into his glove. Would Mom find it gone? It didn't matter—yesterday would be the last time he was bullied. Now he'd show him, now he'd take back some power.

You're gonna be a monster like him, Richard thought and dropped something when the bell rang out and for the first time, he realised he was late.

"Kingdon, pick up your trash," a teacher yelled at the gate, spying on troublemakers, and Richard scooped up his glove, the steel running up the length of the index finger scratched the tarmac, and Richard hurried forward.

I'm not like him, Richard thought again, I don't terrorise people. This is for self-defence.

Richard felt his heart quicken when he heard the laughter, when Simon Tanner picked up a child's rucksack and tossed it onto the bike shed roof with well-aimed practice.

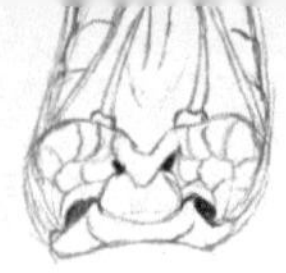

Sticklers for the rules weren't appreciated in his presence.

I'm not gonna kill him. I'm just gonna show he can't push me around anymore, Richard thought. He'd been thinking ALL night, planning without sleep, and now he was exhausted.

What if his hand slipped? What if he killed the bully by accident?

"Hey, shrimp," someone yelled, and Richard felt his feet shuffle forward without his command.

I'm just gonna scare him, Richard thought. I'm not a monster.

"Did your mommy buy ya another computer game? If ya bring that to school, I'll flush it down the toilet, too." Richard was close enough now to smell beer. Simon's tobacco-stained teeth and five o'clock shadow were an instant indicator he should have graduated last year; but after stealing and crashing the headmaster's car, the judge had put him through another six weeks of anger management courses here to stay out of jail.

A chance to get an education and make something of himself.

Some people didn't deserve a second chance.

Richard thought that he could wait out Simon's sentence and then the bully had shaken his hand and tried

288

to break his fingers.

"Let's see how many computers you can play now, rich boy?"

Richard blinked and realised that he was being spat at.

"Hey, ya hear me?" Simon giggled and looked around for a rock.

I could end it now, Richard thought. I could say he pushed me too far and killed him.

I could be a monster too, undeserving of Mom's love.

Hating himself, Richard turned away and marched, head down, defeated, for the school steps.

"That's what I thought, ya little—ow."

Simon stopped talking and yelled again, drawing the teacher's attention as he rolled up his sleeve and pointed to a bloody scab on his elbow.

"He stabbed me," Simon cried. "The little punk stabbed me."

Richard opened his mouth in surprise but felt his lips clamp uselessly together, then somehow he remembered English. "I-I didn't—" Then the buzz of a bug interrupted him.

Dazed, Richard looked up and saw a ladybird land on Simon's shoulder. The sun shone on the dew, running down its six-spotted red shell. When the insect bit Simon

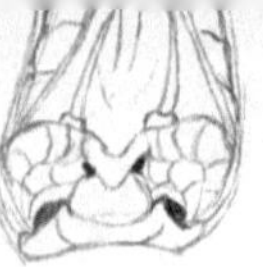

again, the bully shrieked like a kicked dog and screamed for the police.

"Kingdon, what are you—"

Richard didn't hear the teacher till a hard hand grasped his shoulder and spun him round.

"I didn't hurt him, sir."

Richard heard a clink and realised he'd dropped his glove again.

Please don't look down. Is this when I go to prison? Mom would have to visit him. She'd be so ashamed.

"It was a ladybird, sir."

Richard looked up when the sun went away, when the cloud fell out the sky and the sound of a billion bugs beating their wings blotted out the throb of Richard's heartbeat knocking against his eardrums.

The teacher slapped his neck like an African explorer killing a mosquito.

"Ow, wot the hell?"

The teacher swayed and drooled. Suddenly he pitched forward and lay down quietly still as more ladybirds settled on him. They ambled over his body towards his eyes, open in terror, their black jaws clicking.

Some of them flickered as red-coloured lightning travelled down their bodies.

Richard could hear more screams now. Children ran

290

past him, shoulders barging him out of their way as the cloud of ladybirds came closer.

Richard's chest hurt when something grabbed his foot. Simon lay on the floor, his left arm clenched tight against his chest, the small bite on his elbow had blackened and seemed to sizzle like a bad egg on a hot car's bonnet.

"You did this," Simon growled, clawing at Richard with his one good hand. "I'll kill you."

"Let me go, please." Richard wept and wished that his voice was stronger.

He kicked at Simon's arm and started to run with the tide of children rather than against them.

Up the steps, a sports teacher in a grey woollen jumper held an emergency door open, pushing more children inside without care.

"Run, kids," she yelled.

Richard could hear buzzing on his backpack like the hum of a passing train.

No, it wasn't fair, he was supposed to be the one with power. Today was supposed to be a happy ending.

With the thick pulsing cloud of bugs descending on the playground, the sky darkened like an early winter evening.

Richard had never heard a teacher swear, but when

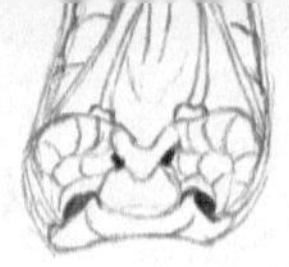

he threw himself the final five feet and into the crowded hallway, he heard a loud bang as the teacher put her shoulder against the heavy door and closed it.

"Quiet, children," she said. "It's going to be alright."

Richard sat there, finding he had no gas in his legs and even though mom had told him to do whatever the teacher said, for the first time, he didn't believe what she said.

Outside, the ladybirds fell across the window like bugs on a windscreen, hungry and looking for a way in.

Now Richard told himself it was alright to be scared.

Only the dead people outside had no fear.

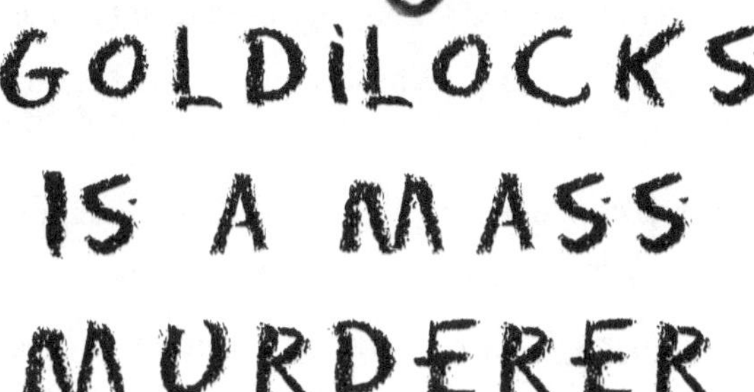

GOLDILOCKS IS A MASS MURDERER

by Neen Cohen

The grounds were emptying as the electronic bell drowned out the excitement of being back at school. An electricity fizzed through the air. Bags were dumped in great piles outside the large pinned back double doors. A sea of teal with bobbing balls of blonde, brunette, and a red no one believed was natural.

Sally's lip lifted against the volume as she entered the school hall. She preferred the quiet of the woods behind the school. She could read all her favourite stories in peace there.

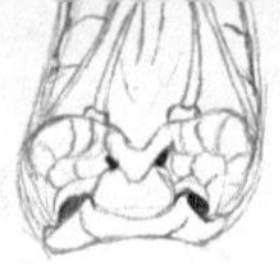

The teachers joined in with their own chatting, loud and animated about their holidays.

"Hey goldilocks." Trisha pulled one of Sally's curls as she walked past and flicked the bandage around Sally's wrist. "What happened? You finally realise no one wants you alive. Didn't do it right though, did ya? You're still here."

"What happened to your mouth? Lockjaw from sucking cock?" Sally's heart beat loud in her chest. She felt her fingers shaking slightly, waiting to see what reaction Trisha would throw at her. Before the holidays, Sally had never retaliated to Trisha's taunts and abuse. It had never dawned on her that she had the power to push back. But everything had changed over the break. She had strength.

Trisha's face went from makeup perfect to bubbling red as her thumb grazed the bruise the makeup couldn't quite hide.

"How dare you. I'll sue you for deformation."

Sally scoffed, shook her head, and walked off. She forced her steps to slow. It wasn't worth showing the seeds of fear she still felt beneath her suddenly cool exterior.

Before the holidays, Sally had dreaded her last year of high school. It meant the end of what she knew.

Even if that was torments and torture.

But the world was now open.

"Oi, goldilocks," Michael said.

Sally growled deep in her throat.

She turned, hands on hips, an attitude that made the school jock hesitate in his step. Her hands trembled as she gripped tighter to her teal tunic, hiding the shake.

He was the missing piece.

She cocked her head as she looked to his left and his right.

"Where's your braindead backup, Mickey?"

"I don't need them to teach you manners."

"Me, manners?" Sally laughed. He was the same height as Sally and almost as thin. His muscles looked impressive only when his two goons weren't around to show how unimpressive they really were.

Michael stepped closer, too close, his face beginning to deepen into a bloody red.

"I'm not your girlfriend. I will hit you back." Sally's words were low and rough.

"In class lines everyone." Mr Jems looked pointedly at Michael as he shooed him back into his class.

Sally felt the sting in her palms as her nails made crescent moons into her skin. She forced herself to take deep breaths; the pressure beneath the bandage on her

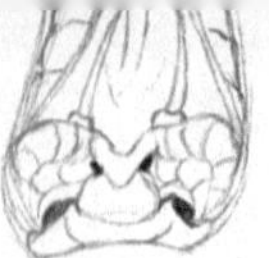

wrist was like a blood pressure cuff. The bite marks beneath itched and scratched, and she wanted nothing more than to take off the bandage.

But no one would believe her story about the wolf, about the strength in her muscles that hadn't been there before. It didn't really matter. She was finding strength in all sorts of ways.

And what once made her feel sick, made her smile.

***

"Hi Sally." Kelly slipped into the seat next to Sally during art class. Sally stopped working on her piece and swivelled to face Kelly.

"Hi Kelly. What's wrong?"

They weren't friends. They weren't enemies.

"Did you really call Trisha a cocksucker?"

Sally swivelled back to her art with a shrug of her shoulders.

"Wow, I wish I could have seen her face."

"It was pretty funny," Sally said.

"What are you working on?"

"Just some doodles." Sally flipped the page in her art book and looked into Kelly's eyes. The girl moved back slightly in her chair.

"Oh, ok. Well, I just wanted to say well done on standing up to Trisha."

"Thanks." Sally would have liked to have been friends with Kelly, but that time was long gone.

She waited until Kelly was back at her own seat before she flipped to her drawing.

A sketch of two bears in the living room of a small cottage. Sally felt a sense of calm she had never felt before as she continued her sketch, filling in details that were burned into her retina.

****

"Have a great afternoon." Sally didn't look at them as she walked past Trisha and Michael in another heated debate of their "relationship." But she made sure they heard her; she felt the eyes following as she walked towards the school gates.

The woods cradled her as she stepped onto the path. The noises from the animals hushed, mere vibrations on the air instead of the raucous excitement that had been her previous background noise. They would come around, or she would get used to the softened silence.

The cottage was easy to find, the cottage from her drawing. For years, it had been her reading cottage. It was

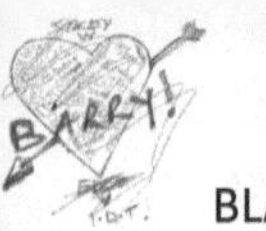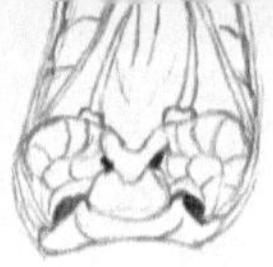

so much more now.

She heard the soft foot treads. Only one set. She could work with that.

A rustle from behind stopped her hand on the front door.

"Trespassing are we, goldilocks?" Michael stepped out from a tree.

"What do you want, Michael?" Sally smiled though her heart raced beneath her chest. Adrenaline and excitement making the bite mark throb again.

"How did you know my boys weren't going to show up today?" He stepped forward. Sally was pleased to see he didn't have his school bag with him, less to worry about later.

"They're in here." She shrugged and pushed open the door for him to enter first.

Three steps in and Michael froze.

Samuel's chest was covered in a bib of blood and guts. His eyes staring lifelessly from his lap, cradled in slack hands. Near the kitchen, Craig's body was a collapsed bag of flesh and bone. If he were stretched out, Michael would see the claw marks covering what was left of Craig's chest, shredding his flesh as easily as scissors would shred material.

"What the fuck is this?" Michael's bravado changed

the moment he saw Sally standing in the doorframe. Her mouth was stretched unnaturally wide, her nose pushing forward, snout-like. The bandage was gone from her wrist, golden blonde fur covering where her skin once was.

"Oh, baby bear, didn't anyone tell you? Goldilocks was a mass murderer."

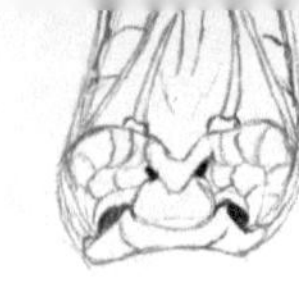

BLACK HARE PRESS

300

WELCOME TO ROSEWOOD HIGH

by Stacey Jaine McIntosh

The blade pierces the animal's chest as I stab upwards, aiming for the heart. The growls and snarling give way to pained cries and after what seems like an eternity but is only a few minutes stops completely, as life is extinguished.

There's a haunting look in the beast's cerulean blue eyes as right in front of me in the deserted school hallway, the animal slowly transforms into a human male.

He looks no older than me.

Shit!

301

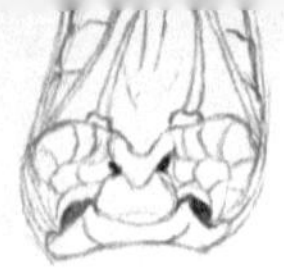

I hadn't expected that. An overwhelming sense of sadness engulfs me, as my mind strays to thoughts of his family.

Slayers weren't meant to show emotion. It's considered a distraction.

Without thinking, I use the hem of my white t-shirt to clean the blade, before rolling up the right leg of my jeans and sheathing the blade in the leather scabbard that I keep strapped there.

All that remains is for me to deal with the body. Thankfully, the hallways remain clear. I cut math to go to the bathroom, only to come across the beastie on my way back.

If only I knew where the incinerator was. I could burn the body.

My locker would have to do.

Picking up the kid's hands in both of mine, I drag him out of the hallway, past three classrooms, and towards the row of lockers.

Noting the combination, I'd been given earlier— three four seven one—I open my locker. Never more thankful than I am now that it is empty and I haven't had a chance to decorate.

Folding the boy up like a pretzel, I stuff him inside and twist the lock before the pressure can force the door

to reopen. I'm leaning against my locker, when the one above me slams shut, bringing me back to the present.

Startled, I take a step backwards and collide with the school quarterback, Mitch Dupree. Strong arms encompass my waist, while wolfish eyes gaze longingly down at me. Ready to devour me whole, if I so much as let him. Not that I will—let him. My life is far too complicated of late to let a boy cloud my judgement or cramp my style. Not to mention people who get close to me have the unfortunate habit of winding up dead and I do not need any more dead friends or lovers to mourn. I have enough of those back at my old school.

Today, is my first day at a new school and now I have to change, and it isn't even home time yet. It's not as if I have forgotten or anything, but sometimes I want a break from the dark clothing I wear to help hide the blood stains, so I break out a white t-shirt. Big mistake. I suppose most will mistake it for ketchup, but I know and just knowing is enough.

My locker now holds a secret. Something that will no doubt get me expelled. A dead teenage boy is stuffed inside. Or at least he had been a teenage boy. At the time when my silver dagger had pierced his heart, he'd been something else. An overgrown wild dog, according to the reports of other students. My bet—given my silver dagger

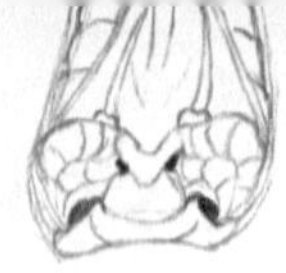

has easily brought about his demise—is on a hellhound. Despite silver being my weapon of choice, the kid couldn't have been a werewolf as they didn't usually show themselves during the day and the next full moon wasn't for another week. Hellhounds on the other hand aren't shy about turning out during the day.

As a slayer, it is my job to slay the demons and other beasties and protect those who cannot protect themselves. A tough gig and one which can be awfully lonely. I have made up my mind not to get close to anyone—potential friends, be damned—yet here is Mitch Dupree holding me and I allow myself just for a moment to daydream about what it would be like to be in his arms for more than a single fleeting moment. The funny thing about all this is, I wouldn't have even known his name if it hadn't been for my English teacher repeatedly calling on him to pay attention in class, rather than talk incessantly to the kid next to him.

"Kinsey Miller." Mitch smiles, straight white teeth almost blinding me. I sidestep out of his embrace.

"Mitchell," I greet as the bell sounds, signalling the end of my first day at Rosewood High.

"You've got ketchup on your shirt," he says, swinging his backpack high up on one shoulder.

Way to state the obvious. I smile back. "I know."

SCHOOL'S IN

There's a swagger in his step as he turns and walks away.

When I turn back to my locker, I see blood seeping through the small grate, dripping onto the floor to form a puddle near my feet. A potential slip hazard, I note. But I can't worry about that now. My first day has officially ended. It's the janitor's concern now.

BLACK HARE PRESS

Mr. Ornell
(when you're late to class)

SUBSTITUTE CREATURE

by T.M. Brown

"Mr Ornell is so gross… he's like half-pig or something," Sophia whispered to Ella. "Ew, do you think his mom *did it* with a pig?" Ella tried to stifle back a giggle but failed. The substitute teacher looked up from his newspaper. *Who even reads the newspaper anymore?*

"Alright, that's enough horsing around back there! Pay attention to the movie and take notes. It's important that you learn about the…you know…economy." Mr Ornell sniffled. It didn't sound entirely unlike the noise a pig might make. He then sank back into his chair and withdrew behind a headline about the latest stock market bubble.

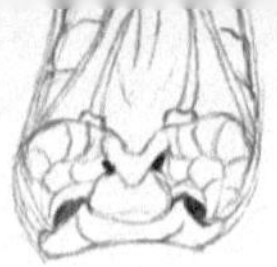

Mr Ornell was, indeed, quite gross. While comparing him to a pig was certainly not the kindest thing to say, his overweight, slovenly appearance inevitably drew such comparisons. Of course, if Mr Ornell were a pig, he was no Babe, Wilber, or Peppa. He was more like one of the hogs you'd see a thirty-second clip about in the local news for setting a county weight record. The collar of his white shirt was stained with sweat. He smelled like potato salad that had been left in the sun for too long.

Sophia rolled her eyes. She didn't see how watching a 1990s documentary about the making of floppy disks was going to teach her anything about the economy. She took out her phone and began texting Ella.

Sophia: OMG. I think Mr Ornell is going to die in class.

Ella: LOL. More like burst!

Sophia: Haha. Right!? For real tho. He's sweating like a lot.

Ella: Sooooo gross!

A GIF of a gagging Jim Carrey followed. Sophia smiled and searched for the perfect response. She was interrupted by Mr Ornell's meaty palm slamming down on her desk. She jumped back in her seat, startled. Her phone clattered to the floor. Everyone in class was staring at her.

"You're supposed to be learning about the economy…" the pig man growled. His face was red and glistened with sweat. His nose was running. He groaned painfully as he bent down to pick up Sophia's phone. It nearly disappeared within his enormous hands. "You can get this back *after* class…*after* you show me your notes on the economy." A sweaty handprint remained in the middle of her desk.

"This stupid movie isn't even about the economy!" Sophia protested. "It's about making floppy disks that haven't existed since, like, the nineties!"

"Well, you'll need to take that up with Mrs Smith." The pig man began waddling back towards the teacher's desk. "I'm *just* the substitute," he said dismissively. Sophia suddenly remembered that she hadn't locked her phone's screen. She needed to get it back.

"You can't take my phone. I read on the Internet that it…that it's against the law!" Sophia shouted. Mr Ornell scoffed. His chins recoiled inward like a compressed accordion. He leaned back heavily in Mrs Smith's chair. It squealed as if it might collapse under his enormous weight. "I can keep it all day if I want to," he said smugly. "You broke the rules." He began scrolling through her phone with his wet, sausage fingers. *What the hell did the pig man think he was doing? She had private things in*

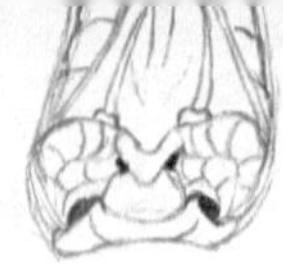

there.

"Hey! You can't do that!" Sophia stood from her seat. "I *know* that's against the rules!"

"She's right, Mr Ornell," Calvin interjected from the front row. He adjusted his thick, tortoise shell glasses. "Just because you can confiscate her phone, doesn't mean you can access her private content." The wiry young man seemed overly pleased with himself. "That's protected by the constitution," he added for good measure. Mr Ornell ignored the students' warnings and continued to scroll through the phone with successive flicks from his fat thumb.

"Seriously!" Sophia screamed. "I'm going to tell Principal Bennet!" The overweight substitute ignored her and continued to stare at the little screen in front of him. *Fine. If that's how he really wanted it, she was going to march over to the principal's office right that moment.* She had nearly reached the door to the classroom when she heard Mr Ornell mutter something under his breath. She turned back towards him and threw open her arms. "Are you ready to give me my phone back or what!? I really am going to tell the principal."

The pig man placed the phone face down on the desk and turned towards her. His already beady eyes narrowed further. "I don't know, Sophia…Ella. Aren't you more

worried that I'm going to burst?" His tone was deathly serious.

"What…ugh…those were, like, private messages. You're going to be in big trouble," Sophia responded. She couldn't believe that creep had actually been looking through her phone. Her mom was going to be *so* pissed. She was sure to get him fired. The pig man struggled up from Mrs Smith's chair. Ella remained seated. She looked shocked.

"No girl, it's you that is in trouble…*big* trouble." Sweat glistened on his furrowed brow. "I've lived for millennia. I will not be ridiculed by some pathetic, suburban whelp…" Mr Ornell's voice seemed somehow distorted—like a thousand whispers trying their best to synchronise with one another. "And, I am *not* going to burst." He shook his head fervently. "Not again…we can control it."

Something moved under the thick rolls of the pig man's neck. Sophia had no idea what Mr Ornell was talking about. He was being weird. He looked really sick. She backed away from him until she bumped against the classroom door. The majority of the class sat in transfixed silence. Two students had taken out their phones and were recording the whole incident as it played out. Mr Ornell turned towards the class.

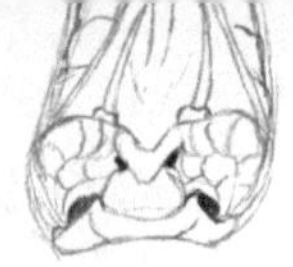

"Who here thinks that I can hold it in?" The substitute's voice continued to grow more distorted. The numerous whispers grew increasingly distinct. "Hmmm…? Who would like a demonstration of immense self-control?" Calvin's hand shot up. There was no other response. The classroom was silent. Something roiled beneath the pig man's pale skin. "Alright, alright…you kids these days are all the same. So, who wants to see me burst?"

At first there was no response. After a few seconds, however, Ella cautiously raised her hand. One by one, the rest of the class followed her lead. There were now a dozen tiny phone cameras trained on Mr Orwell. Something dark slithered beneath his left eye, pushing it momentarily upward. "Alright…" the substitute chucked to himself. His mouth twisted into a cruel grin. "You want something for your Instagram? For your Snapchat?" His bulging gut bubbled with movement beneath his tight oxford shirt. "We'll give it to you…"

Mr Ornell's mouth opened wider and wider until his face split open like a banana peel. Tentacles unfurled from the cavity and began flailing wildly about the room. Similar tendrils burst forth from his fingertips and finally his bulging stomach. Where a blubbery gut had been only moments ago, a void of pure, obsidian black now formed.

Tentacles lashed out and began grabbing students from the front row. They each were reeled, kicking and screaming into the black abyss of Mr Orwell's stomach.

Students ran for the classroom doors, falling over desks, chairs, and one another in their panic. They were too slow for the eldritch tentacles, however. The tendrils moved with lightning speed and frightening efficiency. One by one, the students were dragged into the inky abyss inside of the substitute's gaping ribs. Sophia watched in shock as Mr Orwell swallowed Kyle, Jasmine, Ava, and Shawn. Ella screamed and clung desperately to a desk. The tentacles seemed incapable of breaking her desperate grip. Mr Ornell simply swallowed the desk along with her.

Sophia opened the door and fled down the empty hallway. Just when she thought she'd escaped, however, she collapsed to the floor. A tentacle had slithered its way out of the civics classroom and coiled around her leg. She grasped for something to hold onto but there was nothing within reach. Her sparkly, turquoise fingernails scraped against the beige tile as the tentacle dragged her back to class. The hungry abyss swallowed her whole.

Soon, only Calvin remained. He was still seated at his desk, frozen in place by fear. The tentacles withdrew back inside Mr Ornell's bulging frame. The substitute's

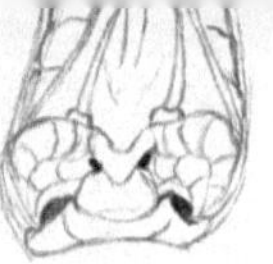

face closed back into place. He removed a handkerchief from his pocket and dabbed his sweaty forehead. He then took the VHS remote off Mrs Smith's desk and rewound the documentary back several minutes.

Mr Ornell cleared his throat and addressed his sole remaining student. His voice was still a chorus of disparate whispers "Alright, class…please continue taking notes on economics."

BRYNHILDR

by Umair Mirxa

Brynhildr walked through the wrought iron gates and up the drive to the main building, trying her best to not meet the eyes of her fellow students. Rumours and whispers had followed her around town, under a dark cloud of suspicion, wherever she went the last week of summer. On the first day back to school, she realised it would only be more of the same. Indeed, she felt certain, the worst of it was yet to come.

She caught up with her best friend, Zarah, on the wide stairs leading up to the building, and immediately felt a measure of relief and calm flow through her. The warmth behind those smiling, hazel eyes as they met her own green pair was the same as it ever had been. No misgivings there. Not a single hint of doubt or accusation. It gave her a reason

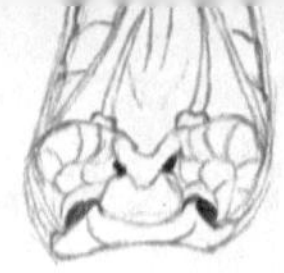

to smile for the first time in a long while.

"You have no idea how good it feels to have you back," said Brynhildr with all the muted brightness she could summon and ran the last few steps up to envelop Zarah in a bone-crushing hug. "Tell me all about your summer. Everywhere you went and everything you did. Meet anyone hot and handsome?"

"I will, I will." Laughed Zarah. "Once you let me go, and I can breathe again. God, when did you get so strong?"

"Gosh, I'm sorry. It's just…I've missed you so much, Z. You won't believe the hell I've been through without you."

"I know some of it from our chats. Social media gave me other bits and pieces when I could find the time to browse. I'm so sorry I wasn't there for you but I'm here now, and I want to know everything. Does anyone actually know what *really* happened to Kevin?"

"Tell you what," said Brynhildr, shifting her feet as she bit her lower lip. "Let's skip first period and sneak off for a bit. I could really use a smoke. Give us time to catch up too, and you can tell me all about Pakistan. Got any hot cousins for me?"

"I am *not* setting you up with one of my cousins. That is just…wrong!"

***

They walked through the school building and out into the grounds behind it, weaving their way across to the patch of woods beyond. It had been, ever since the school first sprang into existence half a century ago, the hotbed for all illicit student activity. A haven for underage smoking and drinking. Each new generation of students passing through the school had come here to experiment with drugs and sex.

Friendships had been forged in these woods. Grudges born and resolved. Many a virginity lost. Romance had blossomed under these trees, and as many hearts broken as there were leaves upon their branches and names carved on the trunks. There had never, however, been a death here before. Not, at least, until last week.

The back-to-school bonfire was a tradition nearly as old as the institute itself. A chance for the two senior-most classes to let loose and have some fun before the gruelling year of study and examinations ahead. Everyone went, without exception. So Brynhildr had gone too, against her better judgement, and now found herself wishing she had listened to her instincts.

"I almost didn't go, you know," she said, leading

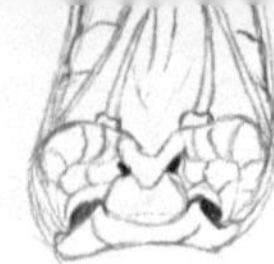

Zarah to the spot where Kevin's mangled corpse had been discovered the next morning, half-buried under the brush. She leaned against a tree, lit a cigarette, and watched her friend circle slowly around the police tape.

"How could you have known something like this would happen? Besides, no one ever misses the bonfire."

"You did. A fine time you picked to go missing, too."

"You know I had no choice, Bryn. My brother was getting married. I only wish you would have come. You *were* invited."

"Yeah, I wish I had too… Listen, Z. There's something—"

"Yes?"

"Never mind," said Brynhildr, stubbing out her cigarette on the tree trunk and lighting another.

"*Oi!* You just had one. What's gotten into you?"

"What do you mean?"

"You're acting weird. We skipped class our first day back. You're smoking more than a chimney, and you keep asking about my trip but you've barely heard a word I've said. Now, out with it."

"I-I can't… there's nothing. Let's head back to school."

"Bryn, stop," said Zarah, stepping in front of her. "Talk to me. What's going on? Did you see something?

318

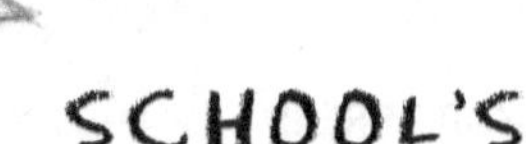

Do you know what happened to Kevin?"

"N-no, of course not, Z. How could you—"

"Look, I don't *want* to believe the rumours. I haven't believed them, not for one second. Now, I don't know what happened here the night of the bonfire but I do know *you*, and you know I love you. You can talk to me. If you saw something, if you know something…"

"Zarah, I…I'm so scared. I-I don't know…"

Brynhildr stumbled through her words, trying to blink away the tears. She looked down at her shoes, and back up again into Zarah's eyes. They were eyes she had known her entire life, and they were pleading with her now. Encouraging her to trust in them. She stared into their depths for a long moment, then accepted the invitation, and poured her heart out to her friend.

***

The clearing had been damp and miserable, in perfect imitation of Brynhildr's mood. She missed Zarah as she plodded around, looking for any excuse to leave early. Earlier in the day, she had rejoiced when several hours of rain threatened to postpone the bonfire. The heavens had, however, ultimately betrayed her.

A couple of beers then, idle gossip with a few

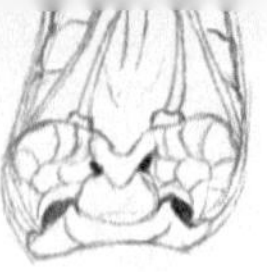

classmates, and being hit on by a bunch of rowdy drunk-too-soon idiots were the highlights of her evening before she decided to call it quits. The simple decision to leave not only brightened her mood but also seemed to cast a charm on the environment around her.

It wasn't her usual route but she decided to walk through the woods and take the long way home. The trees glistened in the night—water droplets on their leaves as diamonds under the full moon's light which illuminated her path. No longer miserably damp but idyllic and cathartic. She stopped more than once, feasting her eyes on the sights before her, bathing in the aromas unique to recently wet earth and wood. A fairy tale experience she wished she could have shared with Zarah, only for the enchantment to be shattered by a muffled scream, abruptly cut off.

Through the trees to her left, thirty-odd paces from where she had first heard the scream, she stopped dead in her tracks. Her first reaction to the scene before her was utter, horrifying revulsion. Kevin stood above a girl—Veronica, from what she could see in the dappled moonlight—lying prone and unconscious on the ground. He had ripped her summer dress nearly to shreds, bunched up what remained above her waist, and removed his own pants. It was even as he lowered himself onto their

classmate that Brynhildr felt something shift deep within herself.

Her disgust mutated and transformed upon itself. It burned through her, a blazing inferno of unbridled rage, and brought with it wave upon wave of incessant pain. Agony as she had never known before coursed through Brynhildr's body, forcing her down to her knees, twisting and remaking her form.

She crawled through the brush, gasping for each breath, clawing at the undergrowth, and felt the breaking of every single bone inside of her. An instinct, born far across the reaches of time, swept over then and took control, and she let escape a howl—primal, monstrous, and majestic—and it echoed back to her through the woods, euphoric upon its return.

***

The headmaster summoned Brynhildr to his office the moment she stepped onto the school's premises the next morning.

She sat before him now, entirely calm and relaxed, trying hard not to let a smile dance upon her lips. It did not matter if she found herself in trouble with the school. Her best friend did not hate her nor was she afraid of her.

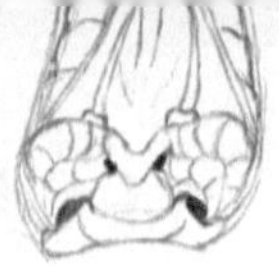

In fact, once the initial shock had worn off, Zarah had been curious and fascinated and had grilled her with a million questions. They had taken the rest of the day off, and even made plans for what they felt certain would come next.

"Miss Klimek," began Headmaster Mehta, his hands clasped in front him. "I am well aware you have already been questioned, both by the police and the school's staff. However, I feel certain you will appreciate why, given my…erm, personal involvement in the tragedy, I might have some questions for you myself."

"Of course, Headmaster," replied Brynhildr softly.

"Very well. I have several witness reports here which state categorically you were seen following Kevin into the woods. Yet, you have continued to insist you neither saw nor heard anything which might shed light upon his fate. I'm afraid I have to say I find your account rather unbelievable."

"Forgive me, Headmaster, but I fear your witness reports are mistaken, if not entirely fraudulent. Kevin may have entered the woods before I departed the bonfire, but it does not imply I had any knowledge of his movements. I grew tired of the evening festivities and walked home. There really is nothing more to say."

The headmaster leapt from his chair, walked around

the desk, and came to stand right next to Brynhildr, leaning over her with a fat finger pointed at her nose. The expression he wore had turned from one of demure grief and stoic resignation to a vile, angry sludge in a frighteningly abrupt transformation. His moustache quivered in sync with his heavy jowls, and he spoke now in short, raspy breaths spit from his tobacco-stained mouth.

"Now, listen here, young lady. You *will* tell me exactly what happened to my son. I have had enough of your lies, and let me reassure you, it will be as child's play for me to ruin any hopes you might have for a career and a successful life. What then might become of a pretty little thing such as yourself, I wonder?"

Brynhildr did not know if it was his tone, ugly and harsh or his ominous demeanour which did it, but she felt the growl deep inside her before it ever escaped her lips. The next moment, she had him pinned down on top of his desk, her hands clasped around his neck. She thought, perhaps, it had been those words: *pretty little thing*. It made no real difference now.

"I killed your son," she growled at the headmaster, even as she choked the life out of him. "I found him in the woods, attempting the brutal rape of an innocent girl. One of his classmates. His *friend*. I caught him in the act, and

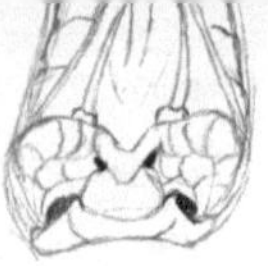

I tore his throat out with my teeth before I *ripped* him apart, limb from pathetic, perverted limb. *You* are no better and shall meet the same fate."

***

Brynhildr rolled back the convertible's soft top and let the wind flow through her hair. It was a gorgeous day, and the headmaster's car was a delight in luxurious driving. They should have found his body by now, she thought. The false trails she had left in her wake had given her enough time to collect her stuff from the foster home and make her escape. She would be long gone before anyone thought to look for her.

Zarah and Veronica were the only two souls who knew what she had done, and only the former knew of her current destination. They alone knew what she had become. Neither of them would ever share her secrets.

Their plans had been well laid the previous night. They would keep in touch discreetly through fake social media accounts, and once the other two had graduated, they would join Brynhildr wherever she had decided to settle. For now, the open road lay before her and promised as many adventures as there were full moons left in her life.

A DANCE WITH DEATH

by Wondra Vanian

Brianna sat in one of the high windows that overlooked the gymnasium. The faculty had declared the bleachers beneath the windows off limits but, since they hadn't specifically said anything about the windows themselves, Brianna assumed that meant it was allowed—which pretty much summed up her high school experience thus far.

She didn't care about the dances, the classes, or the ridiculous cliques; all that mattered to Brianna Chapman was being old enough at the end of it to leave town and never come back. Cedar Park was about as far from civilisation as possible. Most of the houses outside the

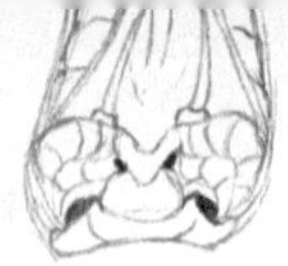

city limits couldn't even get *broadband*.

Brianna just wanted to serve her time and get the hell out. Her best friend, Jade, had other plans. Oh, Jade had every intention of leaving Cedar Park the moment she got her hands on that diploma—but she intended to leave her mark on the place first.

Literally.

If there was a fire set, a building vandalised, or a window broken, there was every chance that Jade had something to do with it. Sheriff Brown and his deputies *knew* Jade Kellert was involved, of course (everyone did) but since they never found a match, a spray can, or a brick anywhere near her, there was nothing they could do.

Not that they didn't try.

Jade would just bat her big green eyes at them, insist she had no idea what they were talking about, and ask to make a phone call. Then, Councilwoman Kellert would show up, looking very annoyed at being drawn away from what was obviously very important work, and the apologies would start.

That was Jade's favourite part. She insisted her mission in life was to make one of the deputies cry before graduation.

Brianna wasn't betting against her.

At that moment, Jade wore the kind of expression

that usually spelled trouble for CPPD. Brianna kicked her feet absently as she wondered what sort of mischief her best friend was planning. If it had anything to do with being a distraction, Brianna was out; she still had another week's detention for being too close to a fire alarm when it was pulled.

"Whatever you're thinking," Brianna told her friend, "don't do it."

Jade grinned. "I don't know what you mean."

Aw, hell.

"Should I be heading for another ZIP code?" Brianna asked warily.

"Probably."

Neither moved. They continued to watch their classmates mill around the make-shift dance floor. Only one couple turned in a clumsy circle, closely watched by overzealous (or was that over-jealous?) chaperons. The rest of the students shuffled around the room nervously, either wondering if they should ask someone to dance or desperately waiting to be asked.

Brianna didn't care much for dances. Or pep rallies. Or sporting events. Or anything else that required her to force a smile on her face and pretend she didn't hate everyone around her. Jade, on the other hand, loved it all. Not the events themselves but the act of going to them.

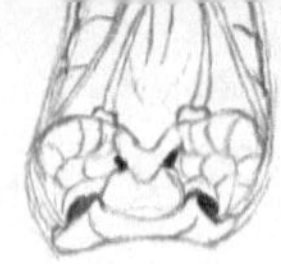

She always said there was something about it being the greatest form of irony a teenager could exercise.

Whatever.

Jade badgered Brianna to go, so Brianna went. Didn't mean she was happy about it.

"Have you had your fill of angst yet?" she asked miserably.

Her friend was spared from having to answer when the vice principal walked up.

Mr Dunham had a soft spot for social outcasts like Jade and Brianna. Probably because he had been one himself, if his checkered pants and paisley tie were anything to go by. He glanced up in their direction and shook his head with a smile.

"Having fun, Miss Chapman? Miss Kellert?"

Brianna looked away but Jade gave the vice principal a toothy grin.

"Hi, Mr Dunham. *Loads* of fun. Best dance yet."

One day, she's going to push her luck too far.

Brianna's attention was drawn from the spectacle her best friend was making of herself when an unfamiliar boy walked into the gym. No, boy wasn't exactly the right word; he looked older than most of the kids in the gym but younger than the youngest teacher, Mrs Welch, who was fresh out of college and insisted her students called

her "Vikki."

He wore all black: a black sweater with the sleeves pushed up and black jeans that rode low on his hips. His wavy hair was also black, and just long enough to brush his shoulders as he looked around the room. A thick black band circled one slim wrist.

Huh. Don't usually see the goths at these things…

But, although the boy wore all black, he didn't look like the goths that trudged through the hallways of CPHS, shoulders bent under the weight of their own existentialism. He didn't look like the emos either, with their kohl-lined eyes hidden behind spiky bangs. He was…something else.

Brianna found it difficult to take her eyes from the boy in black as he made his way across the gym. He was stopped several times by Brianna's classmates, who blushed and laughed and tossed their hair back like meeting a cute guy was some sort of equestrian event.

Was he cute?

Yes…but that wasn't what kept Brianna enthralled. There was something compelling about the boy who made his way patiently through the crowd of eager teenagers, something impossible to name. Maybe it was the way he moved, so slowly and deliberately. Maybe it was the serene expression he wore, like nothing that was

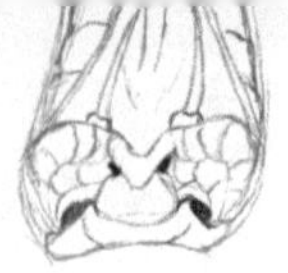

happening around him really touched him. Or maybe it was the way he touched every person's shoulder that he spoke to, leaning in to speak quietly to each before moving on.

Brianna watched their reactions carefully. Some laughed as they walked away. Others looked spooked.

What the hell is he saying to them?

She contemplated going down and speaking to the boy herself but, in the end, Brianna decided it would jeopardise the couldn't-be-less-bothered image she'd spent so long perfecting. Instead, she turned away from the dance floor…

…only to find her best friend clambering down the bleachers.

"Hey," Brianna called. "What the hell, Jade?"

Jade just threw a reckless grin over her shoulder.

"See you in a bit," she called back. "Gotta see a guy about a bomb."

Wait. Did she say bomb?

"Jade…"

"Joking, joking!" Jade laughed. "Party in the boiler room. Wanna come?"

Brianna shook her head. Alcohol made people stupid. Stupid people stood out.

"No, thanks," she told Jade, trying not to sound

annoyed that her friend had dragged her to the lame ass dance, then ditched her at the first opportunity. "I'm gonna bail."

"Don't know what you're missing," Jade said. "It'll be a blast." Then, she hopped over the railing onto the shiny linoleum floor below.

Brianna watched Jade cross the room, with a frustration as old as their friendship. Sometimes, it felt like the only thing they had in common was the hatred they shared for Cedar Park. Not much to base a relationship on.

Better than bonding over shoes.

Well, there was that.

Jade started to walk past the boy in black, but he moved slightly, and they collided. The sound of her friend's expletives reached Brianna up in her perch. Unfazed, the boy caught Jade's arm lightly and spoke, waving a hand in what looked like an apologetic gesture. Brianna waited for her friend to explode (touching was a big no-no) but Jade just lifted her shoulders in her trademark "whatever" shrug and walked off.

Huh. Weird.

She'd seen Jade pop guys in the nuts over less.

The newcomer seemed to have that effect on everyone at the dance. Even Callista Smith—a sure bet

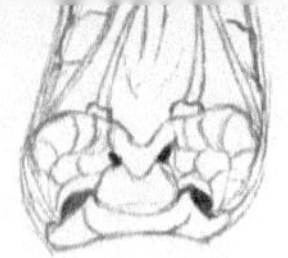

for that year's Prom Queen, who never even looked at a guy if his daddy didn't make at least five figures—practically swooned when he offered her a dance. They swung in an elegant circle, putting everyone else in the room to shame. When Callista's boyfriend cut in angrily, the boy in black merely shook his hand politely and turned to the next girl.

Weird.

Something about the spectacle made Brianna uneasy. Who *was* that guy, anyway? Weren't school dances only open to students?

"Hey, Mr Dunham."

The vice principal had been on his way to the refreshment table, but he turned to give Brianna a friendly smile.

"Where's your partner in crime?" he asked.

"She had to see a guy about a bomb," Brianna answered with a roll of her eyes.

Laughing, Mr Dunham shook his head. "Of course she did. What can I do for you, Miss Chapman?"

Brianna nodded towards the boy. She noticed that he was dancing with "Vikki."

Fucking weird.

"Who's that guy?"

"You wouldn't believe me if I told you," the vice

332

principal answered.

Brianna glared.

Mr Dunham threw up his hands. "If you want to know, ask him." He walked away.

Screw this.

Pushing herself off the windowsill, Brianna jumped onto the bleachers and started down them. She found the boy in black waiting at the bottom. He offered her a hand over the rail, which she took warily.

"You should be more careful," he warned in a cool voice. He released Brianna immediately and took a step back.

A dozen quips crossed Brianna's mind, but one question rose above them all.

"Who the hell are you?"

His dark eyes twinkled. "You don't want to know."

Enough of this cryptic shit.

"Yeah, sure. Bye then." Brianna rolled her eyes as she turned her back on the strange boy.

"I'll be seeing you," he called after her.

A shiver slid up Brianna's spine. There was a certainty to his voice that made her uneasy. Who *said* that?

As much as she hated to admit it, curiosity still buzzed through Brianna's veins. She saw an

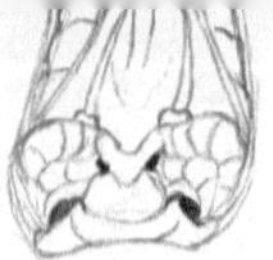

underclassman who looked easily intimidated and stopped the girl.

"You," she snapped. "Who's that guy?"

The younger girl looked terrified. "You wouldn't believe me if I told you."

If Brianna rolled her eyes any harder, she'd choke on them. "Who. Is. He?"

With a look at her friends for support, the girl swallowed hard.

"Death," she said.

Brianna just stared.

"Death?"

The girl nodded. "That's what he said."

Idiot.

"Get out of here," Brianna told the girl. The underclassmen scattered.

"Well," she said to herself, "ask a stupid question, right?"

A small part of Brianna was intrigued by the girl's insistence that the newcomer was Death. Mostly, though, she was sick of high school, dumb teenagers, lame dances, and mind games. Brianna didn't even look over her shoulder as she shoved the gym's double doors open wide and stomped out of the room.

Brianna had only taken a few steps away from the

334

building when she was lifted off her feet and tossed across the parking lot.

Her ears rang and her back burned like it had been struck with a hot iron. Every bone in her body hurt, but her arms and knees, which had taken the brunt of Brianna's collision with the blacktop, hurt worst of all. She'd never had a broken bone before, but something told Brianna that she had more than one now.

It took a long time, lying face-first on the ground, for Brianna to make sense of what had happened. Even when the sound of screaming and the smell of smoke reached her, her mind struggled to comprehend.

I've gotta see a guy about a bomb.

Oh, Jesus. Jade. What have you done?

Brianna tried to push herself up but failed. Definitely broken. Both her arms, at least. She rolled over instead, immediately wishing she hadn't. Some sights could never be forgotten.

Cedar Park High School was engulfed in flames. What was left of it, anyway.

Which wasn't much.

The old, red brick building had exploded outward, showering the already battered cars in the student parking lot with debris. Smoke and flames billowed out of the gaping hole in the school. A siren started somewhere, far

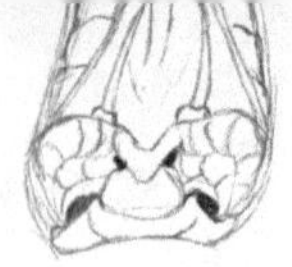

away, and joined the crackling of the fire and the keening wail of a pair of girls who'd been making out in one of the cars when the bomb went off.

Brianna heard the cacophony of noise but couldn't take her eyes away from the fire. She thought there were shapes moving around inside. But, surely, that couldn't be. No one could have survived that explosion.

At that moment, she wasn't entirely sure *she* had.

One of the shapes detached itself from the fire.

The boy in black.

His expression was serene; his hair and clothes untouched by the angry flames. He stopped, turned towards the building, and raised a beckoning hand. Other figures joined him, stepping from the flames as easily as if they were nothing more than an illusion.

But the flames weren't an illusion; Brianna could feel the heat of the fire on her flesh. Yet the boys and girls that stepped through the flames, though shocked and confused, appeared uninjured. One by one, they piled out of the building and gathering in a tight knot around the boy in black. He waited patiently until the very last student had exited the building before moving.

Jade.

Brianna's best friend brought up the rear with "Vikki" and Mr Dunham, looking more sheepish than

surprised. She joined her classmates as they followed the boy in black across the parking lot.

They were all okay. Brianna could have cried with relief, except…*How?* How could they have survived that explosion? It was impossible.

Then the underclassman she'd frightened walked through a steel girder protruding from a Chevy and Brianna understood.

Oh, Jade.

"Death."

The boy in black stopped in front of Brianna. He gently eased her into a sitting position, with a car at her back.

"You'll be okay," he told her softly.

The spirits of her classmates continued their trek, filing past Brianna, one after the other.

"They're…" She couldn't bring herself to speak the word.

He nodded. "Yes."

Brianna could feel the tears streaking down her flushed cheeks, was dimly aware of the pain in her limbs, but was too mesmerised by the dark eyes of the boy before her to care about any of it.

"You're…"

He pressed a finger to her lips.

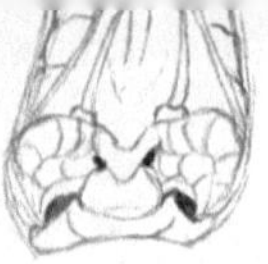

"Shh," he said. "You'll speak my name soon enough. But not tonight."

Brianna went cold all over. He nodded, seeing the acceptance spread through her. Impossible as it was to believe, Brianna believed.

She turned towards the ghostly figures in time to see Jade glide past. Their eyes met. Brianna wanted to go to her best friend, to break Jade's no-touching rule and throw her arms around the other girl—but something told Brianna that, even if she could have stood, it wouldn't have done any good. Jade was already gone.

He rose, brushing dirt from the knees of his black jeans.

"I'll be seeing you," he told her, echoing his earlier words.

Despite the inferno just a few feet away, Brianna was colder than she had ever been. Cold as…

…the grave.

Silent tears ran down Brianna's cheeks as she watched Death lead the throng of students and chaperons away from Cedar Park.

SCARLETT

by Ximena Escobar

Eyes focused on the little "egg-thingy" around the hair root, the rest of her world blurred into dissolution. All but the clasp of two very precise fingernails, as they tweezed the hair and pulled the thing off with a single swipe—perfectly normal scalp-oil secretion stuff according to Wikipedia.

She loved scraping the "thingy" out of the underside of her fingernail. Letting it sit on her thumbnail, ignored. Leave it there to simply exist, as nothing more than a tiny presence in the corner of her eye, whilst she rehearsed her arguments on same sex marriage or the legality of abortion—the whole class listening with admiration. Always from the comfort of her bed and always aware of the little oily secret like a value only known to her.

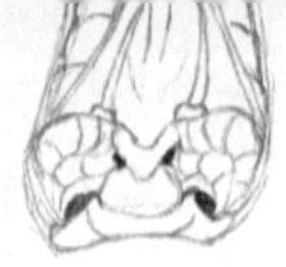

Paste it on her upper lip and feel its moisture. Let it harden slowly as the seconds pass unnoticed. Do it all again and see how many she could collect before someone interrupted her. (The thought of covering her whole face; the thought of a mask of little translucent thingy curdles as she basked in the soothing weight of being *alone*, was the ultimate satisfaction.)

Scarlett sighed at the thought of having to return to the awful wig place; those women with cancer and all the heads on the display shelves made her feel like a freak, but at least she'd be able to wear her hair down now.

Just one more, she thought, before Mum picked her up to have her extensions fitted.

She'd got away with hiding her bald patches in a ponytail for quite some time, but then the End-of-Year Festival happened, and she got her hair wet. Luckily, neither Jessica nor anyone else important noticed them; only probably Lila Roberts who didn't say a word the best of times and maybe FA, the chick with the fat ankles. All eyes were elsewhere, because Jessica had aimed the bucket at her breasts and she ran into the building covering the back of her head instead of her nipples—which, ironically, resulted in an unexpected popularity boost. Nonetheless, she couldn't face going back, so she told her mum everything and got to stay home the last two days.

She's always been jealous of you, darling. And now you've blossomed, turns out you're prettier than her!

Pasting the thingy deliciously on her lip, Scarlett got up carefully to look at the visual in the mirror. She could almost see the sunlight filter through its dense transparency—if she turned her profile to the window at just the right angle. Hair like spider legs was stuck to her clothes; she carefully picked one up, twirling her fingers around both ends of the hair. Pulling it to a full stretch, she used it to scoop up the thingy and watched it hang from the hair like an insect egg, or a grain of couscous stuck to the underside of a fork. But it fell, lost in the high-pile carpet.

Leaning closer to her reflection, she inserted the fully stretched hair between her lower central teeth and prodded as far under the tooth as possible. Eyes closed to the soaring pain, she slid down a blissful climax of release.

Only looping the gum could take it that step further, a sensual but also visual peak of sensation. It took her some time to encircle the little gum protrusion in the middle of her front bottom teeth, but persistence delivered and she soon revelled on the sight of it whitening, bulging above the belt of hair as she pulled the crossed strands in opposite directions. She marvelled at her hair's strength, wondered if it would resist the necessary pull to sever the gum completely, stick the little piece of "watermelon" on her

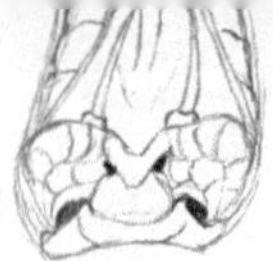

cheek, under her eye—a crispy piece of pink apple flesh to lap onto the back of the hand or the eyelid, or her cleavage. She did… Her gum throbbing as eyes stared at the chunk of gum stuck to the hair—blood running profusely, welling up in her lower lip.

Licking it off the hair, she looked at her tongue, sticking out like the frog who got the fly. She couldn't help but laugh at her reflection—swallowed the gum as blood ran down the corners of her mouth. Something about it had an air of "the Joker"…a "who laughs last laughs longest" kind of vibe.

***

Everyone saw the great hair, but nobody noticed the weight in her pocket. Now the boobs had promoted her to sitting with a new group of girls for lunch, the mandatory blazer sure came in handy—in case she needed to visit the toilets. Today, however, was an "out day," as she'd come to refer to good days like these—conversation flowing nicely with her friends picking her brain about the Philosophy and Ethics essay, something she did have an interest in—especially the debate about the death penalty. So much so, she ended up staying with the group for the duration of lunch break.

Not that "not good" days were strictly "bad," but they were certainly *wrong*; if she took notice of what her mother and the wig lady said about her "self-destructive" habits, and that part of herself which wanted to be accepted. More than accepted, appreciated. It was all about finding a balance; a hair-thin tightrope edge to balance on without falling to the "dark side" but without losing herself either. If there was one thing Scarlett was sure of, it was that she wasn't like any of these girls. She liked her "demons" much better and she wasn't willing to give them up altogether.

"Catch you later guys," she said, suddenly craving a little time on her own. A little time on her own within the shape of a good "out day." A little time on her own to skim the irregular border of "wrong," tease it, to satisfy the balance. "Gotta deal with a library situation."

Pressing her palm against her pocket, the craft knife still inside it, she gave her friends the V-sign with the other hand and walked in the opposite direction as they headed to their classes. She didn't have to worry about missing twenty minutes or so of Citizenship; plus, a late mark would give her a little bit of extra kudos to go with her higher place in the classroom.

Except, Jake Bradley and Cole Knowles appeared around the corridor, and they elbowed each other.

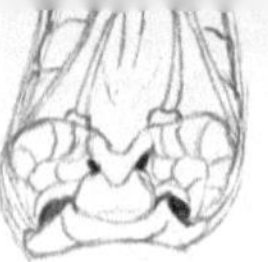

She didn't have time to flick her hair or look at her feet or do whatever she was going to do. Jessica appeared behind them like a sudden ray of sunshine, and that was that. A spur-of-the-moment reflex, a spur-of-the-moment confidence—or rather, forgetfulness—drove her to call Jessica. She wrinkled her nose like Jessica wrinkles her nose when she smiles, and pulled an invisible string with the circular movement of her index finger, like Jessica does.

"Hey, Jess!" Like she didn't know they attended the same school.

They hadn't said a word to each other since their first term in secondary three years back. And neither of them had even acknowledged to each other that Jessica had been the one who spilled the bucket on her last summer, even if she had made sure the whole school knew it had been her. But—she *had* said "hey" three times since school was back, as well as commented on her Snapchat once over the summer, and that was enough for Scarlett.

Jessica looked right at her and headed decidedly in her direction, eyes smiling with bright, confident sparks.

Scarlett knew already to regret it—all of it—kicking herself for her stupidity as she anticipated the bucket-of-cold-water apathy, the brush of Jessica's cruel shoulder as she walked past her, greeting whoever was standing behind

344

her—ridiculing her in front of the boys. She, the boys, and whoever was behind her laughed, the words "wet t-shirt" and "Scarlett Johansson" bouncing from amongst the hideous murmur. Scarlett could only raise her arm and wave to an invisible friend, laugh like she'd suddenly remembered something hilarious as she ran past them and around the corridor. Heat and coldness burning her inside—an invisible pistol of humiliation chasing after her, threatening to collapse her into a puddle of tears.

***

The girls' toilets were still busy, but she walked straight into a cubicle, sat on the toilet as the bell emptied the room—already feeling better as she listened to the water running, the tanks filling, hand dryers blowing, rubber soles screeching like a promise. Until the last swing of the door gave her the cue to stand up and pull her tights down—a fortunate "rain or shine" trend.

She pulled out her craft knife; pressed the blade into her shin. The little cut like a gateway into a separate plain of existence, the other side of the line, just enough that she was still almost completely in the good side. It didn't hurt in a bad way and only fed her with extra self-awareness, enhanced her, wrapped her in a ballgown of *Scarlettness*

that would see her through the rest of the day—a feeling akin to praying; the secret relationship one has with God. Except something called her from the source of her pain and anger, wrapped her like a hair around the gum, and pulled her further into the farthest depth of the "in" so deliciously, she finally understood her mother's concern.

She quickly pulled her tights up, flushed the toilet so she didn't hear anyone come in; but she saw Jessica's shoes appear through the gap under the cubicle door. *"Anybody who is anybody"* wore those, but hers were the original brand, something her mother refused to buy Scarlett out of principle. Scarlett waited for the sound of the door or the tap or whatever but, instead, complete silence waited too from the other side of the door.

"You coming out then, babe?"

Scarlett froze.

"I'm talking to *you*, Scarlett Johnson. You wanna vape?"

Vape? Did she say vape?

"Hey, I don't bite. Thought we should have a chat for old times' sake… I didn't mean to blank you back then."

Scarlett's heart grew a tail and wagged. It was sad, frankly, that her basicness cared so much about Jessica yet, she, the true Scarlett, the noble Scarlett, didn't in the slightest. That part of her that needed to exist in society.

That pathetic part of her that needed Jessica to like her, was stronger—She always had to be the boy, always the supporting role, the backing vocal. Year 6 Jessica made sure Scarlett knew she'd only been invited to her birthday because her mum made her, seeing as they lived two houses from each other. Now, if not apologised, she'd shown signs of maturity. To be truthful, Scarlett had put her down too, once or twice, about her grades, and ever since they stopped taking her "shutters came down," as her mum always said they did. Maybe she had a part in it too.

She opened the door, imagining her new place in the back of the classroom.

"Don't worry, babe, I do it all the time."

"I'm not worried," said Scarlett, expecting Jessica to move out of the way—but she stepped in and shut the door behind her, sliding the latch sideways to a lock.

Scarlett's pupils focused on her unique smile, the little pink bell like a clitoris under her top lip. Jessica consciously wrinkled her nose to lift it over her gums and show it off—only she could turn a lip tie into something sexy. Her mother always said it was the ugliest thing, but Scarlett had always thought it was real pretty, and she went through a phase when she pulled the underside of her own lip in an attempt to have one. She has a flaccid piece of skin hanging in there but it's not visible. (Sometimes it beats,

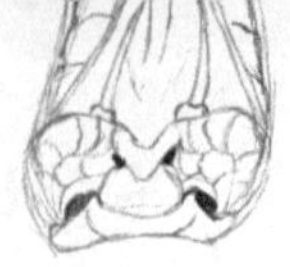

wanting some attention, but for the most part, it's dead meat.)

Without further ado, Jessica pulled an e-cig out of her blazer's inner pocket. They didn't say anything, they just vaped. Laughing quietly at the situation. A chuckle here, a chuckle there—vapour replacing the laughter they didn't allow themselves. (Scarlett always laughed when she was nervous.)

"I like your hair," said Jessica.

"They're hair extensions," said Scarlett.

"I know."

Scarlett felt herself blush.

"I saw you from the window. You left wearing a baseball cap, came back looking all gorgeous. Like…Oh my god…You know all the boys were *already* fancying you after the…you know… t-shirt incident."

"Yeah."

"Sorry."

"Never mind."

"It wasn't you… The *situation* was just funny, you know? It's all about laughing. If you laugh, nothing can get to you."

"Yeah, I have a skin condition…*scalp* condition. But it's better now."

"Honestly, just have fun, babe. Yeah? That was

always the thing about you, always so serious."

The pair said nothing for a few long—very long—seconds. It was easier hiding in a kiss than facing whatever it was that was going on between them. Soon they were blowing vapour into each other's mouths, their tongues spiralling entwined. Scarlett's first kiss, in fact, but she thought she came across like a pro. Jessica's fingertips climbing like spider legs up her shoulder, tangling themselves in her hair. Creeping up and opening, rubbing her head with circular movements—slowly closing into a fist.

Scarlett revelled in the pull upon her scalp, that slit tearing open like a portal of strength. She inserted her fingers in her pocket; the tip of her tongue feeling for the bell under Jessica's lip as darkness whispered, tickling her deliciously, that *nothing* else matters but whatever she needs, and that if she needs anything, it's to give that bitch a taste of her own medicine. Whose voice it was, she didn't know; but that was her favourite company. The *only* company, as she waited like a rabbit for the pounce.

Jessica pulled her hardest, but the hair extensions stayed partially attached. A grin of frenzy freezing in her face as she did—the pang of craft metal blade bulging her eyes as realisation slipped like cement drying in her veins. Scarlett's smile stretching high above her gums, her

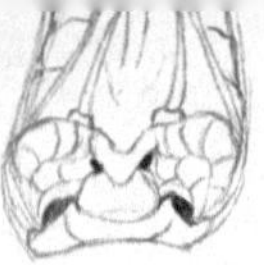

wrinkled nose reflected in Jessica's frozen lake eyes, and the mess of her hair too, like someone who's had a good time. For once a good reflection of her in those eyes.

Knees gave into gravity. Scarlett grabbed her by the hair and positioned her back against the toilet, watching the life flush out of her, gasping for breath like a fish out of water—the knife still stuck in her neck. She pulled her top lip that she folded it over her nose—the little pink bell looking at her, waiting to be cut out like mother when she trims the chicken thighs. She stuck it on the bridge of her own nose, a sizeable chunk which she could see with each eye if she shut one at a time, more worthy of attention than the rest of Jessica, as her weight pulled her to the chessboard floor.

Scarlett laughed. She laughed out loud. Lol. Zero fucks given. Look at her now, all crooked in the corner of the cubicle. It was the freest she'd ever felt her entire life; being able to just be, no matter what anybody thought of her.

She pulled a clump of hair out from under the loose hair piece still attached to her head. Man it felt good. The little root thingies like a lovely bouquet of flowers to smell.

She tweezed each out, swiping them off deliciously with her nails, as the blur of Jessica's corpse lay forgotten in the background and a lovely collection amounted on the

350

back of her hand. Little translucent oily acrylic thingies she craved to transfer onto Jessica, most hard and defined like cocoons, but others a disappointing mash.

There was so much more she could do to her…so much more they could exchange if the bell weren't about to ring. She exited the cubicle and looked at herself in the mirror—her chest pumping as Jessica's own little bell sat on her nose like a ladybird.

Ripping her shirt open, she transferred it to her breast, watching it rise and fall as she breathed—blood coursing through her veins like a torrent of pride—the sight of her half-ripped hair as liberating as the crimson on her hands. She so looked forward to all the time she'd have for herself in jail, in blissful solitude; some of the best people, respected thinkers and writers, did their time behind bars, and that knowledge was enough for her. For that other part. For the little pathetic part who cared about what "the world." thinks

The cubicle door ajar, Jessica's shoes poked out delightfully. These visuals. She'd carry these visuals like little ounces of *more*. Like she carried the little pink of reassurance, the tiny mollusc of self-worth out through the door and into the corridor, on her chest. The boys were waiting; their phones at the ready to photograph her. (Their faces when they saw her—*that* was a photo-worthy sight

351

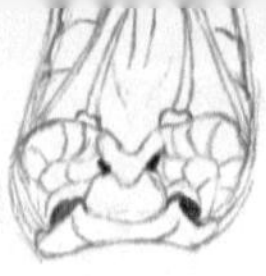

alright.)

Scarlett laughed. She laughed her head off. She always laughed when she was nervous, but this was just laughing last, laughing better. The boys' screams muffled in the echo of her laughter, the doors opening, slamming, the bell ringing.

Scarlett just kept walking, her fingers digging into the underside of her lip, pulling the dangly excess flesh as far as she could bear, as horrified faces emerged and then shrank back into their classrooms. Another little spot of herself to fill; another little corner to bring to existence. A larger little wardrobe of self-awareness to hide in, separate from everyone else. *And be who you are.*

PAYBACK

by Zoey Xolton

I'm startled into wakefulness by a god-awful loud bashing on my bedroom shutters. The metallic sound sets my heart racing, and my eyes immediately train onto my infant daughter asleep in my queen-size bed beside me. *She's safe.* I reach for my mobile phone, sliding it from the windowsill. It's 3 a.m. *Fuck!* I think to myself.

The bashing stops just as suddenly as it started and the house falls eerily quiet once more. My breathing shallow, I slip from bed, pull my hatchet from under the mattress, and creep out of my room—closing the door behind me—all without disturbing the baby. Another sound…I identify the source immediately: tapping on the glass of my kitchen window. I tip-toe down the hall, listening, straining my ears for the next sign of danger.

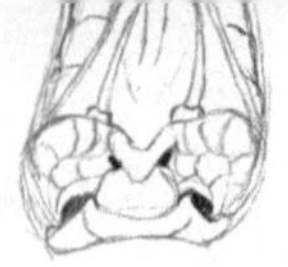

Moments later, I hear the unmistakable sound of my wheelie bins being dragged down the driveway. *What the actual—!* I race to unlock the front door, peering into the dark street beyond my security screen. I heave a great sigh as I catch sight of four teenagers—two girls and two boys, still in the local high school uniform—dashing across the road, down towards the park by the underpass. My bins are ridiculously, and inconveniently, left stranded in the middle of the road. *They could cause a fucking accident! Stupid shits!*

I ride the come-down of the 'fear wave,' as the immediate threat of danger has passed. Now I feel my irritation and rage growing in equal measures to take its place. Still anxious, I lock the security door behind me— to protect my daughter—I have no choice. Hatchet in hand, I stalk out into the street and grab hold of one of my bins. I return it to its rightful place by the garage, before going back for the second. In the darkness I can hear the teenagers' girlish, ridiculous laughter. They're watching me, no doubt, marvelling at how truly brilliant and funny they are.

Yeah, because harassing and terrifying a single mum, home alone, with a baby is funny!? Fucking arseholes. I never used to pull this crap on people as a kid. *What's wrong with the world these days?* I fucking hate

teenagers.

As I drag in the second bin, I stop at the edge of my rental property and in frustration shout into the dark: "You little fucking bastards! You think this is funny? What the fuck are you even doing out at this time? It's a school night! Don't you have anything better to do? Do your parents even know where you are? Leave me and my family the fuck alone, or you'll regret it!"

I am met with more laughter, and then rocks sail over the colour-bond fence, hitting the brickwork of my cheap rental home. I feel my seething fury grow, rumbling within me, ready to explode. I am tired of being woken up, and frightened, in the bullshit-early hours of the morning. I'm tired of having to guess whether it's these stupid little shits, or if it's more real, sinister criminals trying to break in. I've been robbed often enough in this neighbourhood that I live, and run, on fear and adrenalin. I'm a nervous, anxious, strung out wreck. *I'm so fucking over it! I've had enough!* And then, like a lightbulb flickering on in the night, I have an idea.

I'm going to make those little spineless fuckers pay…and I'm going to knock out two birds with one stone while doing it!

***

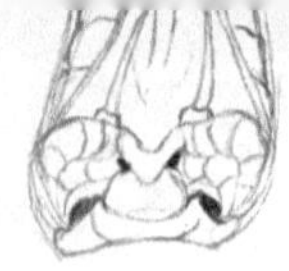

With a malicious smile I prepare my 'peace offering.' Gloves on, I tear open the bright yellow packet covered in warning labels. I unscrew and pour, shaking and mixing to ensure there is no trace, or evidence, of what I have done. I hold up the bottle of clear liquid to the light and my smile becomes a sinister grin. I pop the frosty cold bottle in a gift bag—along with some clean unmarked shot glasses—pen a quick note, and pop back outside.

In the nearby distance, I can hear laughter once more. I look about, the street is empty and otherwise silent. Only idiots, or people with a death wish, come out after dark here. It's a drug den shithole. *This is my payment, Dark Lord, for this first year, and for the next three to come.* I leave the offering on my brick letterbox in plain sight, tape the note to the top of the letterbox so it will be seen, and then disappear back inside. I close the door behind me, and for the first time in a long time, I feel a little more safe.

I wait, ear pressed to the wood and listen. Sure enough, I hear sneakers on the pavement, followed by those rage-inducing giggles. But I wait.

"What's this?" I hear one of the boys say.

Seconds later.

"It's a bottle of fuckin' vodka!" Laughs one of the

girls, clearly stoked, judging by the tone of her voice.

"Holy fuck!" says the other.

"There's a note," says the first male voice. "It says: *I'm sorry I yelled at you kids. I'm just exhausted. I get that you're just having fun. If you could leave me and my baby sleep, the drink's on me.*"

"Fuck yeah," responds one of the girls. "We should screw with people more often if they're gonna pay us in booze!"

Gritting my teeth in anger, I wait until their chatter dies down as they disappear down the street, victorious—no doubt, back towards the underpass. Dank and cold, the concrete covered in graffiti, the ground always littered with broken bottles and spent needles…it's clearly a 'cool' kids hangout. When I'm sure they're off the road and out of sight, I duck outside, quiet as a shadow, and collect my note and the discarded gift bag.

Climbing back into bed beside my baby girl, I reach my arm over her protectively and fall asleep with a smile on my face.

***

I'm woken by a chorus of screams and the sudden but relentless wail of sirens down our street. I hear voices and can see red and blue lights flashing underneath my

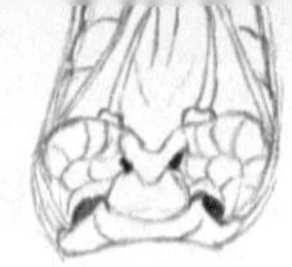

door. Clutching my baby to my chest, I shield my eyes with my free hand as I open up the house and amble across my overgrown lawn towards the street. The road is cordoned off in both directions, barricades have been erected, and several police cars, as well as two ambulances, are parked by the pathway that leads down to the underpass.

"Excuse me," I say aloud, voice still croaky with sleep. "Excuse me?"

An officer on patrol turns to face me; he looks me up and down, standing there, blinking in the morning light in my mumsy powder-blue nightgown, baby in my arms.

"Stand back please, miss," he says. "This is a crime scene. No pedestrians or vehicles beyond this point."

I cover my mouth with my hand in shock. "What's happened, officer?"

He sighs and shakes his head. "A young woman walking her dog early this morning came across four teenagers in the underpass."

"My goodness! Are they okay?" I ask, looking pointedly to the ambulances and stretchers.

"No, miss. They're deceased."

"My God," I say as I bounce, shushing my baby.

"Underage drinking, like so many of them do," says the officer. "Looks like maybe they upset the wrong

358

person. Seems their liquor was poisoned. There's blood everywhere. Doesn't take a genius to figure out what it was either."

I wait, as if with bated breath, horror schooled carefully on my exhausted features.

"Rat poison," he continues. "They were foaming at the mouth, bleeding internally…it's a horrific way to go. Poor shits must have really had it coming."

"And so close to my home," I say. "I'm already so frightened living here, just my baby and me. Break-ins, drugs…and now this? I feel sick."

"You didn't happen to hear, or see, anything last night, did you, miss? We've got no leads. No prints. Just a mess, I've been told."

"No," I say. "I mean, most nights there's something going on around here, but I have my shutters down and alarm system on. I never go out after dark."

The officer smiles, and in an uncharacteristic act of empathy, he places a hand on my shoulder for a moment. "It's a bad neighbourhood, miss. Keep to yourself and look after that little one."

"Thank you," I say, lower lip quivering slightly. "I will." With a nod and a polite grimace, I turn on my heel and head back inside. I close the door behind me, and a grin so wide as to be almost painful splits my face. *Those*

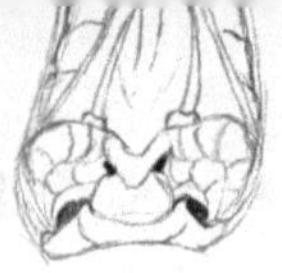

little shits won't harass anyone ever again.

With a bounce in my step, I enter the lounge.

"Hello, Everly."

A bone-achingly beautiful man with long black hair awaits me.

"Dark Lord," I utter, dropping my eyes and bowing my head.

"You've done well," he says, his silver-blue eyes alight like burning stars.

"Thank you, Your Darkness," I say.

"You're paid ahead," he says. "I'm very impressed. You have four murder-free years of peace to enjoy with your daughter."

I sigh in relief and smile. "Thank you."

"One life for every year of hers, that was our agreement for your miracle pregnancy."

"I won't let you down, Dark Lord," I assure him. "Your next soul will be on time, you have my word."

"I have no doubt of it," he says as he approaches. He strokes Lilia's dark locks affectionately. "And how is our child?"

"She's well, Dark Lord. Healthy and strong, with eyes just like yours."

Lucifer places a lingering kiss on my forehead. "You have proven yourself, Everly. You needn't fear the night

any longer. I will have demons guarding your home from this day forward."

A tear spills down my cheek in sheer gratitude. "I don't know what to say."

"Raise our daughter in the Old Ways, lover, and call upon me as it pleases you."

The Fallen Angel smiles devilishly. "Till next time," he says, and then in a swirl of black mist, he is gone.

I collapse into the couch with a blissful sigh. The local high school's siren sounds the start of classes, and I don't even try to suppress the gleeful laughter that escapes me.

I fucking hate teenagers.

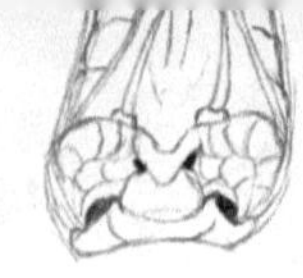

BLACK HARE PRESS

362

SCHOOL'S IN

AUTHOR
BIOGRAPHIES

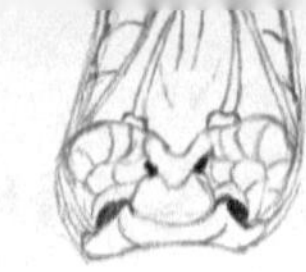

ALISTAIR CROWE

Author of Locker 429

Alistair Crowe, like all humans, was born from the darkness of the womb into the world. Unlike most, he returned to the darkness. As such he has written multiple articles credited as staff, acted on television (uncredited), and worked in radio where he was credited, but it was the overnight shift so no one listened to him. He decided to step from behind the scenes and publish, which allows him to write in solitude, yet remain behind the scenes. The aim of his writing is to enlighten, frighten, horrify and entertain in equal measure.

Twitter: @CroweAlistair
Website: www.alistaircrowe.com

AMBER M. SIMPSON

Author of The Honoured One

Amber M. Simpson is a dark fiction writer from Northern Kentucky with a penchant for horror and fantasy. Her work has been featured in multiple anthologies, as well as online. She assists with editing for Fantasia Divinity Magazine, where she's gotten to work with many talented authors from all over the world.

Website: ambermsimpson.com
Facebook: authorambermsimpson

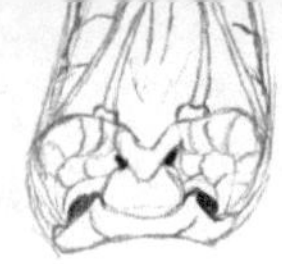

ARCHIT JOSHI

Author of My Baby Shot Me Down

Archit Joshi is an author who loves writing character-driven stories. He also works as a content writer and is eager to add several writing styles to his arsenal. His fiction has been published in many reputable anthologies and magazines, with forms including short stories, drabbles, and 10-word micro-fiction.

Instagram: @architrjoshi

CATHERINE KENWELL

Author of Monster

Catherine Kenwell is a Barrie, Ontario author, mediator, and brain injury awareness advocate. After 30 years in not-for-profit communications, she sustained a life-changing brain injury and was subsequently restructured out of her job. She is published in both horror and creative non-fiction genres, and writes extensively about mental health, brain injury and invisible disabilities. Her community involvement includes public speaking, small indie business promotion, and is chair of the City of Barrie's Accessibility Advisory Committee. Catherine's work has been published in Chicken Soup for the Soul, and in horror anthologies from Black Hare Press, HellBound Books, Books of Horror, and Trembling with Fear.

Website: www.catherinekenwell.com

CHRIS BANNOR

Author of I'll Bring You More

Chris Bannor is a speculative fiction writer who lives in Southern California. Chris learned her love of genre stories from her mother at an early age and has never veered far from that path. She also enjoys musical theatre and road trips with her family but is a general homebody otherwise

Facebook: chrisbannorauthor
Website: www.ChrisBannor.com

DAVID GREEN

Author of Making the Grade

David Green is a writer based in Co Galway, Ireland. Growing up between there and Manchester, UK meant David rarely saw sunlight in his childhood, which has no doubt had an effect on his dark writings. Published in places such as North West Words, The Devil Made Me Do It, Nymphs, and Ancients by Black Hare Press, David is aiming to release his debut novel in 2020.

Twitter: @David Green
Website: www.davidgreenwritercom.wordpress.com

BLACK HARE PRESS

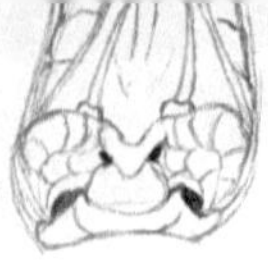

DAWN DEBRAAL

Author of School Daze

Dawn DeBraal lives in rural Wisconsin with her husband Red, two rat terriers, and a cat. She has discovered that her love of telling a good story can be written. Published stories with Palm-sized press, Spillwords, Mercurial Stories, Potato Soup Journal, Edify Fiction, Zimbell House Publishing, Clarendon House Publishing, Blood Song Books, Black Hare Press, Fantasia Divinity, Cafelit, Reanimated Writers, Guilty Pleasures, Unholy Trinity, The World of Myth, Dastaan World, Vamp Cat, Runcible Spoon, Dark Christmas, Siren's Call, Iron Horse Publishing, Falling Star Magazine 2019 Pushcart Nominee.

Amazon: amazon.com/Dawn-DeBraal/e/B07STL8DLX

DENVER GRENELL

Author of Corridor

Denver Grenell is a writer of horror & dark fiction who lives with his family in the small rural town of Featherston, New Zealand. A life-long horror hound who got back into writing after a long break, he is now making up for lost time, furiously expelling every idea that has collected inside his skull over the years. His stories are soon to be featured in Crystal Lake Publishing's Shallow Waters anthologies and Black Hare Press' Ancients & School's In anthologies.

Instagram: @beware.the.moon
Instagram: @degrineer

GREGG CUNNINGHAM

Author of The Cutest Couple

Gregg Cunningham has had several short stories publishing by Zombie Pirate Publishing in anthology books such as Relationship add Vice, Full Metal Horror, Phuket Tattoo, World War four, Flash Fiction Addiction and Grievous Bodily Harm. Most recently, his work has been accepted into Black Hare Press Dark Drabbles series including Monsters/Angels/Worlds/Unravel/Beyond and Apocalypse, with his latest (and best) short story included in their Deep Space anthology.

HENRY HERZ

Author of Zombie Boarding School

Henry Herz edited Beyond The Pale, featuring stories by Peter Beagle, Heather Brewer, Jim Butcher, Rachel Caine, Kami Garcia, Nancy Holder, and Jane Yolen. He authored 22 short stories, including Gluttony (Classics Remixed), Zombie Sonnet 43 (Monsters), Ghost Father (Beyond), and Sins & Virtues (Angels). He authored 11 children's books, including: Monster Goose Nursery Rhymes, When You Give An Imp A Penny, Mabel & The Queen Of Dreams, Cap'n Rex & His Clever Crew, How The Squid Got Two Long Arms, Alice's Magic Garden, 2 Pirates + 1 Robot, The Magic Spatula.

Website: www.henryherz.com

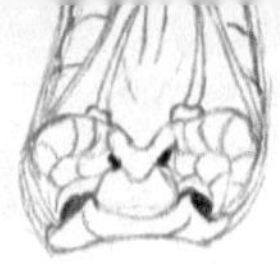

BLACK HARE PRESS

J.W. GARRETT

Author of A Brand New Me

J.W. Garrett has been writing in one form or another since she was a teenager. She currently lives in Florida with her family but loves the mountains of Virginia where she was born. Her writings include YA fantasy as well as short stories. Since completing Remeon's Quest-Earth Year 1930, the prequel in her YA fantasy series, Realms of Chaos, she has been hard at work on the next in the series, scheduled to release August 2020. When she's not hanging out with her characters, her favourite activities are reading, running and spending time with family.

Website: www.jwgarrett.com
BHC Press: www.bhcpress.com/Author_JW_Garrett.html

JO SEYSENER

Author of the Foreword

Jo Seysener is a mum of three crazies, a scatter of chickens, a decrepit kelpie and a rambunctious GSD. She lives with her husband near Brisbane, Australia. When she is not exposing her kids to cult story books from her childhood, she can be found in the kitchen experimenting with new flavours and pairings. She adores alpacas.

Facebook: joseysener
Website: www.joseysener.com

JOHANN VAN DER WALT

Author of The Girls' Bathroom

Johann works in the television industry as a freelance writer, producer and video editor. He has written two children's books, Frankie learns to Fly, (Minimal Press, 2018) & Bhubesi (Minimal Press, 2019), and two poetry collections, one published in South Africa, Parlement van uile, ("Parliament of owls" Naledi, 2020) and another collection published in the States, This Road Doesn't Lead Home, (Red Mare Press, 2020). Johann lives in Johannesburg, South Africa.

JOHN CLEWARTH

Author of Master of the Hunt

Whilst mainly writing chillers for children and young adults, including the People's Book Prize finalist, 'Firestorm Rising' and 'Demons in the Dark', John Clewarth has had over 50 short adult horror stories published in the independent press, under the pseudonym, John Saxton; including a horror collection: 'Bloodshot'. His work has also featured in the podcasts, The Wicked Library, Creepypasta and Tales to Terrify.

Twitter: @johnclewarth
Facebook: John Clewarth - Author

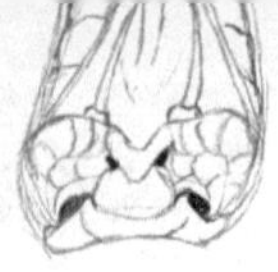

BLACK HARE PRESS

K.B. ELIJAH

Author of The Secrets of Locker 4D

K.B. Elijah is a fantasy author living in Brisbane, Australia with her husband and three cockatiels. A lawyer by day, and a writer by...also day, because she needs her solid nine hours of sleep per night (not that the cockatiels let her sleep past 6am). K.B. writes for various international anthologies, and her work features in dozens of collections about the mysterious, the magical and the macabre. Her own books of short fantasy novellas with twists, The Empty Sky and Out of the Nowhere, are available on paperback and Kindle now.

Website: www.kbelijah.com
Instagram: k.b.elijah

KIMBERLY REI

Author of Miss Lily

Kimberly Rei has been writing for as long as she can remember. At five years old, her parents gifted her with a set of Children's Classics that she had no hope of reading. Yet. The potential alone sparked a love of words that has never wavered. Kim has taught writing workshops and edited novels for Authors You May Recognize. She has published several short stories and now can't stop chasing paper dragons. She currently lives in Tampa Bay, Florida with her wife and an abundance of gorgeous beaches to explore.

LUIS MANUEL TORRES

Author of A Game at the Nurse's Office

Luis Manuel Torres was born in Puerto Rico, lived in Boston Massachusetts for thirteen years and currently lives in Springfield Mass. He has a love for stories in all forms they come in, from books to television and video games. His work can be found in multiple anthologies with Zimbell House Publishing and Black Hare Press. He is always working on multiple writing projects. His debut short story collection Midnight Animals is now available on Amazon.

Twitter: @Luis1989Manuel
Blog: luisitowrites.wordpress.com

LYNNE PHILLIPS

Author of The Principal is Missing

Lynne Phillips, a retired teacher, lives in the beautiful Northern Rivers Region of New South Wales Australia. Her stories, across all genres, have been published in anthologies and various online magazines. Her priority is spending time with her family. Her passions are reading, writing and keeping fit.

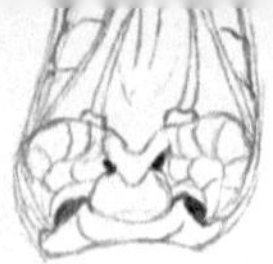

BLACK HARE PRESS

MATTHEW WILSON

Author of Bite of the Bug

Matthew Wilson has been published over 200 times in such places as Horror Zine, Star*Line, Zimbell House Publishing and many more. He is currently editing his first novel.

NEEN COHEN

Author of Goldilocks is a Mass Murderer

Neen Cohen is an LGBTQI and speculative fiction author. Several flash fiction and short stories have been published through Black Hare Press, Little Quail Press, Camden Park Press, and NBH Publishing. She has a Bachelor of Creative Industries and is a member of the Springfield Writers Group.
Neen lives in Brisbane Australia with her partner, son and can often be found writing while sitting against a tree or tombstone.

LinkTree: linktr.ee/neencohen

PATRICK WINTERS

Author of Bad Seeds

Patrick Winters is a graduate of Illinois College in Jacksonville, IL, where he earned a Bachelor of Arts degree in English Literature and Creative Writing and achieved membership into Sigma Tau Delta, an international English honors society. Winters is now a proud member of the Horror Writers Association, and his work has been published in the likes of Sanitarium Magazine, Deadman's Tome, Trysts of Fate, and other such titles. A full list of his previous publications may be found at his author's site.

Website: wintersauthor.azurewebsites.net/Publications/List

PAULA R.C. READMAN

Author of Darkness of the Soul

Paula R.C. Readman is a self-taught author. She learnt her craft from 'how to write' books her husband purchased from Ebay. Since 2010 she's had 34 short stories. a short-read crime novella The Funeral Birds, a collection of short stories Days Pass like a Shadow, and a Gothic crime novel, Stone Angels published. To find out more about Paula and her writing check out her blog.

Blog: paulareadman1.wordpress.com

S.O. GREEN

Author of Lovecraft Club

Simone Oldman Green lives in the Kingdom of Fife with husband, John. They have been published by Dragon Soul Press, Otter Libris, Rogue Blades, Storgy Magazine, L Ellington Ashton, Iron Faerie, Eerie River and Black Hare Press. They also won 3rd Place in the British Fantasy Society's Short Story Contest 2018 for the feminist post-Apocalypse piece, 'Travesty'. Writer, vegan, martial artist, gamer, occasionally a terrible person (but only to fictional people). They thrive on the unusual, which might explain why there are so many cats.

Website: https://thebasementoflove.blogspot.com/
Twitter:@SOGreenWriter

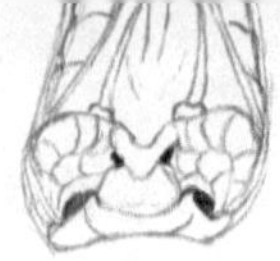

BLACK HARE PRESS

SABETHA DANES

Author of Cyberoach

Sabetha Danes is an eccentric introvert located in Central Texas, in a Stars Hollow-esque small town. Her default language is sarcasm, and is fueled by coffee. As a lifelong bibliophile, she reads and edits all genres but specializes in fantasy and cozy mysteries. Her degree in interpersonal communication helps her over-analyze characters that are only found in stories. She spends her days with her daughter and dude walking trails and drinking coffee.

Website: aconitecafe.com

SARAH JANE JUSTICE

Author of I Was Asleep

Sarah Jane Justice is a South Australian creative whose work has been commended in the fields of poetry, prose, spoken word and original music. She performed at the Sydney Opera House as a national finalist in the Australian Poetry Slam in 2018, presented her work at Adelaide Writer's Week in 2019, and has had both poetry and prose published in anthologies and literary journals from around the world.

Facebook: sarahjanejusticewriting
Website: sarahjanejusticewriting.com

STACEY JAINE MCINTOSH

Author of Welcome to Rosewood High

Stacey Jaine McIntosh was born in Perth, Western Australia where she still resides with her husband and their four children. Although her first love has always been writing, she once toyed with being a Cartographer and subsequently holds a Diploma in Spatial Information Services. Since 2011, she has had a vast number of stories and a few poems published online as well as in various anthologies. Stacey is also the author of Solstice, Morrighan, Lost and Le Fay and she is currently working on several other projects simultaneously. When not with her family or writing she enjoys reading, photography, genealogy, history, Arthurian myths and witchcraft.

Website: www.staceyjainemcintosh.com

STEPHEN HERCZEG

Author of Joshua's Lament

Stephen Herczeg is an IT Geek based in Canberra Australia. He has been writing for over twenty years and has completed a couple of dodgy novels, sixteen feature length screenplays and numerous short stories and scripts. His horror work has featured in Sproutlings, Hells Bells, Below the Stairs, Trickster's Treats #1 and #2, Shades of Santa, Behind the Mask, Beyond the Infinite; The Body Horror Book, Anemone Enemy, Petrified Punks and Beginnings. He has also had numerous Sherlock Holmes stories published through the Belanger Books - Sherlock Holmes anthologies.

Amazon: amazon.com/-/e/B07916SQQS
Facebook: stephenherczegauthor

BLACK HARE PRESS 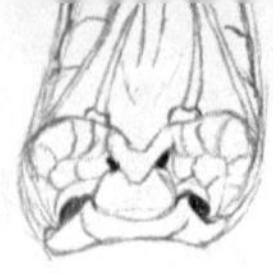

T.M. BROWN

Author of Substitute Creature

Trevor Brown, who writes under the pen name T.M. Brown, serves as an officer in the U.S. Army. He currently lives in Colorado Springs, Colorado with his beautiful wife, Anna, and his two dogs, Fry and Zapp. Although Trevor has long held a passion for speculative fiction, he has only recently taken up writing for publication. T.M. Brown's first novel, The Gloam, will be published by Terror Tract in the autumn of 2020.

Amazon: amazon.com/-/e/B087Z13DST
Facebook: RavenousShadows

TIM MENDEES

Author of The Girl Who Hated Shakespeare

Tim Mendees is a horror writer from Macclesfield in the North-West of England that specialises in cosmic horror and weird fiction. He has recently had stories appear in over twenty publications and has had many more stories accepted for forthcoming projects. He has two novellas, Miracle Growth (Black Hare Press) and Burning Reflection (Mannison Press), coming soon. When he is not arguing with the spellchecker, Tim is a goth DJ, crustacean and cephalopod enthusiast, and the presenter of a popular web series of live video readings of his material. He currently lives in Brighton & Hove with his pet crab, Gerald, and an army of stuffed octopuses.

Website: timmendeeswriter.wordpress.com/

TRISHA MCKEE

Author of School Girl Crush

Trisha McKee resides in a small town in Pennsylvania where love has proven to be a problem. Her work has appeared or is forthcoming in publications such as Tablet Magazine, The Oddville Press, Crab Fat Literary Magazine, Night to Dawn Magazine, Deep Fried Horror, 4 Star Stories, and more.

UMAIR MIRXA

Author of Brynhildr

Umair Mirxa lives and writes in Karachi, Pakistan. His first published story, 'Awareness', appeared on Spillwords Press. He has since had stories accepted for publication in anthologies from Zombie Pirate Publishing, Blood Song Books, Black Hare Press, Iron Faerie Publishing, Clarendon House Publications, Fantasia Divinity Magazine & Publishing, and The ReAnimated Writers Press. He is a massive J.R.R. Tolkien fan, loves everything to do with mythology, fantasy, and history, and wishes with all his heart that dragons were real. When he's not writing, he enjoys reading novels and comic books, playing video games, listening to music, and watching movies, TV shows, and football as an Arsenal FC fan.

Website: umairmirxa.com

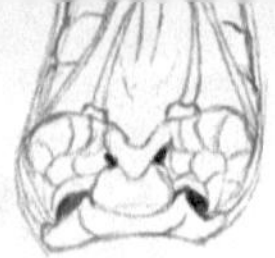

BLACK HARE PRESS

WONDRA VANIAN

Author of A Dance with Death

Wondra Vanian is an American living in the United Kingdom with her Welsh husband and their army of fur babies. A writer first, Wondra is also an avid gamer, photographer, cinephile, and blogger. She has music in her blood, sleeps with the lights on, and has been known to dance naked in the moonlight. Wondra was a multiple Top-Ten finisher in the 2017 and 2018 Preditors and Editors Reader's Poll, including the Best Author category. Her story, "Halloween Night," was named a Notable Contender for the Bristol Short Story Prize in 2015.

Website: www.wondravanian.com

XIMENA ESCOBAR

Author of Scarlett

Ximena is writing stories and poetry. Originally from Chile, she is the author of a translation into Spanish of the Broadway Musical "The Wizard of Oz", and of an original adaptation of the same, "Navidad en Oz", both produced in her home country. Since 2018 she has published several short stories in various anthologies and online platforms, and is now slowly working on her own collection. Ximena has a degree in Arts & Communication Science and lives in Nottingham with her family.

Facebook: Ximenautora
Twitter: @laximenin

380

ZOEY XOLTON

Author of Payback

Zoey Xolton is an Australian Speculative Fiction Author. She likes to daydream, and write stories about the beautiful and improbable, the dark and fantastical, as well as the adventurous and utterly romantic! Whether it's fairy tales, fantasy, horror, paranormal romance, urban fantasy, or science-fiction…she dabbles in it. Zoey has featured in over 100 anthologies to date, and is currently working on progressively longer stories. She prays you enjoy, and fall in love with the deliciously tempting tales, and the characters that she brings into the world. Writing is Zoey's guilty pleasure…perhaps reading her work will become one of yours?

Website: www.zoeyxolton.com

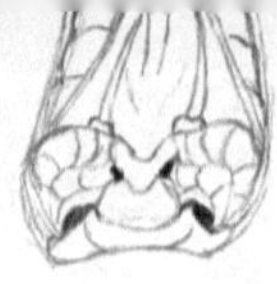 BLACK HARE PRESS

SCHOOL'S IN

ACKNOWLEDGEMENTS

When we embarked on our Black Hare Press journey back in late 2018, we never envisioned the huge support we'd get from the writing community. We have been truly humbled by the number of submissions we've received—more than 5,000 in our first year alone—and have loved reading every single one.

So, thank you to everyone who crafted tales just for us—from the tiny tales in our Dark Drabbles series, to the longer stories—we thank you from the bottom of our hearts.

To our families and friends, collaborators, random strangers who took pity on us, and everyone who has helped us on the way: we couldn't have done it without you.

And to you, our discerning reader, we and these talented writers did it all for you. We hope you enjoyed these tales, and if you did, don't forget to leave a review.

Thank you all—see you next time.

Love & kisses
Ben & Dean

www.blackharepress.com

BERTOL
BR

cherry picker
arlett
Chicaaaa !!!

PUBLICATIONS